WILDFIRE

FOR ROSE

ENDORSEMENTS

Wildfire for Rose captures the spirit of the Wild West as well as the enduring spirit and hope of the people who chose to settle there.
—**Sue A. Fairchild**, professional editor

Andrew Roth blends historical accuracy, exciting adventure, enduring love, and inspiring faith in his first novel—*Wildfire for Rose.*
—**Susan Lunsford**, Academic Program Coordinator

WILDFIRE
FOR ROSE

ANDREW ROTH

PUBLISHING THE POSITIVE

ELK LAKE PUBLISHING INC

Plymouth, Massachusetts

Cover and Interior Design: Derinda Babcock

Editor(s):Cristel Phelps, Deb Haggerty

Author Represented by Hartline Literary Agency

PUBLISHED BY: Elk Lake Publishing, Inc., 35 Dogwood Dr., Plymouth, MA 02360, 2019

Library Cataloging Data

Names: Roth, Andrew (Andrew Roth)

Wildfire For Rose / Andrew Roth

226 p. 23cm × 15cm (9in × 6 in.)

Description: Lost and alone after his father is killed by Confederate night riders, Jason heads west to fulfill their dream. Along the way, he meets and joins a blended Cheyenne family with the same dream--raise horses.

Identifiers: ISBN-13: 978-1-950051-68-7 (trade) | 978-1-950051-69-4 (POD)| 978-1-950051-70-0 (e-book)

Key Words: Western, horses, Cheyenne, Santa Fe Trail, wagon trains, coming of age, historical romance

LCCN: 2019940500 Fiction

DEDICATION

To Laurie, my best friend.
None of this would be possible without you.
I love you.

CHAPTER 1

My teeth chattered in the predawn gloom, and my eyes darted to the edge of the forest, searching for movement. Were they chasing me?

Cold fingers jabbed through my meager covering of leaves, and a shiver racked me, forcing me to huddle closer to the tree at my back. I had nothing—not even a coat.

Wrapping my arms tightly around myself, I realized I did have something. I had my faith in Christ. Pa always said that if you have Jesus, you are never alone.

I pressed my back against the rough bark of the huge, old elm tree on the hills above Westport Landing and watched the sky lighten. Skeletal limbs stretched above me, scant protection against the chill. Tiny buds poked from the branches but no leaves yet.

My stomach shriveled against my spine. I hadn't eaten in three days. Dirty and cold, only my faith kept me company on my lonely vigil. My stomach growled, signaling time to move on.

Hesitating, my gaze swept the line of deep shadows along the distant woods, probing for anyone lurking. Had I lost them? Were they even following me?

The events of the night when Pa lost his life nagged at the edges of my mind, but I pushed them down, not wanting to ponder them. The pain was still too fresh. But I needed to get out of Missouri, that much I knew. Nothing remained for me here.

Shivering in the morning gray, I watched the sun creep over the eastern hills. A mist rose from the ground with the ascending orange ball, the vapors dancing slowly above the wet grass. My ears strained to catch the slightest sound, but silence draped me like a wet blanket, taunting and useless.

Great armloads of last autumn's dried grass covered me, but the intense cold still found me. Somehow, these long, brown stems had escaped the wrath of winter's storms. It kept off most of the chill—but not enough.

The sickening thuds of the two shots as they struck Pa still sounded in my ears. Numbness filled me as I looked into his lifeless eyes right before they closed for the last time. Fear descended upon me like summer storms upon the crops, sudden and drenching. Miraculously, I was not hurt, but I would not think of that now. Again, I wrestled with my thoughts and shoved them away to consider later.

I trembled, not sure if the sensation was from the morning cold or from my troubling memories. What would I do next, now that Pa was gone?

His words of encouragement whispered in my head. I could see him still, kneeling before me when I was younger, grasping my shoulder, our eyes locking. "If you have the Lord, you can find contentment. St. Paul discovered the secret of contentment in any situation. God is always with you."

That was like Pa, constantly teaching me.

I sat there, watching the shadows retreat into the depressions of the land as the morning fog hovered lazily above the fallow fields. Dew glistened with the rays of the mounting sun. I shot a final glance toward the foreboding woods and gritted my teeth. In spite of the cold and fear, an unexpected, overpowering desire to sing welled within me. Softly, I began, the words wrenched from me as the incredible beauty and freshness of a new day blossomed before me. God's creation demanded praise.

Starving, cold, dirty, and alone, I sang worship songs to Jesus. My voice quivered, my throat dry. But as the words continued to come from my lips, my voice gained strength as soon as I confirmed I was not being followed. Soon I felt better as my heart became full. I sang to the Lord. What a beautiful sunrise!

I remembered King David singing to the Lord, and I smiled, encouraged to be in such good company.

Despite my fears, I felt renewed, resolved to trust the Lord. I was not alone. What could man do to me?

Pushing the piled grass and leaves from me, I stood. My stomach growled in protest, and I looked down at my empty belly. I'd better find something to eat, I mused, patting my complaining stomach with a dirty hand.

I brushed the last few dead blades of grass from my stained pants and walked down the gentle slope toward town—my best hope of finding food.

Glancing over my shoulder, a habit I'd picked up these last three days, I saw nobody.

A dirt road at the bottom of the hill led toward Westport Landing. Kneeling beside the small irrigation canal running alongside the road, I drank from the shallow ditch. The gritty water tasted awful, full of silt. River water, no doubt. I drank more, though, not knowing when I would get the chance again.

I thought about the well on our farm and its sweet water. Pa and I dug that well ourselves and lined the hole with native limestone. Pa had been remarkable at building with stone. He'd fitted a rock into place and then leaned against the half-constructed wall, peering up at me on the rim of the well as he wiped the sweat from his brow. "Ireland is full of rock, so it is also full of rock walls and rock houses. You build with what you have."

Pa came from the old country as a lad and always wanted a bit of land for himself. He grew up with stories of America being the Promised Land. A land flowing with milk and honey. I guess that depended on how you felt about slavery.

Studying the dirty water at my feet, hope surged through me, boosting my spirits. Again, I glanced over my shoulder and peered to the west. If this was truly river water, I must be near the border. Perhaps I could evade the night riders.

I walked west in the middle of the dirt road, the early morning sun at my back. I was leaving Missouri and hurried to do so. Although a border state, there wasn't a lot of support for a Union man in Missouri. My mouth watered when I caught the smell of frying bacon. My stomach roared and I put my hands to my belly, attempting to silence the beast.

My nose led me to a grove of trees across the irrigation ditch. I narrowed my eyes, peering into the dim morning light. Vaguely, I could make out a number of wagons parked under yonder trees. The smoke of many fires drifted above the treetops. It looked like a wagon train and a large one at that.

I shifted and chewed my lip. I wasn't looking for a fight. As long as they didn't ask me about my personal politics, I figured to offer work in return for food. As the clouds bloomed pink and rose, I studied them. "Jesus, please let me find someone who'll give me something to eat. I have nothing but my trust in you."

I wiped my hands on my pants leg and jumped the small irrigation ditch. Teamsters bustled about with camp chores. Blue smoke mingled with the tree branches as the smell of food intoxicated me. The clatter of a busy camp filled my ears.

The first wagon I came to appeared empty, but a small fire burned and a battered coffeepot rested on the coals. A skillet with bacon and bread perched atop a nearby rock.

I considered the vacant camp site, my gaze surveying everything with caution. Had the night riders come this far looking for me?

An old man walked a team of huge red oxen into camp, their powerful chests swelled with muscles. The pale man wore teamster's pants tucked into tall boots, and his thin frame stooped at the shoulders.

He stared when he saw me. I could well imagine what he saw. A scarecrow in rags, dirt and ash smudged across my face. I was big and strong for seventeen, but I'm sure I'd leaned down these past three days.

I spoke quickly, not wanting him to think me a thief. "Mister, I'm terribly hungry, but I want to work for something to eat. Can I cut wood or help you harness your team? I'm handy with tools, too, and can mend broken things, if you have a need."

He just stood there, gaping at me. The smell of that skillet so near my feet tantalized my senses—pure torture. I wanted to sit down right then and eat everything in that pan. But I waited.

Finally, the old teamster straightened, his eyes studying me from under bushy brows. "What's your name, boy?"

"Jason Malone. I'm hunting work or anything I can do for a bite to eat." I didn't want to say where I was from, fearing he'd heard about the burning of our farm.

He hesitated a moment longer and then looked around at the other wagons. They, too, had men moving about, and some were starting to harness their teams. He glanced back at me and put a hand to his bearded chin, rubbing it briskly, as if thinking about something serious.

The big oxen stood patiently, their ears twitching in the semidarkness.

"Jason Malone, you go ahead and eat some of that grub. I don't feel much like eating this morning anyway. I'll hitch this team in place. Then we'll talk."

I stepped over the fire and moved toward the big oxen. "No, sir." I shook my head and grasped the lead rope. "Pa always said 'you work first and then you get paid.' I'll not take your food without earning it."

The old man squinted at me but didn't reply. Together we led the team to the front of the wagon. It took only a few minutes to push the beasts into position and help yoke them. Then we hitched them to the big wagon.

I wanted to keep my mind from that bacon and bread, so I started asking questions. "Is this a wagon train bound west?"

He moved a bit slower than I, which surprised me. I was new to this, but he would've been doing it for a long time by now.

The teamster shook his head and snorted in disgust. "No, this isn't a train of pilgrims. We're taking freight to Santa Fe. This is a big train, almost a hundred and ten wagons. Wilmington's the captain, though he has no liking for me."

He didn't elaborate and I didn't push the issue, although my curiosity sparked.

"How long you been with this train?" I reached under the neck of the nearest oxen and grabbed the guide line. Pulling it between the animals, I took it back toward the seat and secured it.

The man didn't say anything for the longest time. I wondered if he'd even heard me. His scowl deepened. When I'd figured he wasn't going to answer, he finally spoke. "I've only recently joined this wagon train. I was part of another train for years."

He didn't continue, and I decided not to pursue that line of questions.

"What's your name, mister?" I asked, steering the conversation to safer ground.

"Call me Cal." He motioned for me to follow him. "Help me round up my other team."

I glanced longingly at the frying pan by the fire before I followed Cal to the livestock corral. Hundreds of oxen, mules, and even a few horses clustered together while men pushed among the animals, selecting particular ones.

My gaze flickered over the horses out of habit, but there was nothing here but strong draft stock. I found none with the lines and look I searched for.

Cal entered the throng of warm bodies, and I followed close behind him, welcoming the rising heat from the massed animals. He searched for his oxen, his grizzled head turning hawk-like in the early morning.

Whether it was the uneven ground or the milling, shoving oxen, Cal stumbled and almost went under the herd.

My hand shot out to steady him. "Hang on there, old timer."

He glared at me and jerked his arm free. "I'm all right," he snapped.

He pointed to a large, red oxen and then looped his lead rope round another's horns.

We returned to camp and again hitched the pair in place with a yoke worn smooth by many years of rubbing oxen necks. The little exertion required to hitch the team had winded the old man. He looked tired and worn out, and the day had only begun.

Cal turned to me. "I can manage the rest from here. You sit and eat. There's plenty of coffee in the pot and a cup on the wagon seat." He walked to the rear of the wagon and busied himself with his gear.

I scrambled to the fire and sat cross legged on the ground, eagerly reaching for the iron skillet. I shoveled hot bacon and bread into my mouth, chewing it slowly, savoring every bite. As I ate, I watched the men around us hitching their animals in preparation for departure.

Chewing the last of the bacon, I retrieved the cup from the wagon seat and was pouring coffee when I heard a rider come alongside the caravan. He stopped near the old timer, concealed behind the wagon. I watched, my interest aroused. Steam rose from my tin cup and I held the warm mug in both hands as the stranger barked at Cal.

"Well, old man, I'm glad to see your team is hitched in time. We'll not wait for you. You be ready when we pull out or you'll be left behind. I'll find someone else to drive this wagon."

The harsh man's commanding voice was clear, but I didn't like its tone.

Cal sighed. "I know, Wilmington." I noticed he avoided eye contact with the wagon master. "You've made it very clear that I'm being tested," the old man added as he securely bound his bedroll.

The unseen Wilmington chuckled gruffly, and I heard the creak of his saddle leather. "You're indeed being tested. If you can't cut it, you're through." Wilmington's voice rose as he spoke. "I'm not going to mollycoddle you on this trail. I stuck my neck out to give you a chance to drive when no other wagon master would hire you."

"And I'm obliged you did, but I've been over this trail a hundred times," Cal countered as he stowed the last of his belongings in the wagon. "I'll be all right. Besides, I've taken on a boy to help me. Don't worry. I'll not slow you down."

"You've taken on a boy?" Wilmington bellowed at this news. "You'll have to pay him from your wages. I'm not hiring him. Is that clear?"

"Of course." Cal spoke softly, resignation thick in his voice. The wagon captain's horse thumped heavily, and I knew he'd been turned away. I listened thoughtfully to the retreating hooves.

I stared into my mug. What had I gotten myself into?

Swiftly, I cleaned the few camp dishes in the irrigation ditch and helped Cal complete his chores. He hadn't said a thing to me since breakfast. Did he know I'd heard Wilmington? I couldn't be sure.

The rest of camp was on the move, and with shouts and the crack of leather whips, the wagons began rolling. There seemed to be an order as they fell into place, one behind the other. Cal mounted his seat and waited. I looked at him from the fire ring, unsure where to be. A lone tendril of smoke rose from the ashes. Cal hadn't said anything to me about a job, so I stood there, uncertain.

"Thanks for breakfast. I hope you do well on this drive. God bless you." The old man seemed to not hear me. He looked after the other wagons pulling out from under the grove of trees, then rubbed the back of his neck with one hand and looked down at me.

"Listen, boy. I have nothing and can't offer you much. I don't know if they'll leave you out on the prairie if I'm not with you. This could be dangerous, but if you need a place to be, you can come with me. I can feed you but little else."

Well, I didn't even stop to consider all that he'd said. When you have nothing, food is a lot. Old Cal said he could feed me, and they were heading into Kansas, which meant they were leaving Missouri behind. That sounded good to me.

I stepped to the front wheel and looked up at the old teamster. "Count me in."

CHAPTER 2

"Thank you, Cal. I promise to be a help." I reached for the whip at his feet and walked to the front of the oxen teams. Grabbing the front bow, I yelled and we started out, the last wagon in line.

I felt a lot better after breakfast, and now I had a plan. Three days on the run with my burned down cabin and a fresh grave for Pa behind me. The farm hadn't really been our land, just rental property we hoped to buy.

Three days behind me and now I was a teamster on the Santa Fe Trail.

We skirted Westport Landing. Dogs barked and children waved from porches and behind whitewashed fences. I waved back, thrilling at my opportunity to leave Missouri.

I glanced skyward and smiled, knowing who was responsible for this unexpected piece of luck.

The river swirled with muddy waves that licked the shores where the wagons crossed. I shaded my eyes and peered ahead, surveying the rolling hills of Kansas as they stretched above the opposite bank. After I got across the Missouri River, I'd be free from slaveholders' ideas. Kansas was a free state. I wondered about Pa and how he'd have felt standing there beside me looking out on open prairie and land he could've owned one day.

I owed him this, I thought. I cracked the whip and clambered atop the wagon as it rolled into the chilly water.

Cal held onto the wagon seat with both hands, his thin face taut. From the corner of my eye, I could see he clenched his teeth as the wagon jostled and pitched across the rolling river.

With a lunge, the swimming oxen found their footing and heaved, water streaming from the wagon as they dragged it ashore. I dropped once more to the ground and watched the oxen teams strain as they moved through the mud.

I paused on the rise above the Missouri River and looked back. Balling my fists, I shoved my hands into my pockets. Missouri lay beautiful and wooded below with rolling hills and brown fields. Little houses, neatly manicured orchards, and white fences seemed to define a picturesque scene, yet I knew the sickness that dwelt there—the desire to get ahead at the expense of another man—a man owned by another.

I had lived there these last six years. Pa and I had moved here from Pennsylvania after Ma died, but now I was seventeen and leaving Missouri behind. Would I ever see it again?

I loved the deep woods of Missouri, but the folks had not liked Union men when it came time to talk of war. Missouri was a slave state, even though it remained with the Union, but most folks frowned on men who didn't favor slavery. So, Pa and I did not have friends.

Chewing the inside of my cheek, I scanned the road that followed the river, angling to the north. I felt at a crossroads, anxiety filling me with the significance of this decision. Should I go west as Pa had instructed, into the unknown? What lay out on the plains for a man like me? Would I discover what I searched for out there? Or should I follow this dirt road to the north, find employment in a factory making goods for the war effort? If I go north, no chance awaited me to locate a ranch, but if I went west … who knew?

To the east and south lay war and conflict. Something unseen pulled on me, drawing me to my destiny. I nodded and gritted my teeth, accepting Pa's advice, trusting him once again, despite his absence.

With a sigh, I turned my face westward and looked up at Cal as I walked beside the oxen. He watched me, a curious gleam in his old eyes.

I nodded at him but said nothing. Could he guess the loneliness in my heart? Could he read the worry in me as I hurried to put Missouri behind me?

I glanced away, hoping he sensed nothing. I had a dream to accomplish. Pa had commanded me to pursue it, to fulfill it.

I looked at the oxen. They were slow animals but strong and could live easily off the grasses of the prairie. Besides, if they got injured or could no longer pull a wagon, they provided good meat.

By midday, the whole wagon train stood on Kansas soil, but we didn't stop to eat. Cal didn't get down from the wagon seat like the other teamsters, and at times he scowled, his face pale and set in hard lines. I said nothing to him about it, wishing to leave the old man alone with his own affairs. Instead, I faced west and took stock of Kansas.

I'd never been this far west and was surprised to see Kansas looked mighty similar to Missouri. Deep woods towered along both sides of the river bottoms, and rolling hills stood on all sides of me. The blue sky was similar to the sky I'd seen yesterday. Early spring had brought a carpet of green grass to the Great Plains, but the grasses along the trail were not yet rich and thick like they'd be later this spring. Early April could still be bitterly cold, but the chances of severe storms was slight. I'd heard the buffalo loved the grass in Kansas. It would soon be good grass for our livestock too.

Wilmington rode by our wagon late in the day, mounted on a big white gelding. He gave me a sharp inspection as he passed. He didn't greet Cal or me but looked somber and serious when he saw Cal on the wagon seat. Most of the teamsters walked beside their oxen or rode the seat only for short periods of time. Cal had been there all day.

Westport Landing behind us and the great Kansas plains before us, I felt excited to be leaving so much pain and grief behind. What would God have in store for me now, I wondered?

All that Pa and I had worked for was gone now, or so I believed. Had our plans and hopes all been for naught?

A meadowlark whistled from a thicket, and I listened, enjoying his song. The endless wind blew gently all day and carried the scent of fresh grass and water. Small streams ran everywhere—obtaining water was, so far, no problem. I wondered what it would be like farther out on the prairie.

I stopped and allowed the oxen teams to pass me then resumed walking adjacent to the wagon seat. Cal stared to the horizon, eyelids half closed against the glare of the afternoon sun. He seemed to rest easier now, some color showing in his cheeks again.

"Cal, how far you think we'll make today?" I figured to start the conversation, him not seeming too chatty.

Ignoring my question, he scratched his ear. "I was some surprised at how fast you agreed to go with us out on the trail. You must not have much back yonder." He hooked a thumb over his shoulder.

I shook my head. "No, sir, I don't. Pa and I were all that's left, and now he's gone. I have nowhere to go except from Missouri and no points south, thank you." A glance over my shoulder confirmed our empty back trail, and I relaxed. I felt better than I had in three days and was convinced God brought me to this wagon train. I would have work and food, for a while anyway.

Cal narrowed his eyes. "You're against slavery, I take it." It was more of a comment than a question.

"Yes, sir. Pa never figured why a man couldn't just do his own work, or if he had too much of it, hire a man to help him. He never saw fit to own another man. That was not popular talk with our neighbors, though." Irritation rose in me at the memory, and I steeled myself for what usually happened next.

Cal surprised me when he grinned. "No, I guess it wouldn't be."

We continued in silence, and I enjoyed watching the sun make a slow path across the sky. The shadows lengthened, and Cal craned his neck to see around the wagon in front of us. He fidgeted on the wooden seat, muttering loud enough for me to hear. "What's he waiting for? We've passed two good camp sites already. What's he looking for? Paradise?" He chuckled at his own joke, and then I saw him scowl and look down, his shoulders drooping.

At the next ridge, I could see where the lead wagons had pulled from the trail. Camp fires gleamed cheerily under trees along a small stream.

The oxen seemed to sense rest was coming, for they picked up their slow pace and soon we found a likely spot.

Wilmington rode by on his white gelding. He reined in when he saw Cal. "Well, good to see you kept up with the wagons today." The wagon master touched spurs to his mount without waiting for a reply, and I heard him laugh. Cal pursed his lips and stiffly climbed down from the high seat.

He stretched, arching his back, and motioned for the oxen lead ropes. I held them tight. "Let me take them to water and turn them into the stock corral. Why don't you gather firewood?"

His bushy brows arched. He looked pleased, I thought. "All right," he agreed and then peered at me sharply. "But don't get too big for your britches. You have a lot to learn." Then he wandered to the creek, searching for firewood. Soon the ground would be scoured for fuel by the many teamsters in the train.

I led the two teams over to where the other drivers watered their stock and waited my turn. A few men gave me a curious glance, but no one said anything to me. After releasing the four oxen into the stock corral, I carried the two heavy bows back to camp, one on each shoulder.

Like I said, I was big for my age. Pa and I had always known work, and there was no one else but us to do it. We'd built, plowed, cut wood, hunted, and always been working from sun up to sun down. I was used to hard work and not afraid of it.

I wished I had Pa's old rifle or my coat or a blanket. Anything to remind me of my life with Pa, but it was all gone. I had nothing but the clothes on my back and the Lord. What had St. Paul said? God's grace was sufficient. Then, it would have to be enough for me too.

I returned to our wagon and found Cal cooking over a small blaze. Beef slices sizzled in the skillet and sourdough biscuits baked in the Dutch oven. The coffeepot simmered on the coals, and I seated myself to wait, my mouth watering.

Cal seemed to be a good cook, and I ate everything he served me. Despite my hunger, I still bowed my head first when Cal handed me my plate.

"Lord, thank you for this man who you've provided to help me. Cal seems like a good man. I thank you for this food and pray you guide our steps all the days of our lives. Amen."

Cal had put his fork down as I prayed. When I looked up, he was staring at me, a scowl on his wrinkled face. He narrowed his eyes as if studying me and then lifted his fork again.

Cal seemed aloof as we ate, so there was only silence around our fire until I could take it no longer.

"Cal, you said you only recently came to this wagon train," I began tentatively, wishing not to annoy the old man. "What train did you belong with before?"

I wished he would open up and talk. I was ready for some dialogue like Pa and I used to enjoy around the supper table. We would discuss a particular horse we'd seen, its strong points and its flaws. Or we'd talk about the farm or what we hoped to accomplish the next day. Sometimes we'd talk about our dream.

The silence this night drove me crazy.

Cal's scowl deepened, and I worried I'd pushed too far.

He picked his teeth with a twig before he spoke. "I was with the Mitchell Train about ten or eleven years, I guess. Before that, I was with Benson. Those were fighting men. I can't remember how many times we fought off Indians."

He straightened a bit, a gleam shining in his eyes as he remembered former days.

"Indians?" I glanced over my shoulder into the gloom. "Will we see any on this trip?" I'd seen tame Indians wherever we lived but never experienced an attack. That is, I reminded myself, not an Indian attack.

Cal warmed to the conversation now and continued to tell me stories of the famous wagon train leaders like Buff Benson and Kit Carson and other tales of the Santa Fe Trail.

"Indians don't usually attack a wagon train of this size. I don't think we'll have any trouble from them," he said at last. I thought I detected a twinge of regret as he spoke. Maybe it was only my imagination.

"How many times have you been over the old trail?" I enjoyed hearing the old timer speak and was learning things of value.

He drew in a deep breath and let it out slowly. "Oh, I have no idea how many times." He narrowed his eyes thoughtfully as he scratched the whiskers along his jaw. "The wagon leaders always keep a journal so as to know dates and loads and deaths on the trail. I've been only a simple teamster these many years, but I've done well."

He peered into the night, a faraway look in his eyes. "I've loved it. If a train gets an early start in spring, like we've done, and if the weather is favorable, we could turn around at Santa Fe and make it back here by winter."

Cal leaned against a log, a cup of coffee in one hand. He hadn't eaten much, but now he talked with eagerness, enjoying the memory of his travels.

"Old Santa Fe was something to see in those days. Pretty senoritas and bright colors and those big Spanish mules. We brought them back, you know."

I nodded and sipped my coffee. Pa had already told me of the big mules from Mexico the teamsters favored.

"Didn't you ever settle down or marry?" I asked, wanting to keep the old man talking.

He shot me a bitter look, and I regretted my question. He didn't answer for a couple of minutes, awkward silence descending sudden and deep between us.

Finally he spoke, but his voice had lost the joy that had come so easily before.

"I lost my wife and baby in the cholera epidemic. That was about ten years before the Bent's gave up their fort on the old trail. They moved about forty-nine or fifty, I figure."

"That was the year of the gold rush. I'll bet you saw lots of people move to California." I was trying to divert his attention from his grief but could tell the spark had left him. I don't even know if he'd heard me. He didn't comment as he stared into the coals, his eyes empty and blank.

After a few minutes, I shifted and tried again. "Will there be guard duty for the teamsters?"

He shook his head. "No. There's little chance of attack this close to the settlements. We'll start guard duty farther out on the plains. Wilmington will decide when." He was silent for a moment and then looked straight at me. I could read the deep sorrow in his eyes.

"Jason, don't mind me. I'm just an old man who's very tired. I've driven wagons on this trail for many years now, maybe too many. It's obvious to everyone that I'm too old to do it alone anymore. Your help is needed, and I know it."

He paused and I squirmed, not sure what to say.

With a grunt, Cal stood. "I'll say good night now." He walked to the rear of the wagon and then disappeared under it with his bedroll.

I noticed something dark, a bundle he'd left on the ground. I grinned when I recognized the blanket.

Retrieving it, I curled with the old log at my back and leaned on one arm, staring into the dying flames. This was the warmest I'd been in three nights.

With a sigh, I rolled over and tucked the blanket around me. Clasping my hands behind my head, I stared up at the sky. The stars glittered and a low wind moaned through the trees by the stream.

My thoughts drifted to Pa, and again I shoved them back, afraid to think on them. I was fed and warm. I would be grateful for that tonight.

I thanked God for bringing me to Cal and then said a prayer for the old man. "Well, Lord, you know all things, and I don't figure it an accident that I'm here."

I yawned and nestled down in the grass, lids half closed as I scanned the heavens. "Show me what you would have me do. Your will be done."

CHAPTER 3

I awoke and for an instant wasn't sure where I was. Then the canopy of darkness and the dim outline of the big freight wagon brought me back. My breath came in small white puffs in the crisp air. I reached an arm from under my blanket and poked a stick into the ashes. Blowing gently, my efforts exposed embers glowing red. I blew again and ash stirred, revealing more live coals. Soon, a tiny flame licked the stick, and a small fire flickered alive.

After adding more fuel, I pushed the coffeepot toward the flame and waited. It'd been half full when I went to sleep.

Finally, unable to put it off any longer, I rolled from my blanket, fully dressed except for my shoes.

Movement at nearby wagons told me the camp was coming to life. I added water to the pot, and folding my blanket, draped it around my shoulders, shivering in the dark. Grabbing the lead ropes, I headed for the stock corral.

I waded into the throng and located Cal's oxen. It took only a few minutes to guide them from the enormous herd of livestock. Other teamsters were doing the same as me, rounding up their animals for the day's work.

I led the four cattle to our wagon, and Cal grinned at me, a wooden spoon in one hand. "Good morning, sunshine." He turned back to the skillet. The smell of frying bacon beckoned.

"I'm glad you finally rolled out of bed," I teased as I tied the oxen to the wagon wheel.

Cal helped me yoke one team and move them into position. He returned to the fire while I wrestled the second pair into place. By the time we were ready to move out, breakfast was ready.

We ate standing up in the manner of the early morning camper and soon emptied our plates and stowed the cleaned dishes in the wagon. Later, when Wilmington rode by, Cal sat on the wagon seat while I stood by the lead team.

The train captain looked us over, his eyes widening. His shocked expression pleased me. Some of the other wagons were still yoking their teams.

As Wilmington moved on, I grinned at Cal over my shoulder. He nodded, chuckling softly in the dim light.

All the stars were gone now except the brightest one—the morning star— shining on a blue velvet back drop, a rosy pink in the eastern sky.

When the wagon in front of us started to move, I cracked the long whip and watched the oxen strain. The heavy wagon wheels turned. Another day of travel began.

Moving helped take the chill from me, but I could still see my breath. Occasionally, I caught Cal watching me as I walked alongside the slow-moving oxen. We'd known each other for only a day, yet I wondered if he sensed the kindred bond I felt growing between us. Did he know how much I needed him?

I looked at Cal from the corner of my eye, not surprised to catch him observing me in return. Did he sense the spiritual differences between us? It seemed we were both watching to see what the Lord would do.

Slowly, the day dawned. A hundred and ten prairie schooners comprised a big train and required several hundred animals to keep the wagons moving. At least a hundred and thirty men were in the train. I even noticed one man with his young son.

When I threw my blanket in the wagon, Cal said nothing. I wondered if I should thank him for his thoughtfulness, but he didn't seem the type to want a fuss.

We passed a farm at midmorning, the only one that day. The sun warmed me, despite the constant blowing wind. I knew this was the mild season of the year, and it would only get hotter as the summer approached. But for now, it was still a chilly day in early spring.

I was surprised how quickly we left the rolling hills and rivers of the eastern Kansas plains. To the west lay endless miles of flat grasslands.

I quickly learned how deceptive this was, realizing I only saw the top of the hills as I scanned the horizon. Between them, folds in the land revealed small valleys and places where an entire town might be hidden from view.

Days passed and the trees were soon left behind. Only a rare sentinel could be spotted along some narrow waterway that cut between the hills. The bare, grassy slopes were all around us and it reminded me of what the ocean must be like, an open expanse that appeared endless in every direction. It made me feel small.

The wind blew incessantly, and time dragged on with infinite slowness. It was as if time had no place anymore. All the teamsters knew it would take months to reach Santa Fe, and they had resigned themselves to monotonous daily travel. The oxen plodded patiently on and the wagon wheels turned. Barring any Indian attacks or other major mishaps, they might winter in Santa Fe. If the weather held and they made good time, they might do a quick turnabout and complete the whole trip in one season before winter's storms made plains travel too dangerous.

This also depended on how fast the teamsters could discharge their merchandise in New Mexico and how fast they could acquire another load for the States.

I liked the easy pace, which allowed me to gather buffalo chips for the night's fire. I had little to do other than keep the oxen moving. Cal rested on the wagon seat, dozing in the sun.

I, too, began to sink into the rhythm and felt at peace for the first time in a while. I fooled myself into thinking my tide of calamity had turned. I couldn't be more wrong.

That evening, I took the tired oxen to water again while Cal worked the dinner fire. A lot of the teamsters shared a cooking fire, but it seemed Cal liked to keep his distance from the others.

We fell into a routine. I would fetch the oxen in the morning while Cal prepared a small breakfast. In the evening, I'd take the stock to water and get them to the rope corral. Cal did the few camp chores and stayed close to his wagon.

He showed me his old single shot muzzle loader, and I sometimes took it and walked off from the wagon a little way, hoping to see something to shoot. It wasn't terribly necessary with us having plenty of food already and Cal eating so little, but it made me feel like I was contributing.

I threw myself into the work of the freight wagon and stumbled, exhausted, to my blanket each night. I was pleased no dreams haunted my sleep. Pa was dead now and I could do nothing about it. Moss won't grow on a rolling stone, and neither will I get bogged down considering past events I couldn't change. But I knew the Lord, and he wouldn't allow me to avoid it forever. He wants to grow us up, develop our character. Sooner or later, I would have to confront my fears.

As the weeks sped past, I wrestled with the nagging thought that I was supposed to reflect on the awful night when I'd lost everything. The idea grew like an itch that demanded to be scratched.

The problem was—I didn't want to. I'd found a place where I was safe, fed, left alone. I liked it. Cal never asked me questions, and the other freighters left Cal and me alone.

But God had other plans.

One day, I walked beside the oxen, my whip dangling over my shoulder. The plodding oxen moved slowly and swung their large heads, patient and determined. One step in front of another. The incessant creak of a turning wheel lulled me.

The wagons stretched out ahead of us and a glance at Cal told me he was dozing again, his head bobbing gently with the dip in the road. I wondered how he could keep his seat with such little weight on him. He leaned with the swaying wagon, even in sleep.

A few puffy white clouds dotted the cobalt blue sky, following us like sheep. The grass swayed gently in the breeze, mesmerizing me. Feed wouldn't be an issue for the animals. Spring lay upon the Great Plains, and green grass spread luxuriantly in every direction.

The lazy day moved slowly, but suddenly, I found my mind going down that ugly rabbit hole of memory I had avoided these past few weeks. I stopped my thoughts from heading that way and thought of scripture instead. *Think on things above*, I coached myself. Pa would want me to think on good things. *Fix your eyes on Jesus.*

Heaven, salvation, the cross, Jesus sacrificing himself for me, redemption, grace. God had a purpose for my life. He had good things in store for me. Be patient. Trials build perseverance.

I thought on these things while the wagons rolled. The distant grass bending before each gentle breeze like the ticking of a clock, the pendulum swinging methodically. My eyelids half drooped.

I woke that night so long ago in Missouri to a brilliant moon shining through my window. The glass was closed against the cold of early spring, but the curtains were pulled back, revealing the moon's vivid light spilling across my floor. I lay there listening, alert to what had awakened me. My shoes lay in the white patch that showed on the floor of my tiny room, every crack visible in the hard wooden planks. All was quiet.

Now, I've been a Christian all my life and no longer wonder when I awaken in the middle of the night, attentive and strangely sensitive. Pa had explained long ago that this was the Holy Spirit presenting someone that needs prayer. Often a mere idea appears to the mind's eye and I pray about it. In any case, I lay awake, vigilant, waiting for I knew not what.

Then I heard the horses. The drum of their running hooves grew louder and then they gathered outside. Flinging my blankets from me, I leaped out of bed and quickly dressed.

Pa's bedroom door opened, and I heard his boots on the hallway floor. Someone outside shouted, "Malone!"

I stopped right there. This was going nowhere good—fast.

I shook my head and glanced at Cal. He still sat on the wagon seat, staring at me with narrowed eyes, his weathered face pinched.

I turned away and focused on the wagons ahead. Shocked, I realized we'd traveled a great distance since the last time I was aware of myself. We were cresting a hill I'd never seen before nor did I recognize the surrounding area.

Embarrassed, I shot another sheepish glance at Cal over my shoulder. He still looked at me intently, and I moved forward to the lead team.

I resolved not to think on those thoughts again. It would not help. It couldn't bring Pa back.

Cal said nothing of the incident, although I knew he'd been watching me. Did he guess my anguish? Did he know why I fled Missouri?

That night in camp, I was surprised to see two men standing by the fire when I returned to Cal's wagon. The oxen were watered and secure in the livestock corral like usual, and now for the first time we had company in our camp.

CHAPTER 4

A large, burly teamster with a thick beard pointed at Cal with a tin cup. "Cal, I haven't seen you since Benson's train. I heard you were doing poorly."

Cal saw me as I stepped into the firelight, his eyes widening. "Thompson, this is Jason Malone. He's riding with me."

I shook the big man's hand. He took a sip from his mug before gesturing to his companion. "This is Baldwin."

I offered my hand to Baldwin. He hesitated then shook it. I studied his thin lips and narrow shoulders. His broad forehead curved over his small eyes.

Maybe he sensed my scrutiny, because he looked at me. "Where you from, Malone?" His voice was high-pitched and nasally. He lifted his cup and blew on it, his beady eyes studying me.

"Missouri." I bent to retrieve my coffee cup. I wasn't about to wait for these newcomers to leave before I enjoyed my coffee. I stepped into the shadows, nursing the warm cup.

"Well, they're at least half sensible." Baldwin chuckled without humor. "Missouri should've followed the Confederacy, but at least they're a slave state."

I said nothing, holding my emotions in check. I wasn't going to give this man's stupid opinion a response. I felt Cal's eyes on me, probably wondering if I'd take the bait.

A man in a red-checkered shirt loomed beside the fire. "I heard that, Baldwin. What do you mean about Missouri being smart because they're a slave state?" The man with the red shirt held his own coffee cup, and to my dismay, knelt beside our fire, making himself comfortable as he peered up at Baldwin. The little crowd was growing.

As if on cue, Thompson and Baldwin sat down.

"I mean Missouri is smart not to lie down for that lying, law-changing Lincoln." Baldwin's whiney voice rose. "The Constitution clearly protects slavery. Who is he to say it's good or bad? Our country was founded on principles and the rights of the people. The Supreme Court upheld that slaves are property, and the government is supposed to protect our property."

"But slavery is immoral. No man should be owned by another," Thompson said, as I noticed two more men joined our circle. They stood back a little, listening.

A few men nodded and murmured assent at Thompson's comment, but then Baldwin rose to his feet. "It's the natural way of things. Slavery is even mentioned in the Bible. It's no sin to own slaves. Besides, our laws defend this right. Lincoln doesn't have the authority to tell people what's right and wrong. He's sworn to uphold the Constitution, not create a new one." His face reddened as his temper heated.

I saw three more men standing outside the firelight, edging closer to hear the discussion.

"Well, I for one am glad I'm not back there fighting in the War Between the States. It means nothing to me. I want to freight goods and let well enough alone," Thompson said, crossing his arms over his chest. "Why does the whole country have to go to war over this issue? Most southerners don't even have slaves."

Baldwin stepped forward, spilling his coffee. "That's not what they're fighting about, Thompson." He stood above the fire now, his weak chin outlined in the light. His small eyes bulged. "They're defending the state's right to withdraw from a Union that does not follow the Constitution. Lincoln is breaking the law and the southern states have decided they no longer want to be part of such a country that allows the president to make up his own policy."

I dearly wanted to say something but held my tongue. I glanced at Cal, hoping he would speak up, but then it occurred to me I didn't know which side he would take. Although he'd asked about my thoughts on the topic, he hadn't shared his political views.

"This country is at war to give all men equal rights. Freedom is for all men, and Lincoln is guided by God in attempting to secure this freedom for black Americans."

All eyes turned to stare at me. I don't know how the words came to my lips. I'd told myself I wouldn't join in this debate.

"Americans?" Baldwin nearly screamed the word. "They're from Africa. They're no more Americans than someone from France or England. Or even these redskins on the prairie." He stood tall in front of me now, trying to intimidate me. He failed.

"America has not brought Africans into this country since 1808, so all the current blacks are Americans. Just like when America fought England for our freedom from their tyranny and heavy hand designed to hold America down, the Union is now fighting to make freedom true for all Americans. It's wrong in a country like ours to have slavery. God has blessed this country, and he would have freedom for all men, regardless of the color of their skin."

I don't know when I realized I was facing the crowd outside the ring of firelight, but there I was. Ignoring Baldwin with his small beliefs, I had spoken my thoughts to the whole assembly.

No one spoke for a moment, the tension thick enough to swat with a stick.

"I think the boy's right. Why should we have freedom when others do not?" I felt a thrill go through me as Thompson spoke up.

Baldwin sputtered. "Thompson, you can't be serious. We're a nation of laws. We follow our elected representatives. They have determined slavery is legal. It's not up to us to change something that has been in this country since it was first formed over eighty years ago."

Thompson shrugged. "Times change. It's our responsibility to change with them." He turned to Cal. "Good to see you again, Cal. Good night." He turned and walked from the fire. Baldwin followed, his voice trailing behind him as he argued with Thompson.

The crowd of men drifted away until only Cal and I remained. He stirred the potatoes in the skillet while I poured another cup of coffee. I sat back on my heels, watching him.

The old man glanced up. "I liked what you had to say tonight."

I remained quiet, sipping my drink. I regretted opening my mouth to that idiot Baldwin. Nothing I said was going to change his narrow mind. A fool is right in his own eyes.

Cal returned his attention to the fire, his wooden spoon stirring the food. "Do your political views have anything to do with what happened to your pa back in Missouri?"

His question surprised me, but it shouldn't have. Cal was clever and I knew that. He had a hunch about a seventeen-year-old boy running alone and hungry across the state.

"Yes. Some men don't want other men holding differing opinions. They figure that if you don't agree with them, you should be shot down like a dog. But God knows a man's heart. It's our Lord that we need to please, not men." I spoke softly, unexpected emotion choking me.

He said nothing to this. The fire crackled merrily as we ate in silence. I heard a coyote yelping in the distance. A slight breeze fanned the night air, making the fire flutter and dance.

"Was your pa in the war, then?" His words startled me after such a long silence. I sensed Cal was genuinely curious but didn't want to offend or intrude.

"Pa wanted to join the war from the beginning but felt he couldn't leave me alone. He'd just decided to join up after spring planting this year, figuring I was old enough to hold down the farm while he was away if he helped put a crop in the ground first. He was killed before we could plant."

We had discussed the war many times, but our mistake had been moving to Missouri.

After my mother died, Pa lost his spark for life. Our dream of owning a cattle ranch with some fine stock for breeding horses had rekindled something in him. Maybe because it gave us a plan to work together. A goal. He would've been content to die except he worried about me. "Paul wrote that it is gain to die, to go to heaven," Pa would say. "I understand what he meant. But Paul said he needed to stick around and teach the Word, and I have unfinished business too. I'm eager to go to your ma and sit at the feet of Jesus. But you're young and need looking after. I must think of you. It's what your ma would want."

He would sigh and look intently at me and then shake his head. "My hope is in Jesus, but he has given you to me to watch over and guide. I still have work to do."

The ranch dream gave us a direction, something positive to think and talk about. So we'd moved to a rented farm in Missouri and tried to make a stake for the ranch. I don't know if he'd really loved the idea or if it'd been more for me. Regardless, it consumed me and drove me to work hard, striving to improve our situation for the promised ranch. Maybe now it was not meant to be.

Wilmington strode into our firelight. "Cal, you'll start guard duty tomorrow night. We're far enough from the settlements that nightly guard duty is prudent. You will report to me after we stop tomorrow, and I'll give you your assignment."

Cal nodded and Wilmington moved to the next glow of camp fires.

"You talk a lot about Jesus." Looking up, I saw the bright firelight play on Cal's wrinkled, tired face. "Do you really think there's an answer to the purpose of life?"

His tone held a note of eagerness, like he secretly hoped I could confirm something he longed for.

"Of course. God is the answer," I said quickly, easily. "Without him, we're just like cows. We're born, we eat, we die. In Christ, though, we have the hope of eternal life. He died for us, that we may know God the Father. God loves us and wants us to love him in return. I give every day to him because he gave his son to me. Without Jesus, there's no reason for living. With Jesus, life has purpose."

He poked a stick into the fire. A swarm of sparks fluttered skyward. "I wish I could be sure," he muttered.

"You can," I said. "God doesn't lie. Jesus is truth. Trust in him."

Cal nodded slowly and then looked up suddenly, a gleam in his eyes. "Jason, I've always depended only on myself. Since I lost my family, I've been angry at God for taking them from me. Now I've met you, and you remind me that God has deeper ideas than I do. He wants to grow me, to have me learn dependence on him."

I sat, stunned by his openness and honesty. He continued to stir the fire, his gaze falling once more to the flames. "I've been thinking a lot about God lately. I'm not going to tell you why, but I've even been praying that he'd send a sign, maybe a person, to come along and speak to me."

I knew what he was thinking. It was not an accident I had joined Cal's wagon.

The old teamster looked up at me again, a sad smile playing on his lips. He nodded and then rose to prepare his bedding.

I sat by the dying fire a short time longer wondering what God had planned for me. Pa was gone. Was my dream of a cattle and horse ranch gone too? Did it even matter anymore?

Maybe because of the debate with Baldwin or perhaps it had been the heartfelt talk with Cal, but that night I couldn't keep my thoughts from Pa.

My father raised me to love God and to try and do what was right. Slavery was not right, but we'd spoken our thoughts in a land where folks didn't agree with us.

That night, the nightmare visited me again like an unwelcome relative, known but not liked.

I heard the rider from the darkness shout Pa's name, and I crouched in my room. Our front door opened, its creaking hinges resisting loudly in the still night as I crawled to my windowsill and peered out.

The front yard was bathed in an eerie, unreal white from the bright moon. All could be seen except the details of the riders, who had flour sacks over their heads with holes cut for their eyes. There were eight of them. Great wisps of steam vented from their panting horses.

Again, the leader yelled Pa's name and I saw Pa standing there in the yard. The masked rider spoke. "Malone, Missouri don't want Union men here. You pack up and leave. We support the Confederate States of America and your ideas ain't welcome here."

We owned an old hunting rifle, but Pa was not holding it. He stood alone, facing them, tall in the moonlight.

Pa spoke but I couldn't remember what he'd said. Or I didn't want to.

The rider in the front of the pack pulled a large pistol from his belt, and the barrel spouted red flame.

The roar of the hand gun rang in my ears, and I opened my eyes, blinking in the gray dawn.

Despite the cold, sweat pooled on my forehead. I shivered and lay there a moment, gathering my wits. Why had I allowed myself to think on those dark days?

Sitting up, I tugged on my shoes and then shoved my folded blanket in the wagon.

As I turned away, I saw Cal kneeling against a rock, gagging and coughing.

"Cal, are you all right?" Something held me back, and I watched him from my vantage point at the rear of the wagon.

He stumbled to his feet and wiped his mouth with the back of his hand. A feeble grin creased his leathery face. "I'm okay, Jason." His voice sounded weak and labored. "Must've been something I ate."

He bent and picked up a few sticks at his feet and then walked around camp, peering into the darkness for firewood.

Dread settled within me, an eerie expectancy choking my heart as I watched Cal. I made my way slowly to the stock corral, a confusing anxiety filling me.

My nightmare had frightened me, but I awakened to another nightmare.

CHAPTER 5

Council Grove proved a good resting place with plenty of grazing and water for the stock. The freight train stopped just past the little hamlet on the banks of the Arkansas River and pulled into two parallel lines. The rope stock corral would be within the protection of these two lines.

I hurried to unhitch the oxen and water them, eager to see the little town. This would be the first settlement I'd seen since Westport Landing. Cal was still sitting atop the wooden seat of the wagon when I returned to camp. He looked pale, and I noticed how shapeless his worn shirt fitted his thin frame.

I knew Cal was in bad shape. The old teamster had played down his discomfort, but I could see the truth in his eyes.

In the days following our first conversation about a savior, Cal had become more curious. Like a sinking man grasping for a rope, Cal took to Bible stories I shared. The aged teamster was always eager to hear of God's promises. With his strength ebbing, he strove to know God.

I'd gathered a few sticks and some buffalo chips on the trail, but when I went to retrieve them, Cal shook his head. "Never mind about a fire tonight. I'm treating you to a dinner at the Hays House."

He reached behind the seat and then crawled down from the wagon, stuffing a thick envelope into his back pocket. He didn't protest when I helped him to the ground. I thought to inquire about the soiled letter but then didn't, leaving his business to him.

We walked up the line of wagons until we reached the outskirts of the town. The small prairie village consisted of no more than seven buildings, weathered clapboard structures or canvas-sided tents. The only exception was the Hays House, a framed building with solid hardwood walls.

Larger than the other buildings, it boasted a spacious dining room. As we entered, I hesitated, embarrassed by my shabby appearance. I wrinkled my nose as I remembered my clothes had been washed only once in the past couple of months.

I caught my reflection in the glass of the front window and almost didn't recognize myself. Long hair hung below my collar, curling at the ends. My clothes were little better than rags and I cringed when I saw a tanned knee peeking through the hole in my pants. No one else seemed to mind, however, so I followed Cal inside.

We sat at a long table, and a plump woman with huge arms unloaded a stack of plates before us. She gestured to a steaming pot. "Plenty of stew. Biscuits and potatoes too."

I scooped two huge bowls of stew, and we ate in silence. My eyes drifted around the clean room, marveling at the glass windows, lace curtains, and real wooden chairs—not benches.

Cal didn't eat much, but I was used to that. He must've seen the way I looked at the pie laying on the sideboard, because he ordered us each a slice.

"Something special," he said, winking at me. We drank a pot of coffee before we left the place. I watched Cal pay the woman for our meals, and then we walked out into the fresh evening air. A dove called for its mate, mournful and searching. Locusts whirred from the cottonwood grove beside the river.

"Thanks, Cal. That's the best food I've eaten in a long time." I patted my stomach.

"What?" He feigned offense. "Don't you like my cooking?"

I arched an eyebrow. "Oh, is that what you call it? I thought you were trying to poison me." I stepped from his side, barely evading the slow arc of his arm. He grinned at me.

As we walked toward camp, I soaked in the sights. The little town on the Kansas prairie hummed with lots of people and activity. Indians, soldiers, teamsters, and emigrant families crowded the wooden sidewalks. A blacksmith's hammer rang out, the dusty street full of wagons and animals.

I nodded to one family, a man with three children and a rail-thin wife. The difficulty of their journey reflected in their hollow, wearied eyes. I wondered how far they'd come to be here in Council Grove. I also wondered how much farther they could endure.

"What do you suppose is their story?" I hooked a thumb in their direction as we passed in front of the trading post. "They look beaten."

"Life's hard, I guess." He smiled at me, the grin never reaching his old eyes. "Don't count them out yet. Maybe they're the tough ones who make it."

I tilted my head and glanced at him from the corner of my eye. He just chuckled. "You and I are both men who understand how hard life can be, huh, Jason?" He looked at me with a sad gleam and then nudged me toward the door of the trading post. "Come on. Let's see what's in here."

"I don't have any money," I protested as he shoved me into the large, crowded room.

"Those rags will fall off your backside and the sight'll scare folks. Let's get you a shirt and pants. You can pay me later." He weaved through the narrow aisles, crammed with piled sacks of flour and beans and then stopped to look at folded stacks of clothes on the shelves.

I scanned the room, amazed at the variety of goods. Leather harnesses, clothing, blankets, guns, tools, knives, furs, pickled items in big jars, and small jars of brightly colored candy—barrels and boxes were stacked everywhere. This store in the middle of this endless prairie held more goods than its counterpart in a bigger town.

As I wandered the store and looked at the various things I couldn't afford, I saw Wilmington and Baldwin enter. The wagon captain moved to the counter and gestured to a clerk. "Make sure these newspapers get to Douglas. Tell him Wilmington brought them in." He handed the papers to the young man behind the counter. Not waiting for a reply, he turned to leave when his eye caught mine.

He stopped and stared hard at me, his eyes cold.

"That's the boy I told you about, Captain. He's a Union man." Baldwin said the words like he was calling me something dirty and lowdown.

Wilmington pursed his lips and nodded but didn't say a word. My eyes met his dark gaze and never wavered. Finally, he turned and stalked from the store.

I heard a couple of teamsters talking near me, discussing a new proclamation the President had only recently signed into law. I edged closer, eager to hear anything of significance.

"I tell you it's true, Larry," the first man said. "Anyone can claim land, a hundred and sixty acres, and if he can live on it for five years, the land is his."

His companion shook his head. "Now why would the government want to give free land away? It doesn't make sense."

The first teamster bobbed his head. "It makes perfect sense if you want to get Americans to leave the crowded east and settle the west. These settlers build and improve upon the land. They'll create farms and towns. I think it's smart and I'm glad Lincoln signed it."

The two men walked out of earshot and I watched Cal pay the clerk for his purchases. Still watching the old man, I saw he hesitated a moment before pulling the thick envelope from his back pocket and handing it to the clerk. Turning, Cal touched my elbow and guided me from the busy store.

Back at camp, I put on my new clothes. My old shirt really was a rag and I couldn't keep it. It was beyond being patched again. But I'd hang onto and repair my pants.

Cal was due on guard duty in a half hour, but I'd been pulling his shift for weeks now. I sat by our wagon, holding Cal's old hunting rifle. We'd decided not to waste our small pile of firewood and reserved it, instead, for breakfast. Cal had already climbed under the wagon and was stretched out on his blankets.

A frog croaked as the sun dipped over the horizon. The wind had died down and the hum of mosquitoes and locusts filled the air. The grove of elms along the river stood motionless in the still night, not even a leaf stirring.

A few scattered stars dotted the darkening sky, a foreshadowing of what was to come.

I watched the pink, orange, and red of the reflections in the clouds as the shadows around me grew. The scene felt peaceful and I scanned the open prairie, enjoying the quiet.

"Jason, what do you want out of life?" Cal's voice broke my reverie. I'd forgotten he lay behind me under the wagon. A bat swooped and climbed into the dim light of dusk. Probably feeding on the mosquitoes.

"You already know what I'm going to say." I didn't look at him. He'd asked me numerous questions about my dream and what I hoped to achieve. He seemed almost obsessed with my future and never grew tired of me telling this story.

Cal didn't respond and I grinned, knowing he wouldn't be satisfied until I told it again.

I chewed my lip for a moment. It was still difficult to say the words out loud. "When last I spoke with Pa, he told me what to do. He'd always wanted a piece of his own land. So, go west and build a fine ranch, he told me. We lived on rented land in Missouri and it always bothered Pa it was not our own. He'd helped raise good horses in Ireland and had an eye for fine stock. He taught me what to look for and said I had the eye, too, like him. We had tried to farm to get some money together to start a ranch, but it never came to anything. After Ma died in Pennsylvania, it kind of took the starch out of him."

Pausing, I looked around. Other men were walking to Wilmington to receive their duty assignments, and I would have to go soon too.

"That's your father's dream. What's yours?"

I nodded at Cal's persistence. He was hidden in the shadows beneath the wagon and I couldn't see him, but I could hear his shallow breathing, as if he struggled through clenched teeth. I pretended not to notice.

"That's just it. It's my dream too. Only I didn't know it until I'd thought on it. But Pa would've been the one to accomplish it. Pa was strong."

I rubbed the back of my neck. "I don't know anymore, Cal. I hope I can do it. Pa told me God has a purpose for me, and my gift with horses is part of it. He told me it was no accident I have the love of good horses in me."

The old man remained quiet for so long, I figured he'd fallen asleep. I was grateful he could get some rest.

I reached for the wagon wheel to stand when he spoke. "I have no family, but I've enjoyed having you along on this trip. I think your dream will come true."

I hesitated and then straightened. What did that mean? How could he know? "I'm going on guard duty. You rest easy." I moved away from the wagon and said my nightly prayer for the old man.

CHAPTER 6

I enjoyed guard duty. It gave me lots of time to think and pray. Besides, the nights on the plains were glorious. I had never seen so many stars.

The wagon captain saw me coming and his eyes narrowed as he studied me. "Watch the stock within the corral," Wilmington growled and looked away.

As I turned, he added, "How's Cal tonight?"

I stopped and faced him, sensing more in the question. One end of his mouth twitched. "Doesn't look like he'll make it to Santa Fe."

I shrugged, playing it off as if his comment didn't hurt. I knew he hated that I stood Cal's guard shift, but I wouldn't give him the satisfaction of seeing the effect his cold words had on me.

He scowled at my apparent indifference, but wasn't done yet. "You know he's driving one of my wagons?"

I walked away, feeling uneasy, his eyes boring a hole in my back. I moved to my position near the stock.

Only the night before, Cal shared that Wilmington had grudgingly given him a wagon to drive when he couldn't find another driver. Cal had no investment in the train. Why he'd been so eager to join this freight train, I had no idea, but I knew Wilmington did not like us.

A few lonely campfires burned low around the wagons, but I didn't watch them. My eyes were on the heavens. The single evening star had multiplied a thousand-fold, and the sky was now covered in tiny, bright lights. How creative God is, I thought. Who else would've conceived the idea of stars? Pa told me God had named each of them too.

As I stood gazing at the sky, my conversation with Cal unsettled me. Pa had left me with a sacred charge to follow my dream, but could I do it? He said God had a special plan for my life.

I kicked at a tuft of grass. Then what was I doing on this wagon train to Santa Fe? Was I putting off the course I was destined to follow? Or was this part of that course? Only God knew.

A little after midnight, my shift over, I returned to the wagon. Retrieving my blanket, I rolled in it and clasped my hands behind my head.

Despite my fatigue, I thought of the trail ahead. Cal told me Old Bent's Fort was located at the crossing of this river, but the fort was burned down and abandoned now. The other teamsters spoke of the train following the Arkansas River for a distance.

I remembered hearing tales of William and Charlie Bent when I was younger. They'd been fur trappers and traders and had a trading post on the Santa Fe Trail near the crossing of the Arkansas.

Yawning, I pulled the blanket higher and allowed my mind to relax. I would need sleep for what lay ahead.

We traveled over the prairie, each day like the last. Never did see any Indians and Cal remarked that I should be glad we hadn't.

"I know you've been over this trail a hundred times, so you must have some good Indian raid stories," I pestered him one evening. "Tell me one."

We were camped on a flat, wide open spot where an attack would be difficult. There was little cover for anyone to use in approaching our camp and I'd been startled when a stagecoach passed us the previous day, heading east. I wasn't sure other folks used the Old Trail.

I'd gotten used to not seeing anyone else on the trail, and the thought of an Indian attack thrilled me.

Cal sat propped against the wagon wheel. Deep shadows lined his face in the glow of the camp fire. Had they been there the entire trip? I didn't seem to recall so many.

I could read the pain in his old eyes, and if it were even possible, he was eating less. Gaunt, pale cheeks hung on his thin face.

"Indian attacks are not important to you now," he said evasively, taking slow labored breaths. "You need to be thinking of your future."

He held a cup of coffee. A thin tendril of steam rose from the mug, and I noticed he never lifted it. I wondered if he simply liked to hold something warm in his hands.

"But I don't know what my future is," I grumbled, disappointed at not hearing an exciting Indian story. "Or maybe I should say I don't know when it'll begin."

I sat on the ground near him, running a cleaning rag through the barrel of his old hunting rifle. Old it might be, but it shot accurately. I'd downed an antelope that very afternoon.

Despite the fresh antelope meat, Cal had only tasted it and then put his fork aside. I'd shared most of the meat with some of the other teamsters.

"You've already begun your journey," he barked gruffly. "I needed help on this trip, and you needed to get out of Missouri. It was my plan to make a final trip onto the plains, and I've done it. I knew I would never reach the end."

I tensed, not sure I wanted to hear anymore.

"The Lord brought us together, Jason. I thought God had abandoned me, but you've proven to be a real gift. Thank you for all your help. Now, what are you going to do?"

I slid the ramrod back into place beneath the barrel and laid the cleaned weapon aside. I sighed. "I don't know. I've been praying for guidance from the Holy Spirit, and nothing's come to me. I don't know what direction God wants me to take."

Bending forward, I took another antelope steak from the fire and tore it apart with my fingers, stuffing little pieces into my mouth.

Cal looked at me with disgust. "Well, you eat like an Indian, I'll say that for you."

I chewed the tender meat slowly, savoring the rich taste. "What do you think I should do?"

He shook his head. "Oh, no. Don't listen to me. I wasted years trying to figure things out on my own, my way. It didn't work. Trust God. Always trust God. I stopped trusting God, and that got me nowhere. Yet, despite my lack of faith, he was faithful."

He paused, squinting at me. "Remember, you told me that he'll show you a path. Well, I believe he will. Be patient and pray. You young ones are always in a hurry. Prepare your heart for the adventure that's coming."

"Adventure?" I stopped chewing and stared at him, intrigued. I was familiar with hard work and doing what I thought God would have me do, but I never thought about it as an adventure. Was it possible I could think about my life that way?

"Yes, adventure." Cal's voice had dropped to a gruff whisper, and I detected his impatience with me, as if he wanted to impart some vital information to me. "God has a plan for you, and it's a good plan, one designed especially for you. Trust him. Your adventure has already begun, but you're used to doing what your pa says, waiting for his guidance. Now you're on your own, and you must make your own decisions. To say you are to begin a ranch is too vague, too simple. You need details worked out. Where will this happen? You can't do it alone and you'll need a partner. What about the initial stock you'll need? A good stud costs a lot of money."

I squirmed under his wise business assault. He asked questions I hadn't thought of. He was right. I'd always leaned on Pa to make these decisions, and now he was gone. Our intent to farm and make enough money to begin a ranch had failed. Did God have another route for me to take?

"Your adventure has already begun," he repeated hoarsely, his voice straining. "You don't realize it. But, you will soon, I'm sure."

He squinted then and his face contorted with pain.

"Cal?" My hand gripped his shoulder. "Are you all right? Is there anything I can do for you?"

I cursed myself for such a stupid question. Whatever he suffered from was beyond my ability to fix.

The pain seemed to pass, and he slowly relaxed again. He looked at me with warm, soft eyes. "You already have, Jason. You have no idea how much you've already done."

He sagged against the wheel, and I nodded toward his blankets, already spread beneath the wagon. "Climb into your blankets, old timer. I'll pull our guard duty. Get some rest." He nodded and without rising, he put his cup down and crawled under the wagon. I glanced at his still full coffee cup and frowned, then went in search of Wilmington.

He gave me my guard station, pursing his lips tightly as he glanced toward our wagon. I didn't bother replying to his questioning look.

I spent the next few hours contemplating Cal's rapid spiritual growth. Mundane topics like weather and food had been replaced with long conversations about spiritual truths. Cal had an intense hunger to learn all about God.

Though not a Bible scholar, I was educated by a man who'd spent his whole life studying the scriptures. Pa had taught me much, and now Cal drank the little wisdom I possessed like a man dying of thirst.

I shifted uneasily in the darkness, my stomach tightening into knots as I considered Cal's challenge to me. How was I going to begin a ranch? I felt ridiculous only pondering this now, so used was I to Pa's help and counsel. I wasn't a boy anymore and I needed to figure out the answers to Cal's questions. How would I actually *begin* a horse ranch? I started praying.

The next day, a gentle, persistent rain began, making everything wet and slippery. Cal sat on the wagon seat, his blanket around his small, bony shoulders. He wore his hat pulled low down and tried to keep me company, but soon the rain drove him under the canvas cover.

The rain didn't feel cold as long as I was walking and steam rose from the backs of the oxen beside me. I tried to dodge puddles in the trail, but my shoes were soaked through. An annoying bead of water danced at the tip of my nose and my hair lay plastered to my head.

The gray sky hovered above like a dirty sheet, but the rain didn't concern me. Cal's condition did.

The Rocky Mountains loomed in the west but gave me no comfort. We would skirt southwest of them soon as we followed the trail through Raton Pass to Fort Union.

There'd been talk of taking the Cimarron cutoff to Fort Union to avoid Raton Pass, saving us a hundred miles of travel, but that way was more dangerous with less water. Wilmington decided we'd take the longer, safer route.

Peals of thunder rolled in the distance, and I saw a streak of lightning a time or two. The storm, a gentle summer rain, held no real danger for the wagon train, but I noticed Cal growing worse by the hour. He'd taken to coughing something fierce, and I saw bloody froth on his lips.

As the sun went down that night, the rain stopped and we camped at the ford of the Arkansas River, near the burned and darkened stones of the old fort.

I took the oxen to the stock corral as I did every evening. When I did so, I glanced over at the remains of the old trading post. The walls were broken in some places and there was no roof. It'd been burned by Bent more than ten years earlier when he'd abandoned the place.

I studied the broken building, an unaccountable sadness filling me. It looked dead. No life remained within it, and I wondered at my confusing sorrow. It was, after all, only an old fort.

I trudged through the mud and the wet grass back to our camp and found Cal sprawled beside our wagon, his hand clutching his blankets. He'd tried to pull them under the wagon, but his strength failed.

I shaped his bedding into a comfortable nest under the big wagon and picked him up, surprised how little he weighed. He shivered but his body felt both hot and wet as I laid him in his blankets.

Fever burned in his old eyes, but he smiled at me weakly. "Don't worry about me," he whispered. "I'm going home. God is waiting for me, and I can't wait to see my savior Jesus. You still have unfinished business. Work hard and build that ranch. It's not only yours and your pa's dream anymore."

I bit my lip, anxiety working through me as I knelt beside my friend. What was he talking about? Was he delirious? I listened to him with only half an ear as I worked to cover him and make him comfortable.

I could hear the teamsters around me setting up camp. An axe sounded nearby, and I knew cooking fires would soon be going. I worried how to make Cal more comfortable. I retrieved my blanket and covered him with it.

I sat with him and quietly prayed. Softly, I sang hymns and the melody made him smile. His eyes fluttered open. "Jason? I came out here to die alone and instead I'm with a friend and the Lord." He tried to chuckle but didn't have the strength. A cough wracked his thin body.

The sun set over the mountains, shadows merging into the dark green grass of the sodden plains. Stars peeked between the floating gray clouds. Muted movements of the teamsters around me kept me company as I sat beside Cal, pensive and vigilant.

This was not the first man I'd sat by and watched die. I had been there, too, when Pa breathed his last.

My heart swelled and my throat clenched. Why was God doing this to me again? Why had I been chosen to watch men die? What was the purpose here?

I continued to pray as Cal went in and out of consciousness. Part of the time he would rest easy and then he'd roll his head from side to side, thrashing in pain. His grasp became so weak that, eventually, it was only I who kept our hands together.

His eyelids fluttered open again. Thompson's camp fire cast a dull glow into the darkness under the wagon. Cal's gaze searched for me.

"I'm here, Cal. Rest easy. I'm here." I pushed his gray hair back from his damp brow and pulled his covers even closer around his frail body.

"Jason, your life is now mine. Live for me and your pa. Live our dream. Serve God. I will find you, Jason. Trust me, I will find you," he whispered, his words barely audible.

I put my ear close to his lips, but he said no more.

For a long time, he lay there, firelight dancing in his open eyes as he stared at the wagon above him.

I knew he was gone, but I waited, hoping I was wrong.

Cal's final words made little sense and I half believed they'd been the delirious ranting of a dying man.

Footsteps thumped in the wet grass behind me. "Cal, where're you fools?"

Wilmington. I exhaled deeply, my stomach twisting into knots. I'd forgotten guard duty.

CHAPTER 7

"I'm under here." With a final glance at Cal, I crawled from under the wagon.

"You never came to me about guard duty, and now I find you in bed asleep," Wilmington blustered, his face reddening in the firelight.

I stood erect to face him. This man had always been so cruel to Cal and me. I didn't understand him. We always pulled our weight around camp, but he'd never given us a chance.

I took a deep breath, calming myself. "I wasn't sleeping. Cal's dead. He just passed away."

Wilmington hesitated and then spoke again, his voice lower. "So, he finally died, did he? Well, he lasted longer than I expected." He looked at his boots then swung his gaze back to me with narrowed eyes. "No matter. You have guard duty now," he ordered gruffly.

I stared at the unfeeling man and wondered again about his hatefulness. "Cal just passed away and you want me to pull guard duty?" Thompson stepped from the darkness and stood beside me. "Captain, I'll pull his duty tonight."

"No!" the wagon master thundered. "We're in Indian Territory and need every man to pull his duty."

Clenching my teeth, I crossed my arms over my chest. "I'll do my duty, Wilmington, but I think this is awfully disrespectful. Cal was a good man." I couldn't keep the bitterness from my voice.

Wilmington stared at me, his eyes glinting in the dim light of Thompson's campfire. He arched an eyebrow and hooked a thumb toward the rope corral. "Watch the stock." With that the big man spun on his heel and strode into the shadows.

Thompson shrugged. "Sorry, Jason." He walked back to his fire.

I rummaged in the wagon for the old rifle. Without a glance toward the small covered form under the wagon, I walked to my post near the stock corral.

The enclosure was made of rope to keep the animals in a certain vicinity, but they easily could've escaped if they'd wanted to. Usually after a long day of pulling heavy wagons, the oxen gave little trouble.

I barely noticed the cold standing near the herd of draft animals as my thoughts whirled. Cal was dead, and not long ago Pa had died. What now? What was the Lord trying to teach me?

In a short time, Cal and I had grown close. He'd been like a wise and caring grandfather, and I knew I'd miss him. For a brief span of time, he'd given me a place to belong, at a time when I dearly needed one. I shook my head, remembering his final words. What had he meant when he'd said he would find me? He'd been out of his head, no doubt. His words held no meaning to me.

I looked up at the huge storm clouds passing overhead. Thousands of tiny lights shimmered above between dark clouds drifting ominously, the storm still threatening. Although I couldn't see the moon, I glimpsed its radiance reflected along the tops of the clouds. Occasionally, they would bunch and blot the light from above.

"What now?" I searched the skies. "Sovereign God, guide my steps. I feel so lost and alone. What's your plan for me?"

I waited, my gaze searching above and within. Expectancy filled me. Surely God would answer.

I clenched my fists and squinted at the clouds. "Please, Lord," I pleaded, my voice cracking with emotion.

I thought of Pa's advice to always lean on scripture. Wait on the Lord. Be still before the Lord. The Lord says, I will never leave you or forsake you. I am with you to the ends of the earth.

Again I prayed, waiting, hoping, yearning for his presence, his peace, his love.

Yet I heard nothing.

CHAPTER 8

Thompson helped me bury Cal a hundred yards from the wagons where Cal could watch over his beloved trail. It took little effort to carry his thin form to the top of the nearby knoll. I wrapped him in his blanket and laid him in the grave we hastily dug in the soft turf. It took only a few minutes to fill it in.

I threw the shovel to the ground and bowed my head. Thompson bowed his as well and I spoke. "Dear Lord, I pray you give this good man rest. Thanks that I got to know him. He loved you, Lord. Welcome him home."

Wagons lurched into line as Thompson and I rushed down the hill. In the dim light, I could make out a couple men at my wagon with the oxen already in position.

Wilmington, with Baldwin beside him, towered above a pile of goods. As I drew nearer, I recognized my gear and some of Cal's stuff.

The wagon leader spoke as we neared. "I'm putting you out of the train. Take Cal's things. You're entitled to nothing more."

I stopped, not surprised. This man never liked Cal. He'd liked me even less. Baldwin crossed his arms and nodded.

Deep shadows sprawled across the prairie. Slowly, the eastern sky grayed as a fine mist began to fall, forcing me to wipe the wetness from my eyes.

"You can't do that, Captain," Thompson protested, advancing a step, looking from me to Wilmington to his wagon. I knew he needed to get his teams yoked and moving. Already the train was in motion.

Wilmington sneered, his gaze hard. "I had a deal with Cal to drive my spare wagon. I had no deal with this boy. Besides, he wouldn't listen to my orders last night until I threatened him. I need immediate obedience from my teamsters for the safety of the entire train."

Baldwin nodded again, a wide grin on his narrow face. I wanted to kick him.

Thompson must've guessed what I was thinking. He looked at me sternly and shook his head. Anger surged inside me, making me want to hit something, but I didn't want to make things worse.

Thompson grabbed Wilmington's arm, drawing attention away from me.

"Can the boy ride with me then?" Thompson glanced at his wagon, but I already knew what Wilmington would say.

"No, he's out of the train. Thompson, get your wagon ready to roll."

Thompson hesitated, his eyes narrowing with concern before he finally turned away.

I tilted my head. "What am I going to do out here alone?" I didn't like Wilmington, but even without Cal, the freight train would be preferable to being left on the prairie. Fear filled me, gnawing at me as it had back in Missouri. Alone again, belonging nowhere, I cringed.

Baldwin chuckled and Wilmington shrugged. "No matter to me." He hooked a thumb toward his partner. "Baldwin here will drive this wagon, and you can rot for all I care, although I will give you Cal's small food stores." Wilmington stared at me, a challenging look in his cold eyes, as if waiting for me to question his authority.

When I said nothing, he turned and marched into the morning gloom.

Baldwin sneered at me again and then strode to the wagon. He climbed up the wagon wheel to the high seat. "Union man," he muttered as he lifted the long leather whip.

He glanced at me from his high perch, and I wondered if he considered using the lash on me. Then he scowled and shouted at the oxen as he snapped the whip over their backs.

I watched the heavy wagons lumber into line and travel off down the trail. The big hulking freighters moved along at a good pace for oxen, and except for one last look from Thompson, were soon just a moving line in the early gray dawn of an ugly day.

I watched them go for a few minutes more and then, realizing the futility, stooped and picked up Cal's gear. I shoved his hat on before hiking back up the knoll and stood beside his fresh grave, not knowing where else to turn.

From this vantage point, I saw the freight train cross the Arkansas and continue down the Santa Fe Trail.

Should I follow them? I could easily keep up with the pace of the oxen. The idea somehow angered me, though. I didn't want to give Wilmington or Baldwin the satisfaction of knowing I was trailing them. How pathetic would that be to sit in the prairie outside the wagons and look in at them? Besides, what would I do for food and water? I wouldn't be able to use the teamster's stores to feed myself.

I pushed the toe of my shoe into the mud. No, I decided, I would not trail them. Pa had always told me I was not alone if I knew Jesus. I looked up at the swollen gray clouds. "You love me. This is not a surprise to you," I said, gesturing at the emptiness around me. "You have a plan for me. There's something you want me to do. Please show me. Whatever you have for me, guide me to it."

I wanted to sit down and cry, but the grass was still wet. I glowered, wondering if I'd made a mistake when I'd joined the wagon train back in Missouri. Should I have taken the road to the north? Had I not understood the Holy Spirit correctly?

I surveyed the plains around me and could see nothing but gray skies and dark prairies. The river poured from the Rockies, and my gaze followed the line of trees that bordered the ribbon of water. Numerous side canyons branched from the larger valley, like fingers from a hand.

I chewed the inside of my cheek. As long as I stayed here, I would have an ample supply of water, but there was no building or tent to shield me from the weather.

Old Bent's Fort stood nearby, but it'd been destroyed years ago. Little remained that could help me.

I had a good view of the surrounding area on this knoll where Thompson and I had buried Cal. I turned to look again at the mountains behind me. The bulk of the Rocky Mountains loomed huge in the distance, but these were the foothills before me, stretching vast and rugged to the taller peaks beyond. I saw some lone trees and many rocky outcroppings, but not a soul in sight. Not even a rabbit or a bird. They would probably be holed up in this weather.

I stared to the east where a dim line above the horizon revealed a shrouded rising sun. Missouri lay that way. Would God bring me from there only to let me die on the cold prairies? God's ways are not my ways, I reminded myself, wondering if he would go to such wasted effort.

I shrugged. Who was I to tell God what he should do? I gritted my teeth and nodded slightly. His will, not mine.

I turned away and searched the surrounding land.

Suddenly, I noticed a thin wisp of smoke curled against the dull sky. I squinted. It seemed to be a couple of miles back in the hills, but I couldn't be sure. Were my eyes playing tricks on me? Distance was deceptive in this weather.

The fire, if it was indeed a fire, wouldn't belong to any friends, but my options were now gone. I decided to investigate. Maybe they had something I could trade for, maybe a horse.

I glanced down at the gravesite at my feet, tied my bundle of gear with a piece of rawhide cord, and started to walk.

The gear under my left arm, the gun in my right, I strode toward the hills not knowing what to expect. There was nothing for me on the prairie, and to stay here meant certain death.

What if another wagon train came by? Surely they would let me accompany them on the way to Fort Union or maybe even Santa Fe. I paused, considering this, then walked on. It could be weeks before another train or stage came along.

I could see the thread of the Arkansas through the cottonwoods and elms as I started into the foothills, leaving the open prairie behind.

Deep ravines carved by heavy rains and rocky outcroppings dotted the land making the going rougher. I understood why the river ford was farther down on the plains. The Bents had wisely chosen the site for their trading post.

I sure missed Pa. My friendship with Cal had delayed some of the loss I'd felt after his death, but now I missed them both.

I shook my head, forcing myself to stay focused. Dwelling in the past would only lead me astray, I knew from experience. Allow the transforming of your mind, St. Paul had cautioned. I knew he was right. To discipline my mind to ponder on good things, encouraging scriptures, or prayer was what St. Paul had meant. Keep my eyes on Jesus.

In an hour, I crouched on a low rise of ground. Ahead of me was a small group of people sitting around a dying fire. I should say dead fire, as only wisps of occasional smoke wafted from gray ashes. Near them lay a body.

From this distance I couldn't make out details but thought them to be Indians. I watched from my perch for another half hour. Nothing happened. They appeared to be content to sit in the rain, so I decided they weren't threatening or warlike.

I straightened stiffly, my clothes saturated from the constant drizzle, and warily started down the low hill toward the small group.

Several in the group turned their heads and saw me approach but made no move to attack or defend themselves. Either they believed me to be no real threat or believed they could handle me. Whatever the case, I walked toward the smoking fire until I stood within thirty feet of them.

I studied them. They looked pitiful, sitting there in the rain. Four bedraggled Indians—an old man, a young boy, a teenage girl, and a woman, probably the mother of the two younger ones—their dark hair plastered to their heads. A dead man lay to one side.

I glanced at him, amazed to see he was white.

I titled my head. The younger Indians showed signs of white blood. The women wore buckskin dresses and the old man and the boy had cotton shirts with buckskin breeches.

I moved closer. When I was within fifteen feet of the small circle, I spoke.

"Hello," I said, my voice loud in the gentle rain. "I am Jason." I tapped my chest while I spoke, hoping they might understand me.

I suddenly felt like an idiot. What did I hope to gain from these people? They looked as bad off as me.

The young girl—she looked about my age—glanced at her companions. No one spoke so she turned back to me. Her finely chiseled features drew my attention and I stared, studying her high cheekbones and her small, pert nose. Wet, raven black hair framed her beautiful face. Her large, dark eyes pierced me in return. I turned away quickly, feeling the heat rise up my neck.

"What do you want?" Her unexpected words, spoken with a highland brogue, caught me off guard. I wanted to ask about the Scottish accent but thought better of it. "I'm alone. I have nowhere to go." The more I said, the more foolish I felt. What was I going to do? I was out on the prairie all alone and hungry, wet, and cold, but these people appeared to be in the same predicament.

"Well, we're alone too. Go on about your business and leave us." The pretty girl spoke, a gruff tone to her voice. I thought maybe I didn't like her much after all.

I hesitated, shifting my weight. "Are you going to just sit here in the rain?"

I didn't want to prod, but I was desperate. Perhaps they could give me some hope or direction. Maybe they knew of some place or shelter.

The girl frowned. "My father has just died, and we're mourning. Leave us now," she repeated and then bowed her head.

"Do you know of any place near here where I can find shelter from the rain?" I persisted. I didn't want to be rude, but I had nowhere to go and was in no hurry to get there.

The girl shot me a scornful glare but said no more. "There are some cliff dwellings in that canyon back yonder." The mother pointed to a side canyon. The old man looked at her sharply, and I read the surprise in his eyes.

I hesitated again, glanced up the little canyon, and then back to the circle of wet people. "Are you folks going there?" I didn't want to be alone.

"My daughter's husband has been killed by Kiowa. We are mourning," the old man explained. I badly wanted to inquire how long mourning would take but chose not to ask.

CHAPTER 9

I looked over my shoulder once more before plunging into the brush-choked canyon. Branches tore at me and rocks and deadfalls tripped me. I had to rest often as I climbed over and around boulders. I kept a vigilant eye on the sides of the little canyon, searching for the cliff dwellings.

The narrow opening of the unimpressive canyon deceived me with its low bushes and a few stunted pine trees. It widened as I traveled on, and a small stream meandered down the center. Probably dry in late summer, it ran strong now between its low banks.

Game trails seemed plentiful. I saw signs of deer, rabbits, and even the markings of a bear.

Finally, up on one side of the canyon, I spotted handmade walls of rock nestled in a deep recess. Carved by countless years of wind and rain, a hollowed space had formed in the cliff face. I scrambled over tangled and fallen debris and came out of the brush on a sandy bench above the little stream.

Tilting my head back, I studied the cliff dwellings. Dark eyes of vacant windows stared down at me, and I shivered, wondering if ghosts of the ancient structure were watching me.

Thunder rumbled, echoing in the canyon, and I knew the storm was still close. As if on cue, the drizzle turned heavier and I wiped the rain from my eyes.

My searching gaze discovered foot holds cut into the sandstone face of the cliff. A crude ladder led to the dry, wide shelf above.

I scurried up these steps until I stood on a low shelf under the protection of the overhanging cliff. Walls of stacked stone formed barriers for individual rooms with the overhang serving as a single roof. Cold and wet, I stood and watched the rain cascade over the cliff above, a thin watery veil between me and the canyon beyond.

In the farthest recess of the hollow, I found a small spring. It seeped from a crack in the wall into a handmade catch basin. Pieces of pottery lay scattered along the back wall and I picked one up, studying the clay pot carefully, wondering if it could still hold water. I might need it.

Six small, dark doorways peered back at me, and I explored each of these little rooms in turn. These walled rooms would provide some kind of shelter.

One of the smaller rooms would serve me well. Dust lay thickly over everything, but I cleaned it out as best I could and then moved my few belongings into the small structure.

In one of the other rooms, I found where an animal had built a nest and was living there still. Probably a pack rat, judging by the nest.

Taking some of the sticks from the nest, I built a small fire back in my little stone room. A ring of rocks marked where previous fires had been, dark stains on the roof revealing where the smoke had filtered from the lodge.

The little blaze cheered me. The roll of distant thunder didn't bother me now as I wiped Cal's gun dry and leaned it in a corner.

Walking to the small spring at the back of the overhang, I rinsed and filled one of the larger clay pots I'd discovered earlier. Returning to my room, I rummaged in Cal's things until I found the battered coffeepot. Pouring water from the clay pottery, I filled the pot and pushed it into the coals. Soon, the boiling water sang and I added coffee.

What a difference a fire and a hot cup of coffee makes! Steam rose from my damp clothes as the fire slowly dried me.

The smell of frying bacon soon filled my small room. There wasn't much of it and it didn't figure to last, but I would enjoy it today. I began to feel better about my situation. I still didn't know what I would do, but for right now, I was satisfied to be fed and out of the rain.

As I began again to consider the Indians huddled in the rain, I frowned. The woman already knew of this place, so they could find it if they wanted. Perhaps I should help them, tell them of the exact location. Would they want my help?

As I sat there sipping coffee, the thought nagged at me. I chewed the inside of my cheek, pondering. I glanced out the tiny window to the wet canyon below. What a dreary day.

I banked my fire and donned my hat. I hated getting wet again just as I was drying off, but I retraced my steps down the stone ladder to the canyon floor.

A dim path, worn deep into the sand, showed along the canyon wall. I followed it, glad to discover an easier route.

They were still there, huddled around the dead fire. I stood beside the old man and cleared my throat. Rain dribbled from my hat brim and I wanted to return to the dry cliff dwelling.

"It's dry under the overhang." I pointed back up the little canyon. "If you want, I'll help bury this man."

The boy shot a questioning glance at his mother. She didn't respond.

The old man grunted. "We will mourn Mackenzie forever. He was a great man and a warrior." He turned to the woman. "Blue Heron, take Scott and Rose and prepare a place for us. This man will help me with Mackenzie."

Without a word, the other three stood and walked toward the canyon. Each stooped to touch the shoulder of the dead man as they passed, deep emotion reflected in their eyes.

The old man pointed to the cliffs across the valley. "We will take him to those caves yonder."

The large, open basin where we stood splintered into countless side canyons. I looked where he indicated and noticed small hollow ledges in the cliff face not far below the rim.

The old man used his hands to push against his knees as he rose and then put a hand to his lower back and stretched. I squelched the desire to help him. With a gesture, he indicated I pick up Mackenzie.

Kneeling, I studied the dead man, noticing his fine features, so like the girl's. His dark hair hung below his shoulders. He looked peaceful. I saw a bullet hole in his red flannel shirt and wondered about his death.

I placed my hands under him and then hefted him to my chest. He was heavy and solid, and I realized this was a much different body than the one I'd buried only a few hours before.

Following the old man into the nearby canyon, I glimpsed the Arkansas River but no Indian encampment, no sign people lived in this area. Why were these Indians here?

The old man moved easier than I would've expected, stepping lightly from stone to stone. My lungs heaved as I climbed the steep hill, and the effort began to warm me. I felt the sweat slide down my chest under my shirt.

He pointed to a shallow recess under the rim of the canyon. I knelt and looked in. It would serve our purposes nicely. I laid the dead man in the hollow, and we hunted large slabs of rock to lay over him. We stacked them deep, protecting the dead man from coyotes and other varmints.

Despite his earlier efforts to rise from beside the fire, the old Indian now moved with remarkable balance. Judging by the size of the stones he hefted, he still possessed great strength. His gray hair hung wet and flat on his eagle-like head. Old he may be, but he moved as one half his age.

When we'd finished, he stopped and stared at the mound of rocks. Rain streamed down his weathered face, but he seemed not to notice.

"Mackenzie was a good friend. May God grant him rest." He bowed his head a moment and then turned away.

Did he say God? Did these prairie dwellers know of God? I promised to find out as we made our way down the steep hill to the valley floor.

I wanted to ask him questions but thought it best not to intrude on his grief. They would keep.

He followed me to the rock cliff dwellings, and I was pleased to see smoke rising from the largest of the lodges. We climbed the stone steps cut into the wall, but I halted on the ledge, uncertain if I should go to my room or not.

He gestured to the dark doorways. "Which room did you choose?"

I pointed to one of the small stone rooms, and the old man nodded, eyeing me curiously.

"You have chosen well. Most white men would have chosen the largest room. White men often want big things. But the smaller room will be easier to heat."

He left me then and bent to enter the room his family occupied. The doorways were very small, and I saw they'd already hung a blanket over the opening.

I looked out over the darkened canyon and wondered what time it was. Then I chuckled. Who cared?

Having nothing else to do, I retreated into my room and squatted before the fire, feeding little sticks to the hungry flames.

My immediate needs were met. I had food and shelter for a while, but what of tomorrow? Why had God brought me to this lonely place? How could I serve him here, and how could I pursue my dream in this remote location?

All right, I thought, I'll just rest and be ready for whatever came my way. "Trust and adjust," Pa always said. God is in control.

The rain increased in the afternoon. By evening time, tired of the confines of the small room, I ventured to the ledge and watched the heavy sheets of rain fall.

It had taken only a few minutes to go through Cal's gear. There was food, a little clothing, ammunition for the gun, and some bedding. I surely missed not having a Bible. I'd always loved to read and study scripture.

I didn't see anything more of Blue Heron or Rose, but the young boy came out and sat near me. We didn't speak for a while, just watching the rain and listening to the occasional clap of thunder. I enjoyed hearing the echo of the powerful thunder bounce from canyon to canyon. God's orchestra, I thought to myself.

"I'm Scott."

He was about twelve. His dark hair hung to his shoulders, hiding his shirt collar.

"I'm Jason."

"I know. You said that earlier. What're you doing out here?" His Scottish accent intrigued me, but I again refrained from intrusive questions. Not yet. "The wagon train I traveled with left me here."

"On purpose?" His eyebrows raised. "They must've not liked you much."

I smiled grimly, remembering Wilmington. "No, not much."

"Where will you go now?" His persistent questions annoyed me because I had no answers.

I scratched my jaw. "For now, I'm here." I figured that was truth enough. "How about you? What brought you here?" The unexpected question fell from me. I'd told myself I wouldn't ask.

He hesitated as he watched the rain for a minute. I could see he wondered how much he should say. "We were wandering, seeking a home. Father was shot by a Kiowa hunting party, but he'd given them the slip and returned to us. He was hard hit, though, and there was nothing Mother could do."

He went silent again for a moment, nudging a pebble with the toe of his moccasin. "The Kiowa couldn't find him, and they left. Father lost his gun, though. We were mourning when you found us."

"Why was he alone when the Kiowa found him?" I wondered aloud, curious.

Again, he hesitated. He hugged his knees to his chest and rested his chin on them. "He was scouting." Scott's reply seemed evasive, as if he were hiding something.

"What will you do now?" I hated to pry, but what if they left? I would be all alone again. Although we were strangers, it felt good to have company.

He narrowed his eyes, still watching the rain. "I don't know. Grandfather depended on father for direction. With him gone, we're not sure which way to go."

His words reminded me of Cal's observation of Pa. Wasn't I the same way, confused as to which way to proceed?

"Can't you return to your people?" Didn't Indians live in tribal bands? I tried to remember all I knew about Indians, which wasn't much.

He glanced at me and shook his head. "It's not that easy. Mother is Cheyenne, but her village was wiped out when she was young. Rose and I are half Cheyenne. We would not be completely trusted by another village of Cheyenne."

I wanted more answers but decided not to push too far. We'd only just met.

I took the conversation in another direction instead. "Scott is your real name? Not very Indian, is it?"

He chuckled and smiled. His white, even teeth flashed in the dim light. "Sir Walter Scott was my father's favorite writer. That's why he named Grandfather Walter."

I nodded, not fully understanding but wanting to be kind.

I returned to my small room when the cold and dark finally drove me inside. I made a little dinner for myself and sat beside my fire, brooding, listening to the rain fall in the narrow canyon.

I sighed. "Okay, God, you have me here and I'm ready. I'll wait on you, Lord. Prepare me for whatever you have. Your will be done."

I looked around the small room made of rock. I should be at peace, right? I was safe and warm. God was going to do a mighty work in me, I was sure. I just needed to be patient. I was in the creator's hand, and all would be well in time. God had my best intentions in his mind and all would be well, if I could just trust and be patient.

I slept horribly that night.

CHAPTER 10

That night, my thoughts were troubled with the memory of Pa's last night. I could still see that bright moonlit clearing in front of our cabin and the men astride their dark horses with flour sacks over their heads. The riders were huge and vivid in the illuminated clearing against the deep shadows of the dense woods behind them.

"Malone!" The rider in the lead shouted. I watched from my window as my father stepped from the cabin.

I saw Pa standing there, facing those brutal night riders. Back straight, he stood tall, not afraid.

"Missouri doesn't want you here. You and your Union-loving son need to leave. We support the Confederate States of America, and slavery is part of the South." He said something about Yankees, but I couldn't remember the specific words. The man shouted with authority while the others sat their horses not saying anything.

Their torches lit the bright clearing with contrasting lights. The incredibly bright moon could not be bested by these hand-held fire sticks.

Pa spoke clear in the still night. "I'm here to stay. We aim to farm a little and eventually raise horses. There need not be any trouble."

"Trouble has come, Malone. And if you won't leave, you'll die." The man held a large pistol, almost invisible against his dark clothing. Moonlight gleamed on its long barrel as it belched flame.

I saw Pa jerk from the bullet. The horses plunged wildly as the rider slowly cocked the Colt again and fired into Pa a second time.

I ran from my room after I saw Pa struck down. I knelt beside him as one of the men threw his torch into the open door of the cabin. Suddenly, they were all riding away, and I sobbed as the last rider fled the clearing, our little cabin going up in a roaring blaze. My father lay on his back and I cradled his head, his pale face staring up at me with piercing eyes.

I couldn't speak. The crackle of flames filled the wooden cabin behind me. Then, with great effort, Pa whispered, "Jason ... leave Missouri." He struggled to catch his breath. "God wants ... something bigger ... than this ... for you." I gripped his hand. "Find our ranch," he wheezed. "I'll tell your Ma ... you've grown so much ... I'm proud of you, Jason ..."

He relaxed in my arms, and I knew he was gone.

The rented cabin was now completely engulfed in flames. There was nothing I could salvage from the blaze. I buried my father in the woods that night and snuck away, hoping not to be discovered. Three days later, I joined the freight train to Santa Fe.

———×———

I awoke in the darkness of my little rock room, cold sweat dampening my brow. The image of Pa and the night riders wouldn't leave me. I reached for Cal's canteen and took a long drink.

Replacing the stopper, I shook the canteen. Not enough remained for coffee.

I chewed my lip and stared at the smoke-stained ceiling. After pushing a few sticks into the embers of my fire, I threw back my blankets. I needed to keep moving. Don't go down that dark hole again, I coached myself as I tugged on my shoes. Despair awaited me there, like a crouching lion, ready to pounce if I lowered my guard. I would not go there, wanting to avoid the pain that was sure to follow.

The nightmare left me feeling anxious and tired. I scratched the stubble on my chin as I stood before my lodge, feeling the early morning chill in the crisp air.

Walking to the spring, I was startled by a figure moving in the shadows. Rose knelt beside the spring, a water skin in her hand.

"Good morning, Rose," I said in a cheery voice, wishing to encourage a friendship with my new companions.

She looked at me, a hint of annoyance in her green eyes. Then she brushed past me and went back to her room without saying a word.

Frustration filled me as I watched her go, the short hairs bristling along the back of my neck. I clenched my teeth. It bothered me being ignored by this young girl.

She was pretty, though, I admitted as I filled my clay pot and returned to my room. A couple of freckles dotted the bridge of her nose, and I noticed a bit of curl at the ends of her long black hair. Did she get that from her father?

I shook the annoying thought of her from my mind and put water on to boil. Then, after cooking a small breakfast, I retrieved my rifle from its corner and went outside.

Birds whistled and chirped in the thickets along the stream, and I saw a hawk circle far above in the azure sky. Yesterday's storm had passed, leaving a vibrantly clear sky behind.

A squirrel chattered at me as I sat on the ledge and cleaned and loaded the old rifle. I decided I would supplement my meager food stores with some fresh meat. Besides, I could use the skins for clothes and moccasins.

The old man came from his lodge and stood beside me, watching me work. I smiled at him, but his dark eyes were unreadable. Soon Scott joined us on the ledge.

"That is a good gun." The old Indian gestured to the hunting rifle.

I nodded. "It belonged to a friend of mine."

I checked the lead and gunpowder in my hunting pouch and descended the stone steps. A wave of excitement swept over me as I walked the dim trail along the stream toward the open valley. It felt good to have something to do. Something that needed being done. There's nothing worse than not having a direction, a purpose, a plan.

The old man and Scott followed me. Pretending to scan the country, I glanced at them from the corner of my eye. They halted when I did, moved when I moved.

Halting when I came to the wide valley, I lifted a hand and shielded my eyes, surveying the land. The river would probably be the best place to look for game. I wended a way around rocks and through gullies, constantly vigilant.

I knew Walter and Scott were somewhere behind me but didn't look back anymore. My shoes were not well suited for walking on the uneven prairie, but I had nothing else. I hoped to make moccasins if I found something to make them with.

The idea reminded me of my new neighbors, and I decided I would share with them if I killed a deer or elk.

Reaching the river's edge, I headed downstream toward the open plains. I tried to walk carefully and make no sound. This seemed impossible. I had hunted back in Missouri and on the plains, but today I sounded loud even to my ears and I couldn't find any game.

After an hour, I halted in a grassy glen, the Arkansas flowing nearby. The old man and Scott came up to me, and I glared when I saw Scott's smile.

Were they laughing at me? I bit my lip and frowned.

A glance at the old man revealed amusement dancing in his eyes as well, and I reluctantly handed the rifle to him when he held out his hand.

"You are very noisy, Jason." The old Indian checked the weapon and then glanced at me, his shrewd eyes twinkling. "I heard you a mile off."

"Well, you think you could do better?" I challenged, angered by his taunt.

The old Indian glided noiselessly into the brush and disappeared. Scott motioned for me to hang back and let Walter get out in front of us. Then, quietly and cautiously, we followed.

Not twenty minutes later, a buffalo came up from the river's edge. The old man quickly raised the rifle to his shoulder. He stood motionless for a moment, and then the old rifle bellowed, a cloud of gray smoke flowing from the muzzle.

The buffalo stood still, apparently unhurt. Then with a slow step, it started forward and toppled to one side.

Scott raised one arm and whooped while we raced forward in time to see the buffalo breathe his last. Walter calmly reached for the shot pouch on my shoulder and deftly reloaded the gun.

I searched the surrounding land. The shot had been loud and so had Scott's triumphant shout. Were other Indians still around? Perhaps the Kiowa hunting party still lingered nearby.

"Is it safe to make so much noise?" I anxiously scanned the hills, thinking of Cal's Indian attack stories and wondering if I would soon experience one of my own.

Walter scouted the ridges too. "No Indians live here, though some travel here to hunt or trade or raid wagon trains. The Kiowa have left. I think we are safe."

The three of us worked together to skin the buffalo. We took the hide and the choicest cuts of meat and turned back to the cliff dwelling, heavily burdened.

As we moved away, I heard the brush breaking behind me and turned to see four scruffy coyotes race from the thickets and pounce on the carcass. They would make short work of the dead buffalo.

That night we feasted. Roasting buffalo steaks over the fire, we got acquainted. I asked the old man if Walter was his Cheyenne name.

"No," he chuckled. "Mackenzie used it and it stuck. My given name is 'Man who moves like ghost through the trees'." He gestured a wavy motion and then dropped his hand off sharply.

"Mackenzie said it was too hard to say, so he just called me Walter." He shot a sad look at his daughter but said nothing more.

The Indian woman nodded, a dull gleam in her dark eyes, then dropped her head. Her grief touched me as I was reminded of my own.

Walter had made a big show of cutting out the buffalo's tongue. Now, he pulled the roasting thing from the fire and bit into it, smacking his lips loudly as he chewed. Scott laughed when Walter licked his fingers with delight. It turned my stomach.

Blue Heron seemed courteous but chose not to engage me in conversation. Was this because of her gender? Not knowing proper Indian ways, I wasn't certain.

Rose simply ignored me. She ate the meat, but never looked up from her meal. Walter and Scott did most of the talking.

I left the meat and the hide with Blue Heron and retired to my lodge, content with the looks of appreciation on my new friend's faces.

The next day I went hunting again, and this time I brought down an antelope. I delivered the meat and the hide to Blue Heron again and was pleased when she smiled at me.

I don't know if we needed this much meat all at once, but I was eager to show them I wanted to help. I figured they would jerk the meat, dry it thoroughly, for future lean times. I couldn't guess what might lie ahead. God was keeping it a secret too.

For two weeks, I left the cliff dwelling early each day and explored the surrounding countryside. I prayed continuously, seeking God's will. Each day wishing I had a Bible.

The Arkansas River wound deeper into the mountains and I followed it, surveying the land as I went. Several other canyons branched from the river valley, but I wouldn't turn aside from the river, tracking it upstream.

After about ten miles, I halted to rest before turning around and making the descent to the plains. It was here I saw a red stallion.

CHAPTER 11

The sound of pounding hooves alerted me, and I stepped behind a boulder as a troop of horses emerged from a distant side canyon. I watched, my eyes riveted, as the band moved toward the river, the sorrel leading the way, his nose searching the air as they approached the water.

A thrill raced through me, but I wasn't sure why. The horses were beautiful. Even at this distance, barely able to make out colors of horses through the dust that hovered around the herd, I marveled at their freedom, their gracefulness as they lined up and drank from the river. With a silent signal, the sorrel stallion raced away, his herd streaming behind him. They vanished in a cloud of dust.

I wondered at the wild horses as I retraced my steps toward the cliff dwellings, not understanding their significance. They were wild animals, beautiful and magnificent, but nothing more. Yet, something about them niggled at my mind.

The land impressed me. I located water in side canyons where springs seeped into tiny rivulets of clear water or tall meadow grass grew luxuriantly. All the side canyons leading from the wider basin showed signs of grazing. Deer, antelope, and buffalo signs were all plentiful with tracks and droppings indicating numbers.

On one of these scouting trips, I discovered the narrow mouth of a canyon with steep sides towering above me at least five-hundred feet from the valley floor. A game trail led into the recess and I followed it, marveling at the rich grass that carpeted the widening little valley. A spring seeped from beneath a boulder, the huge rock looking as if it had fallen from the crags above.

I studied the pasture. Much stock could be kept here, safely enclosed by the tall walls. A man could manage a number of head with little work. The small gap at the opening would have to be fenced. But here the animals would be protected, and it would be impossible for them to stray. Grass and water were in great supply. Pleased with my discovery, I returned early to the cliff dwelling.

Loud, angry voices drifted to me as I approached.

Concealed by the thick undergrowth, I crept forward, hiding in the deep shadows of a giant sycamore tree.

"This is not what Father wanted us to do." I could hear the anguish in Rose's voice. "It was his wish to keep moving."

"We have no way to go on," Walter explained, his voice patient. "We have no equipment, no gear, no supply of food or spare blankets. We've lost everything."

"I don't care. I don't trust Jason, and I wonder what he's doing here. It's strange he appeared out of nowhere right after Father was killed by the Kiowa," Rose argued. "I think we should move on and leave him behind."

My stomach twisted into knots. Leave me? I was just getting used to these people and I didn't want to be alone again.

"No," Walter countered. "He has a gun and is helping us gather food. We need him. He seems very nice to Scott and me. Besides, this is the area where Mackenzie saw Wildfire."

"You're being fooled by Jason. He's no friend of ours. And Father is gone. It doesn't matter now where he saw Wildfire." Rose's voice cracked as she ran into the shelter of the stone lodge.

I stepped from the shadows and attempted to make as much sound as possible. The argument bothered me. Where did I stand with these people?

Walter saw me. With a quick glance at the opening of the dark chamber, he called to me.

"Jason, let's try to get a deer before dark. They like to feed at dusk in this canyon over here." He pointed to a distant opening, and I walked with him, my feelings irritating me.

As we walked, I remained silent. I had worked so hard to help these people hunt and now we had some food. Also, Blue Heron had been making moccasins and clothes for us from the skins. She told me that the buffalo hide made excellent, warm blankets.

So, what was Rose's problem with me? I'd only been helpful to her family.

Walter sensed my foul mood. "You heard Rose?" I nodded. "Why does she hate me so much?"

He halted and looked at me, his dark eyes softening. "It is not really you she hates, Jason. It is the loss of her father and the knowledge that his work was unfinished."

I digested this, trying to understand. "Scott told me that you can't really go back to the Cheyenne. Where do you intend to go?"

He didn't answer but sighed and motioned for me to follow him as he continued walking.

We arrived at the canyon Walter had indicated. A game trail lay before us, and I stepped into it when his hand on my shoulder halted me. He sat on a flat rock.

I watched him, resting the butt of the rifle on my toe. This man always seemed wise, and I wanted to hear that wisdom now.

"When I was younger, I was a wild horse hunter." He placed his hands on his knee and leaned forward. He looked so old, the late afternoon sun shining dully on his gray hair. Then I thought about what he'd said and tilted my head. Had I heard him correctly?

"You hunted wild horses?" My skepticism filled the question. I thought about telling him of the herd of horses I'd seen, but didn't, not wanting to interrupt his story.

"Yes." He smiled at the doubt in my words. "The Cheyenne have many fine horses, and I was very good at capturing them. Horses make a man rich and powerful in the Cheyenne villages. I married a very beautiful girl. She was very proud of me. Later, we had a daughter.

"Our village picked up and moved far to the south to follow the buffalo herds. We needed much meat to see us through the coming winter. While we were hunting buffalo, I found signs of wild horses and chose to follow them rather than stay with the meat hunters. When I returned to our camp, I found it burned and the people all dead. My wife too. My daughter was missing. The Ute had attacked our camp in my absence. We were far from other Cheyenne lands, so no one knew where we were."

He bowed his head, remembering. I remembered my own grief at the loss of someone I loved. I wanted to help him but didn't know how.

"How did you get Blue Heron back?" I hoped my inquiries were not rude, but I was curious.

"There was nothing left for me to do. I did not want to return to the Cheyenne and tell them my entire village had been killed while I was horse hunting. I went into the mountains and found trappers who allowed me to help them trap through the winter. There I found Mackenzie. He was from a place called Nova Scotia. He said he was Scottish, but I never understood what that meant. He was smart and had good ideas. We became friends."

Walter glanced at the sun. I wanted to hear the rest of the story, but he got slowly to his feet and brushed past me, stepping into the game trail.

I stared after him, disappointed. Clearly, he was not going to tell me more right now. I frowned and followed him on the trail to a branch canyon.

He stopped on the edge of a meadow and found another comfortable seat. This time, we were concealed by lengthening shadows, the sun dipping behind the ridges to the west. A long, narrow meadow stretched before us, the tall grass inviting to deer, or so I hoped.

I knelt on one knee and watched the meadow for movement. The rim above had already cut off the sun on the western side of the valley, but there was still plenty of light.

"Mackenzie told me that God would help me with my grief." Walter's unexpected words startled me. I leaned closer, my eyes on the meadow as I listened to his low voice.

"I learned a lot about God and love and strength. Mackenzie shared Jesus with me, telling me of heaven and God's plan for me. He helped me through a terrible time. I blamed myself for my people dying. I wished I had died with them."

"You'd be dead if you were in camp when the Ute attacked," I whispered over my shoulder, wishing to console him somehow. "God kept you alive for a reason."

Walter nodded. "That's what Mackenzie told me." He paused, but I hoped he wouldn't stop there. I waited, wanting more of the story. The shadows crept farther across the meadow and still I saw no deer. A locust whirred in the elms, and a bat swooped, hunting insects.

After a while, the old Indian inhaled deeply. "We brought our winter catch of furs to the rendezvous, and it is there that I again saw Blue Heron. Five years had passed since the Ute took her, and now a Ute warrior was with her at the rendezvous. I knew I could not accuse the man of taking my daughter, for there would be death. So I told Mackenzie, and he bought Blue Heron from the Ute. They later married and had Rose and Scott."

I stood there soaking in his tale, which explained a lot. I chewed the inside of my cheek. There are many reasons why we're not with others of our kind. Here I was on the plains, all alone except for this Indian family.

70

Why was I not with other white people? Because God had a plan for me, I reminded myself. There's a purpose for me being here.

Soon, a fat buck entered the trail, and I shot it. We skinned it out and carried it back to camp. Blue Heron took the skin and meat from me, but I didn't see Rose that night. Scott was his regular inquisitive self, and we talked long into the night, enjoying the fire and each other's company.

My mind raced with ideas. Why had Mackenzie led his family here? How had Blue Heron known of the cliff dwellings? Why was Rose so eager to move on?

I found no answers to these questions and was still reluctant to ask them, not wanting to appear rude or intrusive. Besides, their father had only recently passed away, and the timing did not seem right.

I went to bed that night with heavy thoughts. I still contemplated why I was here, and now, why were they here?

The next day, I showed Blue Heron a hot spring I'd discovered pouring into a small stream that emptied into the Arkansas. Concealed from view, the spring lay among dense foliage and sharp rocks. The undergrowth formed a perfect curtain, and we agreed this would be an ideal location for a bath. The spring was actually two springs, merging to form a small stream. By damming a wide place, we would shape a basin to serve as a bathing pool.

It seemed perfect. Well, except for the smell. Sulfur gas permeated the place, the smell of rotten eggs thick in the air. But we couldn't have it all. I smiled, thinking of the hot bath I would enjoy when the weather cooled.

Blue Heron seemed unduly surprised but interested when I'd mentioned the hot springs. It was as if she didn't believe me. I wondered at this as I showed her my plans to build a rock wall across the small water way and make a bath.

She knelt beside the spring, feeling the hot water, letting it flow over her hand. I watched her, my curiosity getting the better of me again.

"Blue Heron." I hesitated, trying to find the right words. "You've been here before, haven't you?"

She looked sharply at me and then dropped her head, playing with the water. "Yes." She tapped the narrow stream, splashing it softly.

She didn't say anything further until we were almost back to the cliff dwelling. She stopped next to the old sycamore tree where I'd hidden when I heard Rose arguing.

71

"I was taken by the Ute when I was younger. They brought me here. This is the camp they lived in while they traded with the plains Indians at Bent's Fort. I lived here for a month before we moved farther west to Ute territory. I never knew about the hot spring or have forgotten. It was long ago."

She turned and ascended the stone steps to the ledge above. I stood, watching her go.

How many events in life formed our thoughts and memories? I was young when my mother died, and Pa had worked extra hard to make up for it. Then he'd died. Now I only had their memories, the memories of their lives and our life together.

No, I had more than that. I had their faith. They believed Jesus died for our sins and wanted each of us to walk in God's ways, doing good works prepared for us to do before the creation of the world. So, what good work was I to do now? Blue Heron had been taken brutally from her people when she was young and then rescued by a Scottish fur trapper who'd married her. Then he'd died.

What good could come from Mackenzie's death? How would Blue Heron find God's path for her now?

That night, as I sat by my small fire drinking the last of the coffee, I pondered on these things and thought about what was next. Would I waste away in these mountains hunting and exploring until I died?

So much more could be accomplished if I had a horse. I dearly wanted a horse.

I knew Fort Union was a little distance south of us, but how far? I could always go there, but how was I to travel? Walking would surely be tiresome, and I wondered about the distance between water points. Could it be done?

I went to sleep with my thoughts swirling, nagging at me. I tossed and turned all night, never finding a comfortable position.

In the morning, Blue Heron surprised me with new moccasins. Eagerly, I tugged them on. Throwing my old shoes back into my room, I strutted around the rock ledge, feeling the ground through the thick leather. The others stood by, watching. They smiled as I showed off my new footwear, all except Rose.

With these moccasins, I felt like I could fly. They were so light and comfortable. They wouldn't stand up against sharp rocks, but they'd be ideal with the soft dirt and grass of the canyon country.

Leaping from the ledge, I ran through the trees into the open basin beyond. My feet felt the shape of sticks and stones.

I slowed and walked around the open plain, enjoying the morning sun rising over the prairie. Praise songs came to me, bidding me to worship. I began to sing loudly as I sauntered over the grassy field and watched the sunrise.

If I hadn't been watching the sun come up over the plains, I'd never have seen the smoke rising out there.

CHAPTER 12

Shielding my eyes against the morning glare, I stared eastward. A dark plume of smoke drifted lazily into the clear sky. Not a campfire smoke, that was certain. This was much larger.

My stomach tightened with fear. Had the Kiowa returned? Was it a large number of Indians?

Then my pulse quickened. Was it a wagon train?

I raced back to the narrow canyon, and rounding the huge old sycamore tree, I saw Walter and Scott on the ledge. "Smoke out on the plains," I called, trying to catch my breath. "It's not just a camp." I motioned for them to follow me.

We left the confines of the narrow canyon and ventured out into the openness of the river valley, our eyes searching the eastern horizon as we walked. Pointing, I indicated the huge curl of black smoke rising over the silent prairie.

As we stood there, Blue Heron and Rose joined us, lifting hands against the sun's glare. All were silent as we searched for clues. Only a faint breeze stirred the long grasses, bending the smoke column.

After a long pause, Walter shifted, and I realized I'd been waiting for someone to make a decision. Why hadn't I spoken up?

Walter cleared his throat. "It must be wagons on fire. They're on the old trail. It does not seem to be spreading, but smoke that big will soon draw attention. Jason, you must go quickly to see what it is and if you can help."

I'd had the same idea and kicked myself for not speaking sooner. I wasn't a little boy anymore.

"I'll get my gun," I said over my shoulder, my feet already moving toward our canyon.

It took only a few minutes to fetch my gun and fill my canteen. I hurried back to the small group. They were arguing as I approached.

"I'll never become a man without chances like this," Scott pleaded, his eyes on Blue Heron. "Father is gone. I need to learn."

The excitement of the moment was upon me, too, and I knew how Scott felt. I wondered if the glow of adventure I saw in his eyes were reflected in my own.

Walter nodded, but Blue Heron would hear none of it.

"You are too young." She glared at Scott. "I just lost my husband, should I lose my son too? A man should take you to this thing, not another boy. You will not go."

When I realized she was referring to me, I cringed. Another boy? I arched an eyebrow and glanced at Walter. True, I was only seventeen, but I was no longer a boy.

Worry lines deepened on Walter's brow and he scowled. I wondered if he knew he was too old for this kind of thing but agreed with Blue Heron that someone needed to go with Scott, to look after the young boy.

"Mother, I will go with them."

Everyone looked at Rose and I read the surprise in their eyes. It was no secret she didn't like me, but here she'd volunteered to go with me.

She faced me, her green eyes blazing. "I'm going for Scott, not you. You're not my boss."

Astonished, I nodded dumbly.

"That is a good idea." Walter laid a hand on Rose's shoulder. "Move swiftly but be safe. Stay out of sight of Indians or white men. Trust no one."

I handed my canteen to the grinning Scott, and we moved for the open prairie. I saw Rose hug Blue Heron and then ran to catch up with us.

The brush and trees along the river banks afforded cover. We followed the river, taking our time and looking all around. Moving from rock to trees to shallow depressions, we attempted to stay hidden from view.

Scott seemed eager, but something else had come over him. He looked serious as he scouted our area, following my lead. I could sense him trying to convey how grown up he wanted to be.

Rose dragged behind at first, trying to keep her distance, feigning disinterest. But soon she was right beside us, skulking like Scott and me, not able to deny her own curiosity. The excitement of the expedition was contagious.

A mile away, we saw the two wagons, their canvas tops burning.

Belly down on a small knoll, we surveyed the scene before us and scanned the surrounding area. Then, crouching, we moved cautiously toward the smoking wagons.

Four fresh mounds of dirt caught my attention first. The graves appeared hastily dug, tools and goods lay scattered over the ground as if hurried packing had taken place in the dark.

We stopped again on a low hill, scanning the scene. Only one wagon still burned. Two arrows protruded from one of the prairie schooners.

We watched the wagons for another minute and then glanced at one another. "What do you make of it?" I wiped my sweaty hands on my pants, my heart pounding loudly.

"It looks like they were attacked early this morning, dug quick graves for their dead and then fled." Rose pointed to retreating wagon wheel tracks. "Those tracks are only a few hours old. They're heading for Fort Union, I figure."

"What do you think, Scott?" His eyes danced as I turned to him and I could tell he appreciated being included.

"I think Rose is right, but the attackers have already left. They must've been a small party. These wagons were searched by the owners and then abandoned." The young boy pointed to an axe lying on the ground. "No Indian would've left that or the clothes."

"They would if they were in a hurry or still wanted to pursue the wagons for another attack," Rose added, shaking her head. "They could always return for this stuff. We'd better be on our way, too, in case they return."

"I'm not leaving without some of this stuff. It's free for the taking now, right, Jason?" Scott looked to me and I felt suddenly grown up, like the leader.

"It's not going to do these folks any good." I pointed to the new graves. "We might as well take it."

Rose pursed her lips and shrugged but said nothing.

"Gather anything of value we might be able to use and pile it over there." I indicated a distant low point. "Then, we'll move it from here as quickly as we can."

I took one last look around to the surrounding hills. "Let's hope those Indians don't return soon."

Fanning out, we began retrieving the articles of clothing and utensils. The slightly burned wagon still contained things we could use, but only a shovel, a saw, and a scythe with a burn mark on the long handle could be saved from the still-burning wagon.

I bent to retrieve a pile of hastily discarded clothes and noticed the corner of a book. A thrill ran through me as I recognized it as a Bible. I added it to our pile.

When we'd collected our loot, Scott turned to me. "What now? Do we leave everything here as it is?"

"Yep." I tossed the shovel on our heap of goods. "If the Indians return, they'll see the wagons are still here. They might ride off and be done. We can only hope."

Each of us took some of our newly acquired items in hand and started walking toward our small canyon. I glanced back once more at the fresh gravesites and thought of Cal. These people had traveled on the Santa Fe Trail with dreams of their own, but life was over for them now. Were their dreams over, too, or did they live on with family members or friends?

Turning to follow Rose and Scott, I wondered about death. Why do some men live while others die? What had been the purpose of Cal's life? Or even Pa's? Was it so the memory I had of them would somehow shape who I was to become? Would I ever understand what they'd lived for? I glanced up at the nearby hill to the old teamster's lone grave. Cal had said curious things there at the last. Would I ever understand their meaning?

My questions may never have answers, but I asked them anyway. Perhaps life was simply about the never-ending search for answers.

As I contemplated these things, I trudged behind Rose, the unwieldy scythe cumbersome in my arms. In addition, I carried a load of blankets, a coat, other clothes and a coil of rope. I also had my gun slung over my shoulder. Scott carried the shovel and some clothes. Rose, the axe and some food items.

After a half mile from the attack site, we dipped into a hidden fold of the prairie and I called a halt. The load I carried was too heavy to transport far without a rest. Scott dropped his load and collapsed on the ground. Rose set hers down, too, but then quickly moved to the lip of the bowl to survey the surrounding prairie.

Scott glanced at me and I nodded. He moved to the opposite side of the hollow, mimicking Rose's caution.

Lowering my heavy load, I surveyed the area and handed the canteen to Rose. This bowl probably used to be an old buffalo wallow.

Rose took the canteen without a word. I watched her slender throat work as she drank, then glanced swiftly away.

Crossing the little basin, I handed the canteen to Scott as he pointed. "There's a lot of good stuff here. I could use some of the clothes and I found a green dress too." Grinning, he looked at his sister. Rose glared at him. He ignored her look and again surveyed the quiet plains.

I sat near Scott and watched Rose from the corner of my eye. She wasn't very sociable, but her sour attitude hadn't interfered with our task. She'd carried her weight.

A gentle breeze ruffled the grass, making it sway like ripples on a lake. It was beautiful and I glanced skyward, watching white clouds scuttle across the azure canopy. To the west, the Rocky Mountains towered, majestic and grand. I marveled at the glory of God's creation.

I glanced at Rose, a wisp of raven hair blowing wildly across her tanned cheek. She brushed at it impatiently, unaware I observed her. I liked how her long hair danced in the morning breeze.

Suddenly, she turned and caught me staring, and I felt my cheeks warm. She scowled at me and turned away again, her green eyes narrowing with annoyance.

"Hey, look." Scott whispered sharply, bringing me back to my senses. Rose slid across the bottom of the hollow toward his position. I grabbed my gun.

On our hands and knees, we crawled to Scott's side. My eyes followed his pointing finger.

"Cows," Rose whispered with disgust. "Where'd they come from?"

Two cows stood on the edge of a ravine. I craned my neck to see what else might be in that ravine.

The box canyon I'd discovered had good meadow grass and a small spring. If I could get these cows in there, it would require little work to pen them in. The canyon would work as a natural corral.

"Cows? Who cares about old cows? We want a horse," Scott muttered dismally.

"A few cows can build a herd. Besides, we could always eat them if we couldn't hunt." I spoke casually, hoping to conceal my eagerness. I would need their help.

Rose squinted at me. "You want cattle for a herd? We don't. They mean nothing to us."

"Even if we don't use them as a herd, we could always sell them in Fort Union and buy a horse," I countered, thinking desperately of how to gain their cooperation.

Scott nodded. "That's a good idea. But how do we catch 'em?"

"We don't catch 'em. We simply move behind 'em and sort of push 'em back into our canyons. I'm thinking of one that would be perfect for holding stock." I spoke to no one in particular as I watched the cows. A third appeared over the rim of the ravine.

I turned to Rose, hoping she'd read the pleading in my look. She nodded slowly, but without enthusiasm. "All right, Cowboy Jason, what about all of this stuff?" She waved at the goods we'd taken from the burning wagons. In my excitement of finding the cows, I'd forgotten our recently acquired goods.

Scratching my jaw, I nodded. "Rose, you're right. This stuff is more important than the cows right now. Let's carry it back to our canyon and get Walter and Blue Heron to help push the cows."

Rose laughed, and I realized it was the first time I'd heard her laugh. The melody of it thrilled me and then she smiled, adding to the moment. She had a beautiful smile.

"I can imagine Walter and Mother chasing a few old cows on the prairie." Her face looked light and happy for a moment, and it changed her entire look. She always seemed so serious and sad.

We gathered our new belongings and moved out again for the cliff dwellings. I looked over my shoulder at the cows, taking notice of land and markings in the terrain so I could find our way back.

The heavy loads forced us to stop several times on the return trip. Rose and Scott were not half as excited as I was about the cattle, though, and I had to keep encouraging Rose and Scott to continue. I felt my cow herding had already begun.

By noon, we reached our canyon and deposited our goods. Walter listened attentively while I explained about the animals.

"They must've belonged to the wagon train that was attacked. They belong to anyone now." I hoped he would see things from my perspective.

The old man stroked his chin thoughtfully. "Those animals would be a safe bet if we could not find meat." He glanced at Blue Heron and the Indian woman nodded.

I didn't want to use the cattle for meat unless really pushed to it, but I agreed to his suggestion in order to secure their help. "Sure, Walter, if we had to eat one. But let's go. Let's round 'em up and push 'em back here," I said, trying to keep the impatience from my voice.

Carrying the gun and refilled canteen, I led the way back out to the prairie below. Before we'd gone several steps, Walter turned back and picked up the coil of rope we'd just acquired.

An hour later, we stood on the banks of the ravine, which proved to be more like a small valley. By the look of the rich grass and the few small trees below us, there probably was a little water too.

We studied the narrow valley and the small herd of cows grazing along both sides of the narrow ravine. My pulse quickened as I counted cattle. Twenty-two head. Some of them were the oxen necessary for pulling the two wagons we'd found, but the others seemed to be cattle for breeding.

I glanced at Walter and he smiled at me. I think only he understood how important this could be. Scott, Rose, and Blue Heron seemed a little disinterested but were willing enough when we strode down into the bottom and started to push the animals toward camp.

We worked slowly, not wanting to frighten them. The cows were reluctant to give up grazing, probably enjoying the first break they'd had in weeks. I prayed the whole time.

Soon, we realized, one of the oxen, a big red brute, seemed to lead and the other cows were content to follow. Walter roped that old oxen and started toward home. The other cows followed along like sheep with us working behind, pushing strays back into line.

With Walter walking out in front, leading that red ox, we guided the cows into the narrow gap of the box canyon. The work had demanded some running and we were completely done in by the time we'd covered the distance from the ravine. As we pushed them forward, Walter took the rope off the lead steer and the animals moved into the canyon, bending to the rich grass.

The five of us simply stood there, exhausted and panting while the cows fanned out with their tails swishing as they chewed contentedly. Finally, I turned to the others.

"Thanks for helping round them up. I'll have to camp here tonight and make a gate tomorrow. Could someone bring me a blanket, flint, and maybe a bite to eat?" I looked at the tired bunch and knew I'd asked a lot of them, but they turned and started for the cliff dwellings.

Walter laid a kindly hand on my shoulder before he left. I could sense his tiredness, but there was a gleam in his old eyes. "This is a good thing. I think this will help us. I will send one of the children with food and a blanket. Good night, Jason."

The old man walked away then and joined the group treading a weary path back to camp.

After they left, I dragged a couple of deadfalls into the gap and even stacked a few stones as a kind of wall. I would build a proper fence on the morrow. I was tired, too, but so excited I kept working until darkness prevented further action. I would sleep in the narrow opening and my fire would help prevent the cattle from escaping.

I had already prepared for a fire, so when Rose showed up, it took only a moment to get it started. A spark fell from the flint and a tiny blaze leaped amid the piled twigs and pine needles.

After thanking her for the blanket and food, I expected her to quickly depart but was surprised when she sat down. Pleased for the company, I started making dinner for two.

It took no time at all to cook up some venison and the two of us sat there eating, staring absently into the fire.

The sun dropped behind the mountains and the heat of the day diminished. Stars peeped between the towering peaks. I heard the cows chewing and I swelled with pride. We'd done it. The beginning of a herd was tucked safely in this canyon.

Rose sat just inside the ring of firelight, her still face clear in its blaze. The orange light shimmered on her bronze skin and long, dark hair.

I sat across from her, liking the company but uncomfortable with the silence. A curious flutter tickled in my gut as I studied her. My palms felt damp. The unusual sensation confused me. Not able to stand it further, I shifted in my seat, drawing her gaze. "Scott told me how he got his name. How'd you get yours?"

She smiled her rare smile and her white teeth flashed in the firelight. "I was named for a small, delicate flower which was my father's favorite. The mountain rose. He said I reminded him of it when I was born."

Her smile faded then, and a somber look returned, sad memories reflected in her eyes.

"You miss him very much," I said. I was no stranger to loss and I understood the pain.

She didn't say anything for a long time as we watched the flames leap and crackle as sparks drifted into the night sky. "We had a special bond, him and me," she said, finally. "I was his little girl, and I loved him. He taught me to ride and we shared ideas. Even our dreams."

"What are your dreams?" I asked quickly. Perhaps too quickly.

I had been pleasantly surprised she'd stopped to sit by the fire with me and wanted to prolong the moment. I wanted to get her talking, to have her relax and enjoy time with me. But she stood.

"Thank you for dinner. I have to get back now." Rose turned away. I leaped to my feet, but before I could say another word, she disappeared into the darkness.

I watched her go until even the dim color of her buckskin dress was lost in the night. I angrily kicked a log in the fire. Why had I asked her about her dreams? It made her uncomfortable. That was why she'd left.

I sat down again, my thoughts revolving around Rose. Why had she stayed for dinner? Why had she spoken of her father?

I was a fool. Rose never liked me and wanted nothing to do with me. She wanted her family to pick up and move on. But why? Where to?

I had so many questions but no answers. Shaking my head, I wondered about my circumstances. By all rights, I should've died back there in Missouri with Pa. Now I was stuck here in the mountains with some Indians as the summer passed. What would I do for the upcoming winter? I had nowhere to go.

I looked up at the heavens. The few stars I'd noted before had multiplied. A sea of tiny lights now dotted the night sky.

"Dear Lord, you've done mighty things to get me out here. What is your will for me? I know it's not my place to ask what you're doing, but what do you want me to do now?"

I paused, but there was no answer and I sighed deeply.

"God, you are holy, and I'm nothing. Let me trust you and be faithful and walk in your ways. Forgive my impatience. Reveal your purpose in your time, not mine. I love you, Jesus. Amen."

I sat there for another hour contemplating my situation before I rolled in my blankets. As I stared into the glowing fire, all I could see were the delicate features of Rose's face.

CHAPTER 13

Scott and Walter returned in the morning. We dug fence postholes, cut wood for railing, and utilized rock walls where we could. Three days of work completed our barrier.

I took many opportunities to walk among our herd and inspect the animals. Eight were oxen and would be worth nothing except for slaughter or sale. They couldn't help in the breeding or enlarging of our herd and would consume more of the grass in the valley than I wanted. Two more were steers and I chose them to eat first if we needed to. We would have to figure a way to get rid of them. There was no way to get them to Fort Union for sale, but Pa had always told me to start a project with prayer. So I prayed a lot for guidance and wisdom.

As I looked over the herd, Walter came alongside me. The old Indian rubbed his hands together as he surveyed the cattle scattered among the thickets and small meadows. "Well, Jason, you have the beginnings of your ranch right here. How do you feel?"

I thought about that for a moment, remembering Pa. How would he feel? Somehow the idea of starting my ranch lacked something and I wished Pa were here to share it with.

"I'm glad, Walter. This is what Pa and I always wanted." I watched the animals feed on the thick grass—it must be sub-irrigated somehow. The small stream in the side of the canyon wouldn't produce this much water.

"Now, I need some horses." I spoke to myself, but Walter flinched. I looked at him. "What's wrong?"

He smiled, but it didn't reach his eyes. "It is horses that brought us here." He walked away then, and I stared after him.

Horses? Why had Mackenzie brought them here for horses? There were no trading posts or nearby settlements. His comment got me thinking. Walter was often discreet and cautious with what he shared, but Scott might open up.

The next day, I took Scott into an adjoining canyon where I found thick meadow grass. There, I intended to show him how to use the scythe to cut hay.

I cut a wide swath with the long blade, instructing him how best to hold the blade for maximum effect. Scott helped me gather and stack the cut hay, setting it aside for the coming winter. Then, handing the tool to him, I let him try.

His feeble swing made me laugh, but soon he got the rhythm and didn't do too badly. I told him I would ask Rose to come on the morrow and gather hay for him while he cut the grass.

Scott laughed, a grin spreading across his sweat-streaked face. "Rose won't do anything you suggest. She's mad at you."

I tilted my head, nettled at his words. I'd tried so hard to be kind to Rose. "Why? What have I done?"

The memory of dinner with Rose still haunted me. Was she mad at the questions I'd asked? I hadn't seen much of her the last few days—she was clearly avoiding me. Irritated, I sighed loudly.

"Walter told us you wanted a ranch with cattle and horses," Scott explained as he leaned on the bowed scythe. "That the new cows were the beginning of this ranch. Rose was so mad, I thought she'd cry."

I shook my head, not understanding. Scott wiped his grimy hands on his pants before he continued. "Rose has a dream too. She doesn't think it's fair you get your dream while she doesn't get hers."

Scott glanced at the bright sun then moved into the shade of a nearby tree. He laid the scythe down and sat, accepting the canteen I handed him. He pulled the stopper and took a long drink, some of the water spilling out, leaving a path down his dusty neck.

I felt the frown deepen on my sweaty face as my frustration grew. "Well, are you going to tell me her dream or just sit there and drink water?" I tried to sound playful, but I also was prodding him to explain. He shook his head and grinned again.

"Oh, no, not me. I'm not saying anything more. If you want to know about Rose's dream, you'll have to ask her."

He wiped his forehead with his palm. Getting to his feet, he wiped his sweaty hand on his pants leg again. I could see the blisters rising on his palms, but he didn't complain.

I bit my lip. Rose was angry at me, but I felt like the victim. What had I done wrong?

I was tired of Rose's negative attitude toward me. God had brought me out here for something. It was not my fault if I'd found the loose cattle and had a dream of a ranch.

Scott and I worked the rest of the day and stacked a considerable amount of hay. As we trooped back toward our narrow canyon, I caught sight of Walter—who'd been out hunting—walking down by the river.

Handing the scythe to Scott, I headed for the river. "I'll be back soon. I'm going to help Walter." He took the tool and shuffled to our little canyon, a well-worn path now showing the way.

I found the old Indian skinning a buffalo. It was a cow and not as big as the large bull I'd delivered a few weeks before. Walter and I talked of hay and winter and food supplies as we butchered the animal.

Walter gripped a thick piece of the hide, and pulling it from the body, slid his knife between it and the flesh, cutting the clinging sinews. "Do you think you can stack enough hay for your herd to get them through a mountain winter? Snow will come early to these high meadows and stay longer than out on the flatlands." I watched him cut more hide away. He worked masterfully, the knife in the hands of a former trapper. Pulling the skin tight to give his knife more clearance, I nodded. "I think Scott and I can stack enough. I'm going to ask Rose to help Scott tomorrow. I want to scout more grazing land."

Walter paused and stood, arching his stiff back. A wide grin creased his leathery face. "Good luck asking Rose to do anything for you." He chuckled as he bent over the dead buffalo and continued skinning.

"Scott said the same thing," I grumbled. "What's wrong with her? Why's she angry with me?" I looked at the exposed meat of the animal and thought of buffalo steaks. Blue Heron knew how to season the meat perfectly. Maybe we would all feast together tonight, giving me a chance to talk to Rose.

The old Cheyenne didn't look up this time. "Life is full of many challenges. People are born. People die. Sometimes good times, sometimes bad. But what helps keep you going, what helps keep a person looking ahead, is a dream—something to focus on and make you believe there is good ahead of you. Mackenzie said the Bible calls it hope."

He finished one side, and I helped him roll the body over. His words puzzled me, but I'd learned to wait on Walter. He would explain if he thought it was important.

He looked at me then, his wrinkled face tensing as he chose his words carefully. His eyes scanned the horizon before he continued. "Mackenzie had a dream. It carried his family through many dark times. It helped Blue Heron heal as she works to forget her family being killed by the Ute and also her captivity. His dream carried his children through lonely years where they have learned they are neither Cheyenne nor white."

The hide pulled up easier now—the job was almost complete. I turned to look back at the narrow opening of our canyon and saw Rose and Scott walking toward us to help carry the meat and hide.

"Hurry, Walter, before they get here," I whispered. "Tell me Mackenzie's dream. What motivates Rose and why is she mad at me?"

He glanced at the approaching pair, and I could tell he considered the distance and time. They would be within hearing range soon. Walter sighed and straightened, the bloody knife still in his hand.

"He knew of a wild stallion that roamed these parts. We called him Wildfire. He is the color of rust on an old beaver trap. He wanted to catch that stallion and ranch, raising horses."

God has a funny sense of humor. The Indians and I shared a similar vision? My dream, instilled in me as a young boy from my Irish father, was to raise and breed horses. He'd painstakingly showed me the meaning of bloodlines and form. We'd spent hours discussing quality in a horse and looking over an animal for distinct points of breeding. Pa had inspired in me the desire to be a horse breeder without any real financial hope of ever achieving this goal. It had taken me years before I understood how poor we were and how unlikely our horse ranch was. To buy a quality stallion would cost more than I'd ever earn. But to catch a wild horse? The idea had not occurred to me. I thought of the red stallion I saw with the wild horses. Should I tell Walter? If that horse was not the one they searched for, it would break their hearts. I hated the thought of getting their hopes up and decided to hold my tongue.

There were no wild horses in the east. I'd heard about wild mustangs, how their ancestors were brought here by Spaniards. Now, bands of these mustang roamed the open plains and the mountains, acclimating to the harsh environment of the western lands. Could they be captured? Hadn't Walter said that long ago he'd been a wild horse hunter? I'd assumed they were for the Indians to ride, probably not of much quality. But if a stallion possessed the right structure and characteristics, in the hands of a careful breeder …

I chewed the inside of my cheek, considering.

Like Walter pointed out, dreams helped us go on in life. In the face of trauma—what with Ma passing away and Pa and I barely making ends meet—we'd lived on this hope, that one day God would give us the ability to have a horse ranch. To grant the desire of our hearts.

I knew that if it was God's will, nothing could prevent it from happening, in spite of my lack of finances.

Whether or not the actual dream ever came true wasn't the point, I guess. It's the idea that one day it *might* come true, that one day our dream could be a reality. It gave a person hope to continue working when things overwhelmed them. It gave a person something to strive for.

"Mackenzie always said things would get better," the old Indian continued. "That dreams would come true." He peered at me, and suddenly I understood Rose. With the death of her father, she wondered if it was the death of their dream. The plan of catching the wild stallion was a tangible connection with her dead father.

Was it any different for me? Did Pa still live in some small way because our ranch was beginning to take shape?

"She resents your dream coming true." He finished speaking just as Rose and Scott walked up.

I stared at the girl and she wrinkled her pert nose at me. "What're you looking at?" she snapped, her tone saucy and challenging.

I felt sad for her. The death of a dream is almost as bad as the death of a loved one. Doubly hard if they're in the same person. "Hello, Rose," I said softly. My heart ached for what she was going through.

She tilted her head, surprise showing on her face when I didn't respond in anger as she expected. She looked confused as she turned her back on me, helping her grandfather.

I resolved to do everything in my power to resurrect her dying hopes. Whatever I could do to help her go on in life, to continue dreaming of a good thing, I promised to do.

We cut the meat into manageable chunks. I'd already caught sight of coyotes skulking in the brush along the river's edge and knew once we left this spot, little would remain of the buffalo carcass.

When we'd finished, I walked slowly back to the cliff dwelling with my share of the heavy load, purposely falling behind the others. I wanted to spend time with the Lord.

As the others moved farther ahead, I began to pray. "God, you're the master of the universe and have carefully chosen this time for me to be on the Great Plains. It's not an accident that I was left here alone to meet these good people. As you are blessing me with the beginning of my ranch, use me to show them hope in Christ and to help them find their dream again. May I be used by you to encourage them, to work for them, to be their partner for the making of their dream. You have blessed me, and I pray you will bless them. Use me for your glory. Amen."

That night, we feasted on fresh buffalo steaks. Throughout dinner, I tried repeatedly to catch Rose's eye. She, however, kept her eyes averted and would have none of it.

It would not be easy to rekindle Rose's dying dreams. Perhaps her hope was already dead and I would need a miracle. Regardless, I resolved to give it my best and do what I could to help my new friends.

———<>———

In the morning, I explored the nearby canyons and discovered an additional one that could be used as a pasture for a herd. Though the mouth of the canyon was wider, there were more piles of rock debris that could easily be incorporated into a barrier to keep animals contained. The grass within was excellent, too, despite having no water source within the canyon.

I immediately set myself the task of creating a suitable wall with one opening into the canyon. A small gate could easily be constructed later. The wall would not be straight across the canyon mouth, but that was not important. The barrier would twist and run from one rock pile to another. The canyon would be effectively fenced but without an adequate water supply.

Also, like the previous canyon we'd fenced, the inner walls would be impossible for a cow to scale. A man on foot might possibly climb the steep and rugged walls but never a cow. The box canyon would be an excellent pasture.

The heat of summer was well upon us during this work, but it had to be completed. I appreciated Scott's help. Walter, too, would help at times, but I saw little of Rose. Blue Heron worked tirelessly to feed us and prepare furs for blankets. We had acquired a goodly amount of clothes from the burned wagons, but the winter would be cold. We would need plenty of furs for blankets and beds.

One day, after Scott and I finished the rock barrier for my next holding pen, we walked down to the river to wash up. The smell of sulfur drifted to us as we passed the hot springs. Although the bathing pool had been cleared and shaped with walls of stones, there had been no need of it yet. But colder weather was coming.

Singing birds perched in all the trees and overhead, puffy white clouds drifted across the sky. The grass down in the river valley had turned a dull brown where the grass in the higher meadows was still green and luxuriant.

The Arkansas River rushed by quickly on its route to the Mississippi and played music with a roar and a splash as it rounded boulders in its way. I found a game path to the water's edge and followed the trail through the trees and undergrowth to wash up after the hard day's work. Despite the heat, the water was cool and pleasant. Snow melt from the higher mountains fed this river.

I thought of the hay we'd stacked. While Scott helped me with the rock wall, Walter had encouraged Rose to help him cut and stack hay. She'd reluctantly agreed. They were a slow-moving pair at the task, but I couldn't complain. They were, after all, helping me.

I knelt to scoop a handful of the fresh water. The cool river water soothed my dry throat. Scott knelt beside me and splashed water over his head. Then, with a grin, he splashed me.

We pulled off our shirts and bathed in the little eddy along the river's edge, and my mind again began to wander. I'd need to figure out a way to get the oxen from my herd to Fort Union. I wrestled with this problem as we gathered our shirts to move back toward high ground. Then, I saw the track.

Pulling my shirt over my head, I knelt and studied the dirt, not believing what I saw. My heart pounded and tried to burst through my chest as I leaned closer.

There, clearly outlined in the river mud, was a horse's hoof print.

CHAPTER 14

"Whaddya see, Jason?" Scott moved beside me, peered over my shoulder, and gasped. Bending quickly, he put his hand gently to one side of the impression, judging the age, I guess. Then he lifted his head and looked ahead, finding another print. He straightened suddenly and ran for the cliff dwelling.

I followed as quickly as I could but saw no reason to run. If the print had been made by passing Indian ponies, they were probably long gone by now. By the time I got to our camp, the shadows were deep and the sun slanted far to the west. Scott was talking excitedly with the others.

"We only saw the tracks of one, but I'm sure there'd be others. We can see 'em in the morning." He reported to Walter, but Rose and Blue Heron were paying rapt attention as well.

Walter turned to me. "You saw the tracks? Only one?" Hope and fear reflected in his dark eyes.

I shrugged. "I don't know. It was just a hoof print. Do you think it's an Indian hunting party? What's the big deal?"

With a whirl, Rose turned on me, her slender form leaning as her green eyes flashed. "You have what you want, but this is something we're interested in. You only care about yourself."

Her Scottish brogue was more pronounced in her anger. She spun on her heel and fled into her room but not before I saw the tears in her eyes.

I looked from Walter to Blue Heron, confused by her reaction.

"What did I say?" Would I never understand Rose?

Blue Heron gave me a weak smile, her dark eyes somber and pensive. "It's all right, Jason. It's not you she's mad at really." With an encouraging nod at me, the Indian woman followed her daughter into the room.

Walter didn't say anything more, but Scott spoke up. "Jason, this is good. We've found horses. Walter is the best wild horse tracker in the world, and we'll capture this herd. We can close a canyon like you and start our ranch." He turned to Walter, his dark eyes gleaming. "Right?"

Walter looked at Scott and frowned, a weary look in his eyes, but I saw something more there. I saw fear.

"Wait," I interrupted. "How do you know they're wild horses?" My excitement grew as I realized the importance of the horse print. "If these are wild horses, this could be what we've been waiting for."

Scott nodded. He turned expectantly to his grandfather.

Walter sighed and shrugged. "I'm old, Scott. I'm too old."

The boy's eyes suddenly blazed. "Don't say that. You're not too old. We need you."

The old Cheyenne said nothing, just stood there with stooped shoulders and pursed lips.

The crackling of the small cooking fire drew our gaze during the awkward silence. One by one, we turned to the flame, staring into its glowing embers, searching for answers. We all seemed lost in our own thoughts.

A short time later, I left my friends in the gathering darkness and retraced my steps back down into the canyon, walking slowly out into the basin beyond. The sun had dropped behind the western mountains, but some light remained. I looked down the valley and watched a pair of deer feeding by the river.

So they'd come here for horses, and when the opportunity presented itself, they're held back by fear and doubt. Mackenzie was gone and with him the driving force, the leadership, the focus of their dream. The dream wasn't dead with Mackenzie, only the direction was lost. How to make them see the goal still lived?

I'd taken to reading the Bible I'd found each night after dinner. Tonight, though, I wanted to be outdoors—alone with the Lord.

I walked slowly and thoughtfully toward the river. The sun had set, and I knew soon the breezes off the nearby mountains would cause the temperature to drop. Despite the heat of the day, the nights were always cool in our canyon.

I found a flat rock and sat down. Letting my eyes roam across the basin, I thought about what Scott had said about fencing another pasture. Why not use the one I had just fenced? It had plenty of grass. I sat there, half thinking about the wild horses and half thinking about God. What did the Lord want me to do?

There would be time to trap a bunch of horses. Walter certainly had experience for that, despite what he said about his age. Scott, Rose, and I would help him. Blue Heron could run the home camp, preparing meals and the like. I prayed for wisdom and guidance. Pa and I had always figured to save money and buy a good stud one day. We'd never be able to save that kind of money, but we hoped anyway. That option was completely dead now.

But trap *wild* horses? The idea intrigued me.

We would have to trap them using creative measures. However, Walter had known this region at one time. Possibly, we could use a method he'd already tried.

My mind continued to sort out ideas and plans. Something else, a force other than myself, seemed to be bringing these notions to me.

A step behind me made me turn. I barely made out Scott's form in the dim light as he moved up beside me.

We didn't speak for a while. I heard the call of a dove to its mate, the roar of the nearby river rumbling melodiously. The whir of a mosquito buzzed at my ear, and I saw the first star of night peaking above the mountains.

I shifted, knowing what I had to say. "Scott, I'm sorry I didn't understand about the horse prints. I thought they were Indian ponies, or I don't know, a hunting party or something. It never occurred to me they were wild ones."

I paused and chewed the inside of my cheek, choosing my words carefully. "I think we can do this. We just need faith. We have to believe God can do anything."

He snorted. "You don't have to sell that notion to me." Scott sighed and shifted on the rock, searching for a more comfortable position. "I know Jesus can do anything. He's brought us you, hasn't he? And no one knows horses like Walter. And no one can ride like Rose."

"Rose?" I blurted, my head coming up. "She can ride?"

I remembered she told me Mackenzie had taught her to ride, but I assumed she'd meant simply to sit on a horse. There's a big difference.

Scott laughed. "Don't you know that no one can ride like a Cheyenne warrior? Rose was taught by the best. The other Indian girls didn't like horses, but Rose took right to them. Father and Walter taught her everything about riding."

I could hear a brother's pride in his voice.

"I think she took to horses because the other girls weren't nice to her," he continued softly. "Not that we often were with other Indians. They didn't trust us, and we weren't really welcome among them. Our white blood bothered them. I think Rose took to riding because she could be alone. She can ride like the wind."

I shook my head, my thoughts racing. "We could catch a bunch of horses. A horse ranch is not far off if we work hard. We just need to put our heads together."

He nodded. I knew he was on my side.

"We need to convince Walter he can do it." Scott nodded again.

The next morning, though, I found the old man stubborn and sullen, not wanting to hear our ideas.

"Come on, Walter," Scott pleaded. "Let's go look at the tracks down by the river. Let's trail that bunch and discover their patterns and where they like to graze and water."

The old man yawned. "No, I'm tired. We have worked very hard lately. I need to rest today."

No matter how hard we tried to enlist his aid, Walter refused. Rose was worse. Where Walter was evasive, Rose showed open hostility. "What are you two fence builders going to do? Catch wild horses? You were lucky to round up some stupid cows."

Her sour face showed her disposition. She left the ledge outside the stone rooms and disappeared into the thick undergrowth of the narrow canyon.

Blue Heron remained silent on the topic but watched her daughter's hasty departure with anxious eyes.

Rose was right, of course. Scott and I went down to the river by ourselves and attempted to make out the tracks of the wild horses. To the best of my knowledge, I made out the tracks of at least twenty animals, and there were probably more. But we lost the tracks where the herd turned into a sandy wash, the prints losing any definition. I was no tracker.

By that time, it was mid-day, and the heat had turned unbearable in the sun, reflecting from the walls of the nearby mountains and beating back down on us. A fly buzzed at my ear, and I swatted at it, annoyed. I looked up the wash where we'd lost the tracks, and then glanced at Scott. He looked tired and hot, a sweat streak cutting the dust on his cheek.

"I'm hot and hungry," I grumbled. "Let's get something to eat, and then we'll come back and give it another go." I straightened and arched my back, stretching my body. My gaze turned toward the canyon where the cool cliff dwellings were, and I caught sight of someone in the brush. Startled, I realized it was Walter.

I averted my eyes and tried to look like I studied something else. A plan formed in my mind.

We walked back to camp, our spirits low, our shirts soaked with sweat. We climbed up the stone steps to the ledge of our rock rooms, grateful for the deep shadows that met us there. Blue Heron waited for us. With a consoling smile, she served us food.

We sat for a while, soaking in the cool of the shadowed retreat and not eager to return into the heat of the river valley. Soon, Walter ascended the stone steps to join us. With a grunt, he lowered himself and accepted a bowl from Blue Heron.

I watched him from the corner of my eye as he ate, sensing he had something on his mind. I wasn't surprised when he spoke.

"Find anything?"

Scott ignored him, but I shrugged. "There's nothing to find. No one could follow those tracks. They disappeared in a wash. It's impossible."

He ate the rest of his food in silence. When he finished, he wiped his fingers on his pants and looked out over the narrow canyon. In a low, clear voice, he said, "I could find them." Scott's neck nearly snapped as he looked at me, hope gleaming in his eyes. I shook my head, fighting to keep my face passive, hiding my elation. "No, Walter. I don't think so. Those tracks disappeared into sand. Forget it. It'd be too difficult for an old man. No one can find them."

He glared at me, frowning, and then continued. "I am sure I could find those tracks. We will go see."

I shrugged again, feigning indifference, but my heart leaped in my chest. A thrill raced down my back. Scott shot me an inquisitive glance, his eyebrows arching. I gave a curt nod but said nothing. Inside, I prayed fervently.

Walter pushed himself to his feet, stretched, and then made his way slowly down the stone steps into the bright afternoon sun.

Scott and I followed.

As we crossed the basin, excitement built in my chest, and I had to tell myself not to get my hopes up. Maybe the old Cheyenne wouldn't find the tracks, either.

The three of us returned to the sandy wash. Walter studied the torn-up ground, muttering under his breath. Little by little, he made out prints and surmised a direction. As we walked farther up the wash, he found where the animals had exited the sandy ravine, a path of cut-up turf revealing their direction.

He looked at me triumphantly, his eyes twinkling. "A child could have found these tracks, although you almost wiped them out with your own."

I shrugged. "I'm no tracker. Never said I was. We need someone with experience to find this bunch." I was secretly pleased with the old man's interest but said nothing to him about that. "Help us find this bunch, and let's see if we can trap some of 'em."

He chewed his lip and studied the horse's trail then glanced from me to Scott. His grandson gave him such a pleading look. I grinned, knowing Walter would have to give in.

But I knew it was more than Scott's persuasive glance that had convinced Walter to join us. He'd been hooked the minute he started searching for the tracks in the sandy wash. I'd gambled the wild horse hunter in him couldn't be swayed once he hit the trail, and it looked like my gamble was about to pay off.

The old man grinned. "Okay. Let us give it a try."

Scott gave him a fierce hug, and I stood there watching, feeling the old aloneness swell within me.

With Walter leading, we made good time following the herd. Within three hours, we'd located where they'd bedded down the previous night.

Clear tracks showed which way the herd had gone this morning, and Walter showed us landmarks so we could locate this place tomorrow. We walked a direct and faster way back to the cliff dwelling. With the sun dropping in the west, we made it back to camp, tired and footsore.

Walter seemed like a new person. There was a spring in his step. He was in his element and couldn't contain his excitement. Anticipation filled the air like electricity during a lightning storm.

We chattered as we ate, and Blue Heron smiled as she served us. She moved quickly, pouring water as she asked us question after question.

But Rose sulked silently. I felt her piercing eyes on me a few times, but she always looked away when I turned to her.

After supper, Rose again avoided us and left the circle of firelight to seek her own counsel.

Later that night, Walter, Scott, and I made plans for a weeklong journey to track this herd, note their grazing patterns, and find out where they liked to water.

With packs of food and a blanket for each of us, we left camp early the next morning.

As I passed the big sycamore, I glanced over my shoulder, taking in my last view of the cliff dwellings I expected to have for many days. Rose stood on the ledge, watching us go, thickets and undergrowth eventually concealing her from my sight as I followed Walter and Scott down the trail.

CHAPTER 15

We marched directly to where we'd last seen the horse's tracks. The sun peeked over the plains behind us when we found the spot the herd had bedded down for the night. With Walter leading, carefully making out their route, Scott and I tagged along, pressing the old man for details as we walked.

Walter squatted, his gaze fixed on the ground as he spread his hand and gestured. "A young stallion trails behind, afraid of the lead horse. Here are his prints. This is a foal, walking close by its mother. Over here, a pair stopped to nibble on these young willow leaves."

Halting in the shadow of a huge boulder, we ate a small bit of piñon nuts and meat and then continued, eagerness driving us through the heat of the day. We found places where the wild herd had stopped to drink at a stream, and Walter pointed out certain tracks, speaking as if he could see events in his mind. Here a small colt ran around his mother. There a horse pushed another one away from her baby.

I was amazed how Walter could look at these simple marks on the ground and relate a story from them. He easily read signs, and apparently, he understood the horses' actions and sometimes even their thinking.

By nightfall, the old Cheyenne announced we were only an hour behind the herd. "We must be very quiet now," Walter instructed. "The stallion could hear any loud sound. We do not want to frighten them. We will need to find a good place to sit back and observe, to discover their patterns. They must have favorite places and that is what we need to know."

With no water nearby, we made dry camp that night. No fire, not wanting the horses to smell our smoke. Besides, it wasn't cold this time of the year, although by morning, a chill would be in the air.

Walter pulled a number of long rawhide strips from his pack and began intricately weaving them together. I watched him, fascinated by the nimbleness of his old fingers.

"What're you making?" I settled against a rock, my eyes straining to see him in the growing darkness.

"A hackamore," he answered without lifting his head. "It is how the Indians turn a horse's head. No bit." Despite the dim light, the old wild horse hunter worked awhile longer before stowing the thing in his pack.

The next morning, we were up and moving before the dawn. The tracks ran through a trail on the side of a mountain and were easy to make out even in the dim light.

Abruptly, Walter halted and studied the trail while I looked back, peering to the east. I couldn't see the open prairie from here, but knew it was there, stretching all the way back to Missouri.

Walter grunted, drawing my gaze. He scowled and stroked his chin, his brow wrinkling with agitation. Then he shook his head and looked up the mountain, as if searching for a landmark.

"What is it?" I stepped closer.

He looked at the tracks in the trail again before he spoke. "Something spooked them. They have started running. We cannot keep up with them if they continue to run."

Scott drank from the canteen and then wiped water from his chin. As he handed the canteen to his grandfather, he said, "What'll we do if they run?"

Walter squinted then shook his head again.

"It's all right," I quickly put in. "They'll slow down soon. We'll catch up." I hoped I sounded more confident than I felt.

Walter looked at me doubtfully. "It is foolish to track horses on foot. It is very difficult. We would do much better on horseback."

I arched an eyebrow at him, surprised by this unexpected negative comment, the first on the trail. Was he losing the thrill of the chase? I worried he was thinking of turning back.

"Well, we don't have horses, so we do what we can," I added, slapping him on the back. "Come on, let's get going."

Walter pursed his lips and looked at Scott. The young boy nodded, his dark eyes shining.

With a shrug, the old Indian trudged into the trail. Scott shot me a worried glance and followed his grandfather.

I bit my lip and peered up at the cloudless sky. I hoped I could keep their spirits up.

Our camp that night was a somber one, full of doubts and anxieties. All of us were tired and sore. Scott showed us blisters he'd acquired on his feet and grimaced as he washed them in a creek. I tried hard to keep the conversation going, attempting to move toward positive ground. I also prayed constantly on the inside. Was I doing the right thing in pushing the Indians so hard? Should we go back to the cliff dwelling? I thought of Blue Heron's cooking, and of course, Rose.

"I haven't ridden a horse in a year," Scott grumbled, rubbing his tender feet.

"Maybe you never will again, if it is not God's will," Walter added, a sour tinge to his voice.

"Scott," I interrupted, hoping to distract them. "How did you come to know Jesus?" His head came up and even Walter turned to look at me. I had their attention.

Scott shrugged, then grinned at Walter. "Walter and Father were always telling me Bible stories. Father carried two books—the Bible and an old copy of Ivanhoe. Father taught me how to read. Rose and I took turns reading aloud. Father and Walter trapped furs, and most nights, at camp, we'd read the Bible around the fire and talk about what we'd read. Or about horses."

He paused and dropped his gaze, pretending to work over his feet again, but not before I noticed the tears in his eyes.

Walter grunted and rubbed his knees, a faraway look in his old eyes.

"Thinking of former days?" I asked, tossing another stick on the fire.

Sparks flew up as Walter glanced at his grandson then returned his gaze to the little fire. "Those were good days. I never learned to read the white man's books, but Mackenzie taught Rose and Scott to understand the markings on the paper. It was good to hear the stories and talk about what they read. God helped me through a difficult time when my family was taken from me."

The old man sighed. Shadows filled the deep lines in his face, and suddenly, he looked very old, older than a body had a right to be. He continued, his voice in a low whisper, as if his memories prompted him.

"The Bible guides me. God's word is truth, sharper than any double-edged blade. It speaks to my soul. I have been saved by the blood of the Lamb."

Walter sounded so tired, bone weary. Was I pushing him too hard?

Silence fell over our camp like a shroud, and the black night pressed in on me. We all stared into the blaze. I wondered if I'd been mistaken to try and capture the wild horses. What if we failed? Perhaps it was too much for Walter and his grieving family. They'd endured a lot already. Another defeat might set them back, way back. Maybe this was too much for them to attempt.

But had I not heard the Lord correctly? Were we foolish, like Walter said, to chase them on foot?

Scott's voice broke the somber silence. "It's always been the five of us. Other Indians kept their distance, not sure if we were one of them or not. It made the five of us very close."

Scott leaned forward and tossed another stick on the small blaze. "It seemed like horses became a way for our family to have purpose, a way we were all connected. Horses and Jesus."

Suddenly, something clicked in my mind. Horses and Jesus. Scott was right. I understood now what drew me to these people. They shared my faith and my hopes. Horses and Jesus was the connection we shared.

I smiled and glanced skyward. "Thanks," I mumbled, knowing who had showed this to me.

Scott rolled in his blankets. Walter appeared to be asleep.

Lying back on my buffalo skin pack, I pondered. These people had gone through tough times, but they were together. I was alone. I felt the hunger in me to belong, to be a part.

Mackenzie's untimely death had left them without a leader, without direction. An unfamiliar void remained where before there'd been a way to go, a path to take. Now, they were lost.

I prayed for success. I wanted to give these new friends what they needed as much as I did—a new beginning.

CHAPTER 16

When I awoke the next morning, Walter was already awake and packing his gear. He nudged Scott with his moccasin. "Get up, sleepy head. We have horses to chase."

Scott threw the blanket back and looked at me, his eyes unnaturally large in the early light of dawn. I nodded and smiled as I dressed and loaded my pack.

A kindred spirit existed between us now. I think it had always been there, but now we were aware of it. We were united in our quest. We each desired to catch horses to start a ranch, and we each wanted to grow in our understanding and obedience to Christ. And, I suspect, we wanted to do these two things together.

Was this to be my new family? Had the Lord brought me out here to become one of the Mackenzie clan?

Perhaps. But first, I would need to earn their trust. Especially Rose's.

For three days, we nagged at the heels of the wild bunch. Walter continuously pointed out hoof prints. By the time we finally caught sight of the herd, I felt like I knew each horse.

Walter motioned us to get down. We crawled on our bellies to peer over the edge of a hill to watch the herd grazing below. The horses had spread out across a mountain meadow and were feeding quietly. Occasionally, the stallion, a sturdy, dull brown stud, would sniff the air and survey the surrounding area. Shoulders scarred from many battles, he was tough and ready for another fight.

He would not be easy to surprise.

We counted twenty-six head in the bunch, including a couple of young stallions, too young to challenge the old leader.

The sight of all those horses just out of our reach made me crazy with excitement. I could hardly contain my eagerness. I laid a hand on Walter's shoulder and whispered close to his ear. "Well? What do you think? How can we trap them?"

He studied the herd a while longer, glancing occasionally to side canyons or deep ravines that cut across the meadow.

"Some twenty years ago, I ran a herd into a dry wash around here and trapped them. I think I know where it is, but how to get them to go there, that is the question. I used fire that time to push them into my trap."

Walter spoke as if to himself. I could tell he was working the details out in his mind, figuring out how to move the animals where he wanted them to go.

I glanced over Walter's back to where Scott lay in the short grass. He grinned at me and I nodded. We both could see Walter was having fun. He was the master at this game.

As the days of our hunt had continued, he'd grown more resolute, more excited to succeed. He seemed to be pleased to discover he still had the ability left in his old bones. Each day, the years of hardship and toil seemed to slip away from him as we followed these wild horses. Now, Walter seemed like a young man again, his voice and actions full of excitement.

Walter motioned and we drew away. We made a small fire for our dinner, downwind from the herd.

Staring into the blaze, I found myself missing Rose. Why? She'd been nothing but contrary to me, but I wished she was with us, sharing the thrill of the chase. This is where she belonged.

I wanted to ask Walter the questions that nagged at me, but I didn't have to. Scott talked enough for the both of us. I simply sat back and listened.

"How can we push this bunch into your trap?"

"I am working on it," Walter growled evasively, tossing another stick on the fire.

"What does the trap look like? Will it hold a bunch of this size?" Scott prodded but Walter didn't seem to mind. I could tell he liked the attention.

"If it was not a good trap for this herd, I would not use it." His old eyes twinkled.

"How will we break them if Rose won't help us? No one rides like Rose."

The old Cheyenne said nothing and looked into the flames, finally ignoring his grandson.

I shifted beside the fire. "I was thinking the same thing. I hope you have these details worked out, Walter." We were forced to rely on the old

Cheyenne's horse knowledge. I wasn't sure how things were going to work out, but I trusted God. A miracle had been needed to pull Walter into the chase, but now here we were.

The old wild horse hunter grunted, and Scott and I looked at him, expectancy filling us.

"Yes," he nodded, stroking his chin. "I think I have it figured out."

Walter seemed to enjoy the suspense, because he said nothing more for a few minutes, allowing the tension to build. Scott started to squirm.

Finally, Walter drew in a deep breath. "There is an old waterway over there a mile or so, if I recall correctly. It has high walls and leads into a box canyon. There are a few places where the herd can escape the wash, and we do not have time to build fences, so we will have to block those paths. I think we can do it if we have help."

"Help?" Scott repeated. "I don't think you can get Rose to help us."

"No, I do not think I can," he agreed, nodding. "But I think Jason can."

I stared at him, thinking he'd lost his mind. Scott laughed outright. "Jason? Rose would never help Jason."

"I don't think you know what you're talking about, Walter." He might know horses, but he was wrong about this.

He narrowed his eyes at me. "No one held this dream of a horse ranch more dearly than Rose. Only you can understand that. You must convince her to help. It depends on you."

My sleep that night was fitful at best. I tossed and turned, worrying that we would never catch these ever-elusive horses.

The next morning, Walter took a stick and drew a map in the dirt, showing the most direct trail back to the cliff dwelling. Only about four miles as the crow flies, but the trip would take me almost half a day to get there.

"You must hurry," Walter warned as he slapped the light pack on my back. "I do not know how long these horses will stay here. The grass is good, but anything could make them move on. Scott and I will scout the wash and figure out which paths will need to be blocked."

He paused and laid a hand on my shoulder, peering into my eyes. "I will expect the two of you tomorrow."

I gulped and nodded. Walter's dark eyes held a glint of hope, but something else too. Worry. I could tell he wasn't sure I could pull this off.

With a backward glance at Scott, I hurried down from the edge of the valley and moved toward our camp.

I walked for hours as if in a trance. I swayed between believing God would encourage Rose to join us and the belief she would never help. I prayed unceasingly, seeking the Lord's wisdom. I asked that he would give me the right words to persuade Rose. I poured out my soul before my God and tried to guess what would happen.

I arrived at the cliff dwelling by noon. At first, Blue Heron seemed worried when she saw I was alone, but I assured her that Scott and Walter were safe. I explained I had returned only to retrieve much-needed supplies.

Rose listened closely as I described the herd and told about certain horses, their characteristics and relationships within the herd. I described their colors and watched her green eyes glow.

I'd discovered her one weakness—she loved horses. She was a natural horsewoman, and her desire to ride coursed through her veins like blood.

The time sped by with my continual chatter about the wild horse herd. I hoped I painted a picture Rose could see in her mind.

After sharing elaborate stories of the herd, I praised Blue Heron for such a delicious meal. "Neither Scott nor I can cook like this, and Walter won't even try."

Blue Heron smiled and then began to bustle around the fire. Rose chewed her lip, her long lashes ringing her narrowed eyes. "So, they're just watching the horses and waiting for your return?" She tilted her head and squinted at me.

I nodded. "Yes, I'm to gather more supplies and join them again. Also, they're hoping you'll join us."

All of my cleverly rehearsed speeches fell out of my mind as I blurted out my true intentions. By the shocked look on her face, Rose wouldn't be persuaded easily.

Her green eyes flashed. "What?" she demanded. "Do you think I'll help you? Forget it." She waved a dismissive hand and turned away. "I'm not interested in watching you succeed further," she said over her shoulder as she moved toward her room.

"That's just it, Rose," I called to her retreating form. "This isn't for me alone. This is the pursuit of your family's dream." I took a step toward her. "I want horses for a ranch, that's true. But you do too. It's what you're meant to do."

She whirled, eyes blazing. "What do you know about my dream? What do you know about family? You're alone."

I stepped back as if slapped. Her words stung.

"My family wanted a ranch and they're gone, but their memory lives within me," I said quietly. "I'll chase this dream in honor of that memory."

I paused, remembering Pa.

"It's the same with you. Your father wanted this for you. Now is your opportunity. Walter is a great horse hunter, and you're a great horse rider. Help us. We can't do this without you."

Cal's words that I would need a partner whispered to me, but I pursed my lips and pushed the thought away. She might help us round up some horses, but I doubted if Rose and I could ever be real partners.

She hung her head, listening as I rambled. I wondered if I'd gotten through to her when she lifted her face, tears rolling down her bronzed cheeks.

But then she shook her head. "Father is dead and with him is the dream." She stared at me across the small fire, and I could see my argument had failed. Hope withered within me.

"No, it's not." Blue Heron stepped forward as Rose and I looked at her. I'd forgotten she was present.

"Your father was a great man, and he did great things to help this family, things you will never understand. I mourn for him every day in my heart. I miss him. Now is your chance to honor his memory as Jason honors his family. Rose, you must do this for your family, but more importantly, for yourself. Hope did not die with Mackenzie—only slept. This has always been what you were made for. Help capture these horses and live the life you were meant to live."

It was the longest speech I'd ever heard from Blue Heron. When she finished, only the crackling of the small blaze broke the silence.

Rose spun and disappeared into her room. Blue Heron smiled, but I saw the doubt in her eyes. Then the Cheyenne woman turned and followed her daughter.

I sat by the fire for a long time, adding fuel despite the warm summer night. My thoughts jumbled and twisted. I was unable to make sense of them. I didn't understand what the Lord wanted me to do. Would we hunt wild horses? If not, had I failed?

Finally, I rose, my legs stiff from sitting so long, and found my way to my room. I stared at the stone ceiling, unable to find peace.

<hr />

With the gray dawn, I crawled from my bed and stood on the rock ledge, wishing I had coffee. The dark canyon yawned below me, reflecting my mood.

Had everything come to nothing? Were all my hopes and expectations gone? Where was God?

The leather door flap rustled behind me. Rose came out, dressed for travel in pants. Blue Heron stepped beside her—a buffalo hide pack in her hands.

Rose glared at me. I looked away, not wanting to see how well the pants fit her slender form. I shifted uneasily.

"I'll go," she said. "I'll help, and I pray this is what Father wanted."

CHAPTER 17

Joy mingled with surprise, filling Scott and Walter's eyes as we entered their camp that afternoon. Morose, Rose stared at them. Her brother smiled at her, and the old Cheyenne embraced her.

Rose had been silent on our trek to meet her grandfather. I respected her desire to be left alone and didn't want her to change her mind.

We clustered together then, and with a nod and a twinkle in his old eyes, Walter filled us in. The horses hadn't strayed. They grazed and rested amid the rock-strewn meadow. The mud-colored stallion was still on guard but did not seem uneasy. He suspected nothing.

With a gesture, Walter beckoned us forward. A thrill ran through me as I crawled to the top of the hill beside Rose. Silently, she surveyed the herd scattered below, her eyes glistening. I studied her from the corner of my eye as she leaned forward on her elbows, taut, eager, her radiant face glowing with anticipation. She couldn't conceal her love of the horses.

Without the use of horses, our task would be very difficult. Walter would light the brush on fire at the edge of the valley below. Our hope was the herd would run from the smoke and flames, toward the opening in the ravine.

Along the way, we'd be stationed to help contain and guide the running herd. If one of us failed to keep them restricted to the dry stream bed, they would escape.

"When do we drive them?" Rose shifted, her voice low. It was the first I'd heard her speak in hours.

"Now." Walter edged away from the top of the hill.

"We don't have time today for that," Rose argued, following her grandfather.

Walter made sure he was out of sight from the horses before he led the way to our gear. I hadn't expected to start the drive this late in the day, either.

"Is there time?" Scott stood beside me, our gazes fixed on the old Indian.

He nodded. "There is a chance the herd will move in the night. We cannot wait. We need to move now. There might not be another opportunity."

"And if they won't be turned?" Rose demanded.

Walter shrugged. "Get out of their way. We want no injuries."

Each of us knowing what must be done, we moved into position. My heart pounded as I took my place. Heat waves shimmered in the dusty, narrow gulley, and I wiped my forehead with my sleeve. Sweat trickled down my back beneath my shirt. My pulse quickened. I hoped I was up to the job of turning the running, frightened horses as they came to me.

I glanced at the sun, judging the remaining time of light. Shadows already stretched across the sand. Soon the heat would dissipate, and the evening cool would descend.

As dusk approached, I fired another prayer off to God, knowing this wouldn't work without divine help.

Walter had walked down the left side of the valley to the deadfalls and brush we'd seen earlier. A fire in that dry tinder should push the animals in the opposite direction.

Scott had been excited when I'd left him. "This is it, Jason. We can do it," he had whispered. His confidence soaring, he had picked up the old rifle and moved quickly toward his guard post.

Rose had looked at me with a look of hope, fear, and a little desperation. I knew how she felt. This was our chance to get horses. Would it work?

I nodded to her, too full of emotion to speak. She must've understood, because she shot me a weak smile and walked away to her position.

My post was the first bend the horses would reach after leaving the valley. As they approached, I was to turn them along another route, a branch ravine toward the box canyon. If I was successful, I would mount a high knoll and watch how Rose and Scott managed.

I stood in my spot surveying the area, shifting to what I hoped would be a more advantageous position. The wash took a sudden turn here, and I must keep the animals in the dry watercourse.

I chewed the inside of my cheek, wishing I had really long arms to block this gap. I picked up two long tree limbs instead. I considered stripping the branches from them, then thought better of it. The leaves would make me look bigger than I was.

As I settled in to wait, I couldn't see or hear anything. Afternoon waned quickly into twilight, and shadows filled the ravine as the sun dipped below the mountains. Only the first, pale star of evening peeked over the rocky ramparts above me—soon would be full darkness.

Had Walter made a hasty decision? Perhaps it was too late today to attempt the capture. Darkness would be upon us soon, then it would be too late to try and herd running horses.

I looked farther down the wash, hoping to catch sight of Rose. If the herd was turned at my position, they would head her way next.

I wiped my sweaty palms across my pants and gripped the long branches tightly. I watched the shadows lengthen. The waiting was killing me. Would we be able to do this before it got dark? There was no way running, frightened horses would see me waving my tree branches in the dark. A thick curl of dark smoke rose over the mountain ridge to my left. Walter had started his fire. The smoke grew, and soon black clouds filled the sky. I watched them slowly drift overhead, praying Walter was all right.

Time stood still. When would something happen? I held my branches at my sides, the tips resting on the ground, feeling kind of foolish with my leafy arm extensions. Would the herd even come toward me?

Suddenly, a pounding of hooves filled my ears. A horse screamed, its whistle piercing the still evening air. They were coming!

I couldn't see them, but my heart leapt into my throat at the roar of running horses. They came around the bend, stretched low, running all out. I recognized the scarred brown stallion leading the pack, his nostrils distended, his head held high.

For a split second, I thought they'd ignore my presence and run right over me, then I waved my tree branches and yelled at the top of my lungs.

The brown stallion ran at me but then turned, leaning far to one side, before righting himself and leading the herd into the adjoining wash.

I watched as every head of the frightened herd followed the brown stallion and rounded the corner into the empty watercourse.

Dust filled the air, and before I knew, they were gone. I heard their sound die away. Dropping my leafy branches, I raced for the top of the ridge.

I reached the crest in time to see the herd turned by Rose. The animals were heading now for Scott's position. The narrow ravine was choked with dust, and I couldn't see individual horses but followed them by the dust plume that hung over them like a billowing banner.

I spun and raced back down the hill to the sandy floor, almost colliding with Walter as he hobbled along the wash.

He saw me, his eyes widening in the gloom as he panted heavily. "Did Rose turn them?"

"Yes," I shouted and ran after the horses, leaving Walter to catch up.

My own breath came in great gasps as I rushed down the winding sandy floor toward Rose. I followed the torn earth the herd had left in their path. The air was thick with dust and deepening twilight.

I rounded the bend where Rose had been placed to guide the herd. She stood there, hands on her knees, panting. She looked up. "I turned them. Oh, Jason, they're so beautiful." Her eyes glowed, and I grinned as I jogged past her.

The heavy report of the hunting rifle caused my feet to stumble. Then I was running again, the sound lending wings to my feet.

Rose fell into step behind me and we ran on, the dust choking me, breathing difficult. I almost had to stop, but I pushed on.

I found Scott standing in the trail, the rifle dangling over one shoulder. He grinned when he saw me. "Jason, they went in the box canyon! They're trapped." The last light of day showed the excitement on his face.

With the final rays of sunlight, we pushed the animals into the box canyon. Now the sun was gone, the valley dark.

Rose stood beside me, and I turned to her. "Get some wood. Let's build a fire in the opening."

Fearing the horses would attempt to escape, we built a roaring blaze across the gap and piled wood on it. Orange light splashed brightly across the rocks, painting the nightscape with vivid color.

The three of us gathered fuel for the long night ahead and waited for Walter to join us.

He limped into camp a half hour later, a wide smile on his lined face. The old horse hunter had succeeded again.

"This is only the first," Walter said with a light in his old eyes I hadn't seen before. "We will catch Wildfire when we find his sign. I am sure he is still in the area. It would take a lot to drive him from these mountains."

I looked at Rose then, and she was smiling at me. I loved when she smiled.

CHAPTER 18

A sense of disbelief filled us that night. Disbelief that we'd actually done it. Rose was the most shocked of us all. She'd poise motionless, like an attentive deer, listening to the distant sounds of the herd. Then she'd relax, and a faint smile would play on her lips.

We sat around the roaring fire, talking of breaking and riding wild horses and which ones were our favorites.

Our fire blocked passage through the ravine from the canyon so the horses would be secure for the night. We talked of the capture and the number of horses we had. I marveled at how the excitement level in our little band had grown so rapidly in such a short period of time. In just a few hours, we'd gone from a bunch of doubtful, skeptical wild horse hunters, to genuine horse owners.

"They came tearing down the wash, and at first, I was terrified." Scott gestured wildly, his face beaming in the firelight. "That old brown stallion was leading the pack with a fire in his eyes. I almost ran from my post, I was so scared. But then I lifted the rifle and fired into the sky, and he turned and ran in here. The herd followed him like they were all tied on a string. Then I was standing here all alone and it was over."

Walter pulled a hackamore out of his pack. I noticed this one was different than the one I'd seen him work on before.

"We will see how many we can cull out of this bunch first," he said. "It will lessen our work to immediately get rid of the ones we do not want to keep. Also, there will then be less animals to feed."

I was surprised to hear this. I had assumed we'd keep every head we'd captured. "Why let any go? Shouldn't we keep 'em all?"

Rose glowered at me. "You're new at this, Cowboy Jason, but we've done this before. Some of these horses will show good lines and be proper for breeding or breaking, but some'll be too old or unhealthy. We don't want to waste our time on horses that have no value for us."

Rose spoke like a rancher. This was business to her, not a pony ride.

I was no tenderfoot when it came to horses, either—Pa had taught me a lot about bloodlines and breeding. However, as I sat there listening to these experts in horseflesh, I felt like a novice.

Pa had taught me a lot, but we'd never owned fine horses. He'd shown me many such animals, but we'd owned none. We'd certainly never captured wild horses before.

I decided then to listen and learn.

The next morning, Scott was positioned to feed the fire and block the herd's escape while Rose, Walter, and I walked into the narrow box canyon with the rising sun. A hazy fog rose slowly from the canyon floor. That was a good sign—there must be water around somewhere.

Our feet crunched on the sand and hard-packed dirt of the wash. Huge boulders were strewn about as if a giant had hurled them there. The canyon was choked with broken slabs of rock and debris with few open areas.

Weaving among the boulders, we passed stunted trees and scant undergrowth. Only a few big trees that had evaded avalanche or fire over the decades remained.

We rounded a giant pile of stone, its jagged outline revealing it had once been part of the mountain above. There in a small grassy meadow, stood the herd.

They'd caught our scent or heard our approach and were watching us as we drew near, their backs to the canyon wall. Bunched and nervous, their eyes never left us.

The mud-brown stallion stood as a sentinel out in front, his fine head up, staring at us, his long mane tossing about in agitation. His forelegs stamped the earth as if he prepared for battle. The scars on his shoulders, neck, and flanks attested to his cleverness and combat abilities.

The brown stallion had earned this herd. Now, we had too.

The herd clustered behind him as we stood opposite them, pointing out specific horses, keeping our voices low so not to further alarm them.

"Rose, tell me if my old eyes see what I think I see," Walter whispered out of the corner of his mouth. "Is that gray a gelding? He looks like he has a brand on his left shoulder."

I strained my eyes, and I did see something on the gray horse but couldn't make it out.

Rose craned her neck. "Yes, it's a brand."

Confused, I bit my lip. "So what? What does that mean?"

Rose squinted at me, but Walter placed a hand on her shoulder.

"The brand means that gray horse has been ridden before and must have gotten loose from a ranch or a wagon train. We probably could rope and ride him quickly. It would surely help." Walter spoke with patience. I appreciated the contrast from the condescending way Rose addressed me.

Rose pointed to a large rock above the herd. "If we could climb there without the herd moving away, I could rope that gray gelding."

I studied the large boulder, then glanced at the slender girl beside me. I could feel my eyebrows arch skeptically at her proposal. Rope the gray gelding from there? I doubted if she could do so but said nothing. The tall boulder towering above the herd wouldn't allow an easy throw of a rope. Could Rose be serious about her intentions?

"Yes," Walter mused, looking at the position of the rocks above the herd. "We will try. I will keep the stallion's attention, and you slip around behind. Be careful. When you rope the gelding, we will move in to help." He handed her the coil of rope and the rawhide hackamore.

Rose gripped the hackamore in her teeth and bunched her long hair into a ponytail. Dark strands curled against the copper skin of her nape. A tingle ran through me as she bound her hair with a length of blue ribbon.

My stomach tightened, and I looked away as she glided into the rocks and bushes.

Walter shifted beside me as we alternated between watching the herd and the top of the big boulder. Walter pointed at a few colts and foals. "We will hope to break and train those little ones. They will be easiest because they are young. But some of them are past the point of breaking to riding. We can still use them for breeding if they are not too aggressive."

We watched them. They watched us. The stalemate continued with the stallion eyeing us warily, stamping occasionally. The herd kept their distance, and we didn't attempt to approach nearer. Walter explained we didn't want to make them any more nervous than they already were.

At length, I caught sight of Rose perched atop the huge boulder above the side of the herd. Directly below her was the gray gelding. She signaled to us with a wave and crept forward on her hands and knees.

She lifted the coil of rope and shook out a loop, holding the lasso in one hand as she eyed the gray. Walter and I readied ourselves to run at them the second the loop hit the gelding.

Rose slowly drew herself up and swung a wide loop above her head. The rope went around once, again, and then a third time. The herd must've sensed her nearness then for a number of them turned to look up at the instant her hand darted forward. The loop streaked through the air.

The rope settled perfectly around the gelding's head. Rising quickly, Rose braced her feet and held the plunging gray.

With a slap on my shoulder, Walter rushed forward.

I hurried to catch up as I watched, amazed that Rose held the plunging horse without losing her footing. Her arms strained, her body moving like a willow sapling as she crouched on the rock, her knees bent. She held the rope around the gray's neck with perfect intuition of when to tighten or slacken her hold. The horse continued to plunge and rear as Walter advanced.

The other horses scattered and shied to one side of the tight canyon during the commotion. Dust rose in clouds as they kicked up sand and moved away from the roped gray. The brown stallion tried to remain between the gelding and his herd, protecting them. His large eyes rolled in fear and anger.

Walter whistled loudly as a signal to Rose and she deftly threw the end of the rope to the old wild horse hunter. He grabbed it midair and quickly wrapped the end around a tree, securing the rope.

I don't know how Rose appeared so swiftly, but there she was, darting among the hooves and dust and throwing herself toward the dancing gray. She ran forward and vaulted onto its back. Her legs wrapped around the belly of the gray horse, her hand gripping the rope around his neck.

Walter released his tight hold on the rope, allowing slack as the horse pranced wildly, desperately trying to dislodge Rose as the loose rope dragged beneath it.

In the excitement of the fight with the lone gelding, I forgot to check the rest of the herd. They'd moved off to one side and watched the show. Why they hadn't run farther up the canyon, I didn't know. Perhaps the stallion felt reluctant to lead them away, still trying to protect one of the herd.

Rose continued to hold the rope in one hand, choking the animal with the loop. It seemed to hesitate in its mad fight. At that exact moment, the Indian girl quickly slipped the hackamore onto the horse's head. With amazing speed and agility, Rose had harnessed the snorting, rearing animal.

The loose rope dragged under the horse's belly and almost tangled around his front hooves as he plunged stiff-legged in tight circles. Rose crouched on the horse, clinging like a burr, refusing to be thrown.

Soon, the gray tired and slowed. Rose used her knees and the reins to guide the animal as they began to move about the torn clearing in a methodical routine.

Rose kicked the gelding, driving him up and down the clearing, darting toward the herd and then away again. The stallion continued to watch, eyes blazing, but Rose was now on equal footing with the herd.

She turned the heaving gray toward Walter and rode to us, reining in the animal beside us. Walter removed the rope and coiled it, putting it over his shoulder.

Rose leaned and patted the gray's trembling shoulder. Her hair was messed and she panted, but a wide grin spread across her sweat-streaked face and her cheeks glowed. She sat on the animal like a queen, and I understood what Scott had said about her riding.

"Good job, Rose," Walter congratulated as he stroked the horse's neck. The gelding stamped and rolled his eyes, but the Indian girl had a firm hand on the reins and held the horse in check.

Walter was right. The gray had been ridden before. I could tell this was not new to him as Rose tugged the hackamore, and the horse obeyed the command, turning his head from side to side.

"One down." Walter held up a finger. "Take some time to ride him and get the feel for him. Maybe we can use him to guide the others. I would like to cull the herd a little today. What do you say?"

Rose seemed happier than I'd ever seen her. She sat astride like someone born to it. Her green eyes sparkled.

She nodded. "Let me take some of the starch out of him, and then we can start cutting the herd." She turned to ride away and called over her shoulder, "Pick one to cull."

Walter and I watched her ride the gelding around the meadow while the herd squeezed into the corner of the canyon. We stopped at noon for a much-needed break.

The afternoon was spent with Rose circling the panicked herd, wearing them down as she attempted to separate two old mares. Scott had been alerted to allow them their freedom. By the end of that day, the pair had been culled.

As the sun set, shadows lay thickly across the narrow canyon and the herd stood wide eyed and nervous, not being used to the constant pushing and an Indian girl riding among them, trying to make them separate and abandon two of their own. I felt sad to see them go, bolting down the dry wash toward where Scott waited. But these two old mares weren't going to benefit the ranch we were building.

That night around the campfire, I shot glances at the gray gelding picketed in the nearby shadows. He was exhausted but seemed calmer now, still boasting a roguish look in his eye. He didn't seem afraid of the campfire, perhaps he'd seen one before. He also didn't seem bothered now by our nearness.

CHAPTER 19

The next four days were filled with grueling work, culling the wild horse band. Any horse that appeared sick or too old, did not show positive blood lines, had short legs, a swayed back, or any other defect or undesirable quality were released. Only animals with promising qualities for good breeding were kept.

We had constructed a gate of bars that could easily be removed when releasing the culled horses. This makeshift gate proved invaluable in containing the wild bunch as we worked them.

I looked at the gray again. Although he watched us continuously, he'd become more and more comfortable with our presence. A few choice handfuls of grass had not hurt, either. Currently, he was the best of our riding stock.

We'd argued about the brown stallion for the last four days. He was a tough animal and showed signs of quality but would never be tamed and might prove to be more difficult than we wanted to deal with. His scarred hide gave proof of his great strength and defiance. He must've fought many battles to prove his dominance within the herd.

As we sat down to dinner one evening, Rose and Walter debated the stallion's presence in the herd once again.

"Some of the younger stallions have his blood and will be easier to handle. We don't need him," Rose argued as she finished her dinner. "Besides, I want only one king stallion on the ranch. Wildfire."

Walter shook his head. "Rose, we have not even seen signs of him. You better get that idea out of your head now and tag one of these young stallions as your stud."

I wanted to believe the horses I'd seen up the Arkansas were Wildfire's band, but I truly had no idea what the stallion looked like. Again, I decided to say nothing, not wanting to raise Rose's expectations.

She only smiled at the old man. "Not yet. I'll be patient a while longer. There's still a chance we'll find him."

The brown stallion was cut out of the herd and released the next morning.

A young strawberry mare had been roped, and Rose and Walter alternated working with her. She wore the hackamore on the second day, and Rose rode her on the fourth. Using the strawberry mare and the gray gelding, we roped and broke two more of the younger stock for riding.

The little red mare showed incredible swiftness and agility. She loved to run, and Rose loved the speed. My blood quickened just to watch her riding across the prairie on the strawberry mare, the pair of them stretched out low.

Rose seemed like a new person, driven yet happy. She kept busy with the stock, and her energy level soared, rarely looking tired—even at the end of a tough day. I found keeping up with her difficult but thrilled to watch her ride, her dark hair streaming behind her like a cape.

We agreed the fifteen remaining head of stock would be transferred to the large meadow where the cattle were penned. With plenty of grass and water there, we would have time to break more animals and possibly begin construction of barns and corrals. Walter plaited additional short ropes of rawhide, so we could use them in handling the horses. We took three more days to move the horses we intended to keep to the holding canyon near the cliff dwelling. Scott and I fenced off a second canyon that was full of good meadow grass. We cut and stacked tons, adding to our stores of feed for the coming winter. The canyon had no natural water source, meaning that keeping stock there long term would be impossible unless this could be remedied.

On one of my explorations into the surrounding mountains, I discovered a good spring above the canyon that flowed directly to the Arkansas. With some work, I believed we could alter the course and reroute the flow to the dry canyon, providing water for the stock. At least through summer, anyway. The stream would freeze in winter.

Now that we had riding stock, I kept thinking about a trip to Fort Union. I puzzled out the details in my head as we worked, and then mentioned my plan one night during dinner.

"The eight oxen I have are not going to help me build a herd. I'd like to sell them and buy winter supplies or at least some things we need for ranching."

I'd assumed we would stay here for the winter, but no one had openly discussed it. I wondered if this is where they planned to settle permanently. For me, I was convinced this was the place the Lord brought me to. I knew I would build my ranch here.

"What things would you need for your ranch?" Walter tilted his head.

I shrugged. We'd gone over this many times. I wondered why he pressed for my wish list again. "Well, I would need some tools for building a house and a barn. Hammer, nails, lumber, lanterns, bedding …" I rambled on, relating various necessary articles for a new ranch. I saw a twinkle in his old eyes as I listed my desired purchases.

"Will you also need a wife?" His look of innocence fooled no one.

I had turned eighteen just a few days ago, and he'd told me it was time to get married. "Braves who do not marry young are stuck with the ugly women," he'd warned.

Rose shot me a sharp glance during this discussion, her eyes searching mine, but she said nothing.

I squirmed and bit my lip. "I'm not interested in picking up a wife at Fort Union," I stammered.

Rose dropped her gaze, intent on her plate. Glancing at her from the corner of my eye, I noticed a little color in her cheeks.

By the time August arrived, we were working every day breaking saddle stock, stacking hay, and hunting for more furs. The cliff dwellings would be cold for a long winter, but they were the best structures we had to live in for now.

One night, Blue Heron made a delicious dinner of sage hen. The tender meat melted in my mouth. We'd taken some flour from the burned wagons months ago, and tonight we enjoyed the last of it, the meat covered in a golden crust.

I licked my fingers and glanced at Walter across the fire. "We need supplies from Fort Union," I began, all eyes on me as I spoke, "if we plan on staying here for the winter."

I paused, wondering if they had a different plan. I hurried on, hoping they didn't. "It's too late in the season to attempt to find new quarters. I'd like to ride the gray gelding and herd the eight oxen to the fort. I need to purchase winter supplies, but I'll return as soon as I can. I'm thinking I need another person to go with me. Any volunteers?"

Scott's hand shot up, his eyes shining, but Walter vetoed his eagerness. "Scott, we need you to build a tank for the water from the spring on the mountain. You are needed to build the ditch that will carry the water to the meadow. I think Rose should go with Jason."

Every head turned to look at Rose's startled face. "Me?" Her eyes widened. "I don't care to go. Let Scott go. Or you go, Walter."

Walter shook his head. "No, I think Jason is right. We will need supplies for winter. You can take extra mounts to carry supplies back here. I do not want to go to the white man's fort. It is time for you to visit a white man's settlement. Besides, you are half white."

Rose frowned, and I read the hurt in her eyes. "I'm also half Cheyenne," she added quietly.

Walter sighed and nodded. "Yes, my daughter, you are. And that is the best part of you. But times are changing. You need to change with them." He paused, letting his words sink in. "I want you to go."

Rose shot a meaningful glance at her grandfather. "Will you also change with these new times?"

Walter chuckled softly, shaking his head. "No, I do not have to. I am too old."

She scowled at her grandfather but said nothing. I could tell she wasn't happy about coming with me to Fort Union—but I was.

I helped Scott for the next two days, trying to bring water to the dry canyon. The spring would be easy to dam to alter the course, but the actual ditch was not easy to build.

We dug a tank in the canyon floor and started trenching from there to the spring on the mountain. I helped dig some of the easy ditches, but the more difficult ones, he would work on in my absence.

Rose worked every day with the four horses we hoped to take to Fort Union. Two would be used as pack animals. The oxen would only be driven one way, so we hoped the trip wouldn't be too difficult going and coming.

The night before Rose and I set out, we celebrated her birthday. Although Indians didn't have specific calendar days for birthdays, Blue Heron had observed a shooting star the night before and announced the next day would be Rose's birthday.

Scott told me this was something Mackenzie had taught them. White people liked to know special days, but the Cheyenne believed every day was special, a gift from the Great Spirit.

During dinner, Scott shared he'd found a wild honey tree and would show me where it was. Wild honey was a rare delicacy.

I enjoyed dinner with my friends and had begun to think of them as my own family, but I hadn't been invited to join. I liked their gentle familiarity and kindness to one another, but I was still an outsider to them.

And yet, something more was happening, I could feel. My feelings for Rose were changing.

CHAPTER 20

We rode with the sunrise. I could hardly eat before we left, my heart racing with anticipation. The last settlement I'd seen was Council Grove. I was eager to see Fort Union.

The oxen took no time at all to cut out from my small herd of cattle. We drove them before us, out toward the open prairie and the old trail.

Weeks of feeding and little work had allowed the oxen to put on some meat and fill out. They should fetch a good price at the fort.

With the morning sun bright upon our faces, we skirted the Arkansas and started following the ruts in the plains carved by countless wagons. The route was clearly marked—there was no way to get lost. The road led southwest toward Santa Fe.

However, getting lost was not really my fear. I was more afraid of Indians or lack of water or even a wagon train coming along and bothering us. There were always many dangers that followed a person traveling on the Santa Fe Trail.

Small dust clouds lifted from each hoof as the oxen walked, heads down and tails swishing. Without wagons to pull, we made good time. A larger group would've gone slower. The oxen moved out with a steadiness that pleased me.

The horses were doing fine, too, with Rose keeping a close eye on them. Having never been trail ridden, it was difficult to say how they'd do on this trip.

Rose had swapped her feminine buckskin dress for pants and a shirt. Except for her long hair, she would pass for a young boy from a distance, although my knowing eye could detect her feminine curves. Old Cal told me about the various stopping places on the Santa Fe Trail. He'd been over the trail a hundred times, knew each place by heart, and exactly how long to reach the next one.

The problem was, he'd died before we'd arrived at Fort Union. I'd no real idea how far we were from that old post.

I remember after we'd passed through Council Grove, we came to the cutoff for the shortcut to Fort Union. This route was more dangerous due to the lack of water but shorter. It'd been a wet spring, and some of the teamsters were for trying that route, remarking on the time it would save the wagon train.

Cal had scoffed and shook his head. "I've been that way before. Not worth the risk."

Wilmington decided not to attempt this shorter route to the Cimarron River Valley. He determined they were not in such a rush that warranted the additional risk. Cal leaned over to me that night and whispered, "That's the first sensible thing I've seen the man do."

Avoiding the Cimarron Cutoff, we traveled up the Arkansas River to Old Bent's Fort, which Cal told me had been abandoned now for over a dozen years. This is where the Santa Fe Trail crossed the Arkansas and started southwest to the Purgatory River and then over the Raton Pass and into New Mexico Territory. That, Cal had told me, was where Fort Union was located.

But how far into New Mexico would we have to travel until we found Fort Union? I couldn't remember any details.

I glanced over at Rose now and stared. What a pleasure to see how perfectly she sat her horse. She looked so natural perched on that strawberry mare's back.

A sudden thought came to me then. How come they hadn't any horses with them when I'd found her family months ago? I knew Rose had been taught the art of riding and breaking wild horses, and Walter was a master at catching wild horses. So where were their horses?

Telling myself I would certainly ask this question around the campfire that evening, we pushed on.

I rode the gray gelding. Of all the horses we'd trapped, this one seemed the most content to allow a rider. We made good time that first day on the trail and found where wagon trains had camped before us at a waterhole on the prairie. The animals were content to graze and stay close to the fire, but we still picketed the horses securely.

I figured we'd covered about twenty miles this first day without really pushing hard. I wanted the oxen looking good when we came to Fort

Union and didn't want to run the meat off them. We would take our time but try to get there soon.

We'd left the gun with Walter, figuring he would need it for hunting. With plenty of food packed, we were set for the trip and planned on buying more at the fort. Prior to leaving, we decided we'd trust the speed of the mustangs if we were forced to flee attack. The oxen would have to be abandoned if it came to that.

Rose gathered fuel for the fire as I prepared a small dinner. "Cal told me there's a café at Fort Union. If the oxen sell, I'll treat you to a nice meal," I promised, thinking of coffee and pie.

Depositing an armload of sticks near the fire, Rose glanced at the tethered horses, wiping dirt and bark from her hands. I watched her from the corner of my eye for a minute, but the pants made her figure more distracting, so I turned away.

Twilight fell as the fire brightened, shadows forming between the folds in the land. I peered east and wondered what was happening back in Missouri. Did the war rage on? Could I have imagined I'd be on the other side of the plains a few short months ago? Yet, here I was.

Abruptly, Rose sat near me, pulling her knees to her chest and wrapping her arms around them. She tilted her head, measuring me with her cool, green eyes. "Jason, if you hadn't been kicked off the wagon train at Bent's Fort, where would you be now?"

I had told her the whole story of Cal and Wilmington. She knew I was a Christian and believed God had maneuvered the events to where I'd met her family.

"I guess I would've gone on to Santa Fe with the other teamsters." I handed her a piece of dried meat. "God used Wilmington's hard heart the same way he used Pharaoh's hard heart in the Bible. All for God to reveal his glory."

She chewed in silence for a minute before she spoke again. "But what are you going to do now? Your herd is only a few head of cows. It'll take thirty years for you to make a profit from them."

I smiled at her. She was learning fast about profit margin and business plans.

"Walter and I have already talked about this. I'll wait on the Lord. He has a purpose for me, and I'll build my ranch where I am. It'll work out all right, you'll see."

I wished I felt as confident as I sounded. I knew God was faithful, but was I? Like Rose said, my ranch was pitifully small and would take years to grow at this rate, but I would try my hardest to trust the Lord. He knew what he was doing, even if I didn't.

Blue Heron had provided mint leaves for tea, and steam rose from our tin cups as I poured water over them. Then I sat back to let them soak. I handed Rose another piece of jerky.

I thought about what I wanted to ask her. "Rose, when I found your family on that rainy day, you had no horses. Why is that?"

She traced the rim of her cup with a finger, a faraway look in her eye. I knew she was remembering that wet, sad day of her father's death.

"Father and Walter had a bad winter of trapping and had to sell our horses to pay their debts. That's why we were down on the Arkansas when you found us. Father wanted to catch Wildfire, break some of the mustangs for sale and keep some for a ranch." She paused and I knew remembering was painful for her. "I guess our ranch is going to happen but without Father." She dropped her head.

I pursed my lips and nodded. I knew how she felt. For hours sometimes, Pa and I would talk about barns and water, cattle and corrals. We loved to plan for the day our dream would come true. I was saddened to think Pa had died before he saw the ranch realized.

"Rose," I said, my voice soft. "Your ranch will always include your father as long as you remember him."

She looked up, her eyes glistening, then laid a hand on my arm. "Thanks for being so understanding, Jason. I know we haven't always gotten along, but I'm glad you're with us."

Her words made me feel uncomfortable. I mumbled something and stood to check on the stock.

I moved among the animals, letting them know I was close. One of the mustangs shied when I put my hand on his shoulder, but the gray gelding stood still. Looking up, I watched the incredible sight above me. Where else on this planet could so many stars be visible as on the Great Plains? Like slivers of silver brilliance, the night sky was full of pinpoints of light, shimmering and shining brightly.

I thanked God I had time with Rose and prayed he would give me wisdom and patience in dealing with her. I knew so little about women.

I wandered the plains for over an hour, praising God and enjoying his creation. By the time I returned to camp, Rose was asleep. I stared at her for a moment, watching the firelight play softly on her copper skin, her black hair tousled messily around her head like a dark crown.

I didn't want to admit to myself I was in love with this girl. I wasn't sure I even knew what love was. I loved my folks but never anyone else I could remember. What did I know about loving this beautiful girl?

I found my blankets and rolled in them. Tomorrow would be another challenging day. I needed some sleep.

We took seven days to ride to Fort Union—the best week of my life. All day, I rode with Rose, except for the opportunities she took of suddenly kicking the strawberry mare into flight. They would go racing across the plains as quick as lightning. The little horse loved to run and seemed to enjoy Rose riding her. The two would run all out, the mare stretching low and her legs pounding the prairie turf. I'd never seen a horse run so fast.

At night, we sat by our little campfires and talked about our dreams and our hopes. God revealed to us a friendship that opened with a brilliance neither of us could deny. I simply loved to be near her. We lived each day with an excitement and a happiness neither had felt, nor expected, in a long time.

I felt things went badly for me for such a long time. Then, in the twinkling of an eye, they had turned around. Had God been testing my faith? Or was he shaping me for things ahead? Only he knew.

Too soon for me, we sighted the small settlement. We halted, our gaze fixed ahead, surveying the tiny post on the Cimarron River. What new things would we find there?

I glanced at Rose, reading the fear on her face. This was new to her.

A desire to protect her swelled within me, surprising me but pleasing me too. I liked the idea, and I sat straighter on the gray's back.

"Don't worry, Rose."

She looked at me, fear still registering in her green eyes.

"Don't worry. We'll be all right. God is with us."

She nodded, and a weak smile touched her lips. "Thanks, Jason. I'm glad you're with me too."

We rode toward Fort Union.

CHAPTER 21

Reaching the fort, I instructed Rose to keep the oxen on the outskirts of the small post as I rode in to find a buyer.

Rose was only too eager to avoid town. The number of men walking around and the long, low military buildings frightened her. She was not accustomed to such things.

Leaving her on the banks of a small stream which fed into the nearby Cimarron River, I turned toward town.

Riding bareback is not easy, especially when you do it all day, day after day. But even with no saddles, riding was better than walking. I rode that gray horse up to a hitching rail in front of the general store and slid off his back.

I stretched and arched my back before tying the hackamore to the rail, and then stepped onto the stoop of the store.

My hand on the doorknob, I glanced back at the gelding. He already had his head down, dozing in the sun. Been hitched to a rail before, I gathered.

I'd not been indoors for a few months, not since the wagon train had stopped at Council Grove. I entered the dimly lit little store eagerly but with a bit of anxiety too. The scent of leather, coffee, and tobacco invited me in. I inhaled deeply, promising myself to get some coffee while I was in town.

A round man with suspenders caught my eye and motioned me over. He had a friendly face and the look of someone who enjoyed people and the comforts of town life.

"Howdy, son. What can I do for you?" He gave me a sharp once-over, but his voice seemed pleasant enough.

"Hello, sir, I'm Jason Malone. I've settled up on the Arkansas. I thought I'd ride down here and get acquainted."

He rubbed his hands together, smelling business, his red face beaming. "Fine. Fine. You'll be needing supplies."

"Yes, I will. But first I need to sell some oxen. Any idea who I should see about that?" He squinted and stroked his chin. "Well, you're in luck. A train is due here tonight. The soldiers told me one was coming in. That means I'll have fresh supplies for you, and they might want to buy your oxen." He glanced out the window toward the south, and my eyes followed his gaze. There were no wagons in sight.

I thanked him for his kindness, and promising to return, I left the store.

My thoughts were so full of the information I wanted to share with Rose, I almost missed the soldier looking at my horse at the hitch rail.

He stood in front of the general store, a curious eye on the gelding. I closed the door behind me and hesitated, uncertain. Should I be worried?

I walked to the horse, his voice stopping me. "Hey, there. You're no Indian. I was imagining an Indian warrior riding that horse bareback with a hackamore. Now why do you ride that way, son?"

One hand on the gray's shoulder, full of mane, I turned to the soldier, noticing stripes on his uniform. He was a big man, mostly in the chest and arms. Lean in the waist and rangy, like a rider. He had a square chin, but I thought his eyes were kindly.

"We caught some mustangs up on the Arkansas and don't have saddles or bridles," I explained as he started toward me. He put a hand out to the horse's nose and rubbed it.

"This horse seems like a good one. Who breaks your animals for you?" He was running an expert hand under the neck and looking at the flanks and legs.

I swallowed hard. "Just some friends of mine who're really good at catching wild horses and taming them for riding." I felt this was truthful without giving too much information. For some reason, I felt reluctant to say that some Indian friends had broken this horse.

He looked at me with a squint. I squirmed, wondering if he sensed my evasive answer. "Do you mean you have more horses? Are you interested in selling any of them?"

Shifting my feet, I hesitated. "Could be." I finally said, "Not sure."

He arched an eyebrow and smiled. "Well, if you ever are sure, the army is buying. We're always in need of saddle stock. Since the war broke out, we don't get new mounts out west."

He finished looking the animal over and turned to me.

"Have your pa come see me if he wants to sell horses." He extended his hand. "I'm Sergeant Reynolds. I handle purchases and supplies."

I shook his hand with a nod. Pa always said to never trust a man with a weak hand shake. Sergeant Reynolds's grip was firm.

He turned to go. On an impulse, I stopped him.

"Sergeant, I'm Jason Malone. I'm trying to put a ranch together up on the Arkansas River. I would appreciate any help or advice you can provide."

He narrowed his eyes and studied me. I knew what he saw. A tall, slender man of eighteen with long, unruly hair way past need of a haircut. Shirt and pants soiled and rumpled, covered in horse hair.

"Boy, do you have folks?"

I chewed my lip, uncertain how much to say. "I live in some cliff dwellings back in the canyons from Bent's Fort. We're catching wild horses, and we have a few head of cattle. We want to ranch the land and make it ours."

I'd not intended to spill my story so suddenly but felt I could trust this man. I hoped I was right.

He nodded. "Well, the first thing to do is homestead the land. Lay claim to the land rightly with the government. It's free to you if you can live on it for five years. I'm authorized to record claims for this region. Second, invest in settling the land. Build on it. Establish your ranch while the land is yours for the taking. Make sure you locate on water. That's what'll make it valuable."

Someone called his name, and the big sergeant looked toward them and waved.

"I have to go, Jason. Why don't you come and see me tomorrow? I'll be in my office. Reports will keep me busy all day." He pointed to a stone and adobe building. I agreed to see him the next day.

He walked away then, and I pulled myself onto the gray and rode back to camp.

Glancing to the south, I saw a snake-like thread of white canvas covered wagons. The expected freight train approached.

I pulled rein and frowned when I sighted a man riding a white horse leading the big wagons. I recognized that big steed. I ground my teeth and kicked the gray.

Wilmington.

So, his wagon train was pulling into Fort Union at the same time I was present. He must be on his return trip from Santa Fe. So what? He did what he wanted. I was rankled the man was here, but so be it. Discharging me from his wagon train was not a crime. As wagon master, he could do whatever he liked.

I vowed to do my best to stay out of his way and rode to camp.

That night, Rose and I stayed up late talking about plans to homestead a piece of property and have actual ownership. This is what I wanted, to own my own land. That was what Pa had wanted too.

Rose didn't understand the Homestead Act, bristling when I told her about Sergeant Reynolds. "I don't trust him. He just wants to learn where we are so he can come take the land for himself."

I shook my head. "No, it's true. I heard about it when I was in Council Grove. President Lincoln signed this new law that gives people free land if they move west. The government wants people to move out here and settle the land."

"You mean steal it from Indians. They were here first." A scowl crossed her pretty face. "Walter told us how white people have tried to take even Cheyenne lands. It is not right, Jason."

No use in arguing with the truth. I sighed. "Well, we're claiming land no one lives on. There's a lot of empty land. Our ranch won't interfere with any Indian lands. Blue Heron told me our land was used in the summers by trading Utes from the west. We need to claim it so that it'll become ours legally."

She shook her head. "Jason, you white men are arrogant. You don't understand that land can be used but not lived on. Indians have camped at our cliff dwellings probably for hundreds of years. Just because no one is there now doesn't mean it's not claimed by a particular tribe."

As her anger increased, her brogue became more pronounced. I decided to move the conversation away from Indian rights and onto the mutual goal of creating a ranch.

"Tomorrow, we'll try to sell our oxen, and then see Sergeant Reynolds. I'd like you to come with me." I figured it best for her to participate right away in the process. "Two heads are better than one. I would like you to hear what I hear."

Rose hesitated, but then agreed. Even though she seemed nervous, she was willing to learn the business of ranching. I was pleased she wanted to participate despite her agitation toward white men.

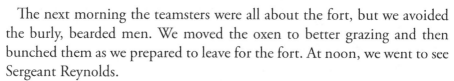

The next morning the teamsters were all about the fort, but we avoided the burly, bearded men. We moved the oxen to better grazing and then bunched them as we prepared to leave for the fort. At noon, we went to see Sergeant Reynolds.

He ushered us into a stark office furnished only with a scratched desk, three mismatched chairs, and a file cabinet. He seated himself behind the desk.

"So," he began, resting his elbows on the desk and leaning forward.

I squirmed and almost smiled. Sergeant Reynolds must've wondered why he'd asked me to come to his office. I'm sure Rose and I didn't look very impressive. We were just young folks looking for guidance and possible business connections.

"So, you want to homestead a place and raise horses?" the sergeant said finally.

I nodded but said nothing.

He smiled. "Well, this couldn't happen at a better time." His look put me at ease, and I sensed Rose relax a bit beside me.

"The army is needful of riding stock. It takes a long time for requisitions to be sent east, replied to, and sent west again. Horses are needed to fight the war, but few are spared for us out here on the frontier. I have authority to purchase additional saddle stock, but it's rarely available. To have you settle on land north of us in an area that we can easily access would greatly enable our procuring horses. What can I do to help you in this endeavor?"

His chair creaked as the big army man sat back and stared at us with genuine interest. He pressed his hands together, touching his fingertips to his chin.

The speed of our discussion stunned and worried me. I could feel Rose's eyes on me, trying to catch my attention. Was she suddenly alert too?

"Why would you want to help us?" I asked. Had I been wrong in my assessment of this soldier? Was Rose correct that he intended to cheat us somehow?

"Your success is in my best interest," Reynolds replied. "You will raise and break horses, we will buy them." He smiled again.

I nodded, his congenial manner relaxing me again. This had to be an answer to prayer. God had ordained this meeting. I was sure of it and of the soldier's sincerity. Rose was not.

I turned to her and read the doubt in her eyes. "This is good, Rose. We can homestead a ranch and catch wild horses. We have a ready buyer. What else do we need?" I felt smug and satisfied.

Her green eyes narrowed. She frowned at me and my heart sank. "It's not that easy, Jason," she said. "We have horses, but to sell them to the army means they must be prepared for army service. The horses will have to be broken to saddle and bridle, ridden by men with boots. We'll need a lot of gear to make this work."

Reprimanded, I slumped in my chair. Her negative response made me feel empty. Would we never move in the same direction? She seemed so obstinate. Or maybe she just understood better than me what was expected of a real horse ranch.

The sergeant leaned forward again and fixed his gaze on Rose. Clearly, here was the business contact he needed to impress. I scratched the stubble on my jaw as I recalled Cal's words about a partner. "All right, young lady, what do you need from the army so that this venture can succeed?"

Rose didn't even hesitate. "Saddles to train the horses with, bridles with bits, and boots so the horses will get used to spurs."

Sergeant Reynolds looked from Rose to me and then back to her again. "We have some used items that I think I can lend you. We have tack and riding boots from soldiers killed in the field. Their gear is in the barn doing no good for anyone. I can authorize you to have them and you can prepare mounts for the cavalry."

Before Rose or I could respond, he stood and thrust out his big hand. "I have other matters to attend to. Swing by tomorrow, and I'll have the gear ready for you. You can tell me then the exact location of your ranch, and I'll record your homestead claim."

We stood and shook hands. "One more thing, Sergeant. How is the war going?" I watched him closely, wanting to know the truth. "The last I heard, the Union wasn't doing well."

He smiled, his eyes brightening. "I'm pleased to be the one to tell you things have changed. General Grant has captured Vicksburg on the Mississippi, and Meade pushed Lee out of Pennsylvania. The Union is doing well." He walked around his desk and opened the door for us. "I'll see you tomorrow."

We stepped out as two troopers entered the office. The door closed behind us and we found ourselves standing in the bright afternoon sun, ranchers with a market for our horses.

In a daze, we meandered up the hill toward camp.

"Does this mean what I think it means?" Rose whispered, her voice full of excitement and hope.

"I believe so. We can sell our saddle-broken horses to the army." My thoughts turned to Pa, and I grinned, knowing he'd be proud of me. Perhaps this was my small contribution to serving the Union.

My heart swelled, and I was in awe. God brought me to this land with nothing but a dream. Now I was a rancher with a promised income.

I glanced at Rose ... and new friends, I thought with pleasure.

All of a sudden, Rose snatched Cal's old hat from me and pressed it onto her head, tucking her long hair under its brim. She laughed as she ran from me.

I chased her, and she squealed, evading my clumsy grasp. She was light and nimble. I couldn't catch her.

She raced for camp with me on her heels. As she rounded the trees near our camp, we skidded to a halt.

Two men stood beside our fire ring. "Captain Wilmington, these boys are funning while we're here to talk business." My heart chilled as I recognized Baldwin.

I turned from the sullen teamster and looked at Wilmington. He stared, his cold eyes on me, a taunting smile creasing his face.

CHAPTER 22

Captain Wilmington seated himself on the log beside our fire and fed sticks to the glowing embers. Baldwin crossed his arms over his chest, a malicious gleam in his small eyes as he watched me, ignoring Rose.

I stood speechless, astounded to see these two men in my camp— the same men who'd kicked me out of the wagon train. I thought of Cal, anger churning in my gut.

I fought the desire to force them from camp. An unspoken peace calmed me then, a wisdom whispered noiselessly in my head.

"Well, boy," Wilmington began, his gaze intent on the fire at his feet. "I see you've made it to Fort Union. I didn't think you would have any real trouble anyway."

I stared at him but said nothing, waiting. "We don't care how you made it," Baldwin interjected. "We're here because we heard you have oxen for sale. We looked them over and we're interested."

"Oxen?" I repeated. I hadn't expected that.

"Yes, we've checked them out. They seem sound. What do you want for them, boy?" Wilmington stood and faced me, reaching into his pocket.

I squinted and glanced at Rose, who watched me, her eyes wide.

"Hurry up. I need to get back to the wagons," Wilmington growled. "Let's conclude our business. What do you say?"

Pa always taught me that demand created price. These men needed my oxen. I wondered what they would pay.

"Two hundred and fifty dollars," I said, and wondered where the words came from.

Baldwin and Wilmington chuckled, rolling their eyes in exaggeration. "Come, don't be ridiculous. Tell me a fair price for these animals and I'll take them off your hands." I could tell the wagon leader was trying to keep his temper under control.

I had these two men over a barrel and didn't mind seeing them squirm a little. They needed these animals, but didn't I need to sell them?

"You heard my price. Two hundred and fifty dollars for eight oxen. Take it or leave it," I repeated, squaring my shoulders.

Wilmington slapped his pocket and bristled, his face reddening. "We'll leave it. I'll not pay St. Louis prices in Fort Union."

"Captain," Baldwin caught the wagon master's arm. "We really need these oxen. We lost some good animals coming over that dry spot, and they have to be replaced."

Wilmington jerked his arm from Baldwin's grip and glanced back at me, his eyes narrowing. "I'll give you a hundred and fifty dollars, no more."

I thought about taking it, then noticed the deep furrows in his forehead. He needed my oxen badly or he wouldn't be negotiating.

I shook my head. "No, I'll not take it. I don't need to sell right away. Another train will be along any day, and they'll buy them." I didn't know if another wagon train was coming over the trail, but I didn't care if these men bought my oxen or not.

The apprehension in Wilmington's eyes told me I had struck close to the truth. Maybe he knew of another wagon train not far behind him.

I felt Rose's eyes on me and glanced at her again, sensing her worry. We could truly use any money we got for these oxen. The income would help us establish the ranch and buy supplies that would see us through the coming winter. Was I foolish to bargain with these men?

Baldwin looked over our horses. "Your nags, are they for sale?"

Rose leaped forward at this, color rising to her heated cheeks. Baldwin had made a mistake, slighting her beloved horses. "These horses are not for sale to you." Her fists clenched and she leaned forward, ready for battle.

"Sit down, boy." Baldwin waved a dismissive hand in her direction, his eyes still on the horses. "You're not part of these negotiations. This is men's business, not for little boys."

Before Rose could respond, I jumped in. "Let's wrap up this deal. Two hundred and fifty dollars and the oxen are yours."

Wilmington stepped beside Baldwin and studied the mounts. He looked them over as the mustangs grazed and then turned to me.

"These horses don't look like much. I'll give you twenty dollars apiece, as well as a hundred and fifty for the oxen."

Rose was furious now. She stamped her foot, and I shot her a warning glance. Wilmington had insulted her with his low offer. Her face went white and then red as she sputtered.

Again, Baldwin cut her off. "These mounts aren't as good as the Captain's gelding here." He gestured to the big white horse and then sighed with disappointment. "But we can use them."

Rose spat, "My horses could run circles around that fat, white horse."

I put a restraining hand on her arm.

Wilmington chuckled again. "My steed would whip any of your scrawny mounts in a race. Watch your mouth, boy, when you talk about my horse."

I saw my chance. "Okay, Wilmington, let's make a deal. A race. If we win, you pay two hundred and fifty dollars for the oxen. If you win, you can have them for a hundred and fifty."

My remark made Baldwin and Wilmington howl, and Rose rocked back on her heels.

"You can't be serious." Baldwin grinned. "The Captain's horse would run away from these little ponies in a half mile race."

Wilmington jumped in. "All right, Jason." I noticed this was the first time he'd used my name. "I'll make a deal with you. But let's make it interesting." His big face beamed with a taunt. "We'll race, and if you win, I will pay you four hundred for the oxen. But if I win, I get them for free."

Baldwin shot his captain a concerned glance, but I was rapidly doing the math in my head. Four hundred dollars would go a long way to building a ranch.

I stuck out my hand to seal the deal, and Wilmington stepped forward, his hand outstretched.

"Wait," Baldwin shouted.

Our heads turned, staring at the thin teamster. "This is a good deal," he agreed with a sneer. "But to make the deal even better, this boy has to ride your horse in the race." He hooked a thumb at Rose.

I blinked. I'd assumed Rose would be riding for me anyway. These two baboons didn't even know she was a girl.

I feigned shock and scuffed the dirt with the toe of my moccasin as Wilmington laughed. "If this boy can beat me, I'll give you five hundred dollars for the oxen." He held his belly with both hands and laughed louder. Baldwin joined him, slapping Wilmington on the back, until the two of them grew red in the face.

Rose leaped forward again, her eyes blazing fire, but I grabbed her arm and held her back. I spoke over her shoulder.

"Okay, the race is tomorrow morning. Five hundred dollars for the oxen if our horse beats your white gelding."

"And they're free if you lose. And the boy here rides your horse," Baldwin chuckled as the two men turned and walked from our camp.

They continued cackling loudly as they retreated until they were out of earshot.

Releasing Rose, we watched them depart. I glanced at her, fear creeping into me. Had I just made a big mistake?

Then, her face brightening, she turned to me. "Jason, this is incredible. We'll get five hundred dollars," she said, her green eyes glowing.

I bit my lip. "Only if you win," I said, nodding toward her. "If you lose, we drove those oxen here for nothing."

Her head tilted and she smiled. "Don't you have confidence in my riding?" She rested her hands on her slender waist.

I nodded. "I have all the confidence in the world in you, but I don't trust Wilmington. We've never seen him race. What if his gelding can beat you?" I was afraid we'd let the emotions of the moment dictate our wager. We stood to lose a great deal.

She pulled my hat from her head and tossed it to me, her dark hair tumbling about her shoulders. "Don't worry about that. No one can beat me when I'm on Strawberry."

Rose walked to the little mare and put her arms around the horse's neck, nuzzling her face against the long mane. Then she turned to me. "Tomorrow, we'll beat that big white horse, you'll see."

CHAPTER 23

News of the race spread throughout the fort like a tumbleweed in a wind storm. By time we approached the general store the next morning, a large crowd of teamsters and soldiers already assembled to watch.

Wilmington stood near his huge white gelding and laughed when he saw us leading the little strawberry mare.

"Baldwin, will you look there. The young boy is a young girl," the wagon master grinned and pointed. He turned to me. "Don't try to weasel out of our deal. This girl has to ride your horse or bet's off."

I nodded. "Of course. She'll ride my horse."

Sergeant Reynolds stepped from the crowd. "I will be judge here today. The finish line will be in front of the store. Private Pickett here will walk with the two racers a half mile yonder where we've paced off a starting line. He will make sure the two horses have a proper, fair start. He will fire his pistol to signal the beginning of the race, and whichever horse crosses this line first is the winner."

The big sergeant indicated the line he'd drawn across the ground and then shot a worried glance in my direction as if to communicate his disapproval at this risky gamble.

Rose nodded at Reynold's instructions, and accompanied by the waiting soldier, strode with Strawberry toward the starting line. She looked over her shoulder at me and grinned.

Wilmington watched them go. "Listen, boy, don't try and cheat me. When I win this race, I get your oxen for free." He wore an ugly sneer. I hoped Rose would be safe. I did not trust this brute.

"And if my horse wins, you pay five hundred dollars for the oxen." I spoke loudly, hoping my words were overheard by others.

He nodded and followed Rose.

Sergeant Reynolds put a rough hand on my shoulder as we stood together, watching the two racers walk away. "I hope you know what you're doing," he muttered under his breath.

I hoped I did too.

The Lord had been in this adventure from the beginning, from the burning of the rented shack back in Missouri, to the death of Pa. He had guided me to Cal, the sickly teamster who'd given me shelter, to Mackenzie's family who had taken me in, finally accepting me as one of their own, and to this race in New Mexico Territory.

Now, here I stood, on a dusty parade ground, waiting for a horse race which could prove to be fatal to our dreams. We needed this money to establish our ranch and begin breaking horses for the army, not to mention the necessary supplies it would purchase for the upcoming winter.

I stood up straight, throwing off my worries. God had been with me all along, I would not doubt his presence now. Whatever happened, win or lose, he was a sovereign God. He already knew the outcome of today's race. I needed to trust him, no matter the outcome.

The crowd grew restless. Baldwin stood at my elbow, the tension thick enough to kick with a boot. He grinned now, and I could see his crooked, stained teeth.

"The captain and I are sure impressed you showed up this morning. I half expected you to chicken out." The sallow-faced teamster chortled. He seemed confident Wilmington would win this race.

"Why would I do that when we're going to beat you?" Although I spoke with assurance, my quiet voice conveyed doubt.

He just scoffed and turned away.

Sergeant Reynolds shot me a concerned glance and then raised an arm and signaled to the soldier at the starting line. The crowd leaned forward and grew silent, all eyes fixed on the starting line.

I shielded my eyes for a better view. Barely discernable in the distance, I saw the two racers and the soldier who was the starter.

Sergeant Reynolds pulled binoculars from a case and studied the racers. I wish I had field glasses, too, I thought, straining to see better.

A shot sounded, and the crowd yelled. Private Pickett had fired his pistol. I jumped at the sharp report, my insides tightening into a knot as I watched the two horses leap into action. The race was on.

I kept my eyes on the two horses running toward me but couldn't tell how Rose fared at this distance. Reynolds nudged me and handed me the glasses.

I took them with sweaty hands. Lifting the binoculars, I saw the two horses zoom into view. They ran side by side, the little strawberry mare stretched low, Rose's dark hair streaming behind her in the wind. Wilmington was slapping his mount brutally with a quirt. I felt sorry for the big, white gelding.

My fingers gripped the binoculars. "Come on, Rose," I whispered, willing her to listen to me, as if my wishes had any control over the outcome of the race.

I lowered the glasses as the racers neared the finish line. Rose leaned low over the little red mare's neck, her mouth close to the horse's ears as she shouted encouragement to her mount. She stuck on the back of the little mare like a burr.

With only a hundred yards remaining, I watched Wilmington cruelly beating the gelding with his quirt, the wagon master's face black with rage as he tried to catch up with Rose. But the girl flew over the ground, the mare stretched like an arrow.

The crowd cheered for their favorites, and the crescendo increased as the racers crossed the finish line, Rose in the lead by an entire length.

If the race were a longer length, Wilmington might have won. The short half-mile distance didn't allow his big gelding to get its stride right, and Rose's little mare proved too fast for the short distance sprint.

Men slapped one another on the back, talking excitedly as the two racers returned, still astride their heaving mounts. Rose patted the pony's neck with admiration, a wide grin on her tanned face. My heart swelled with pride as I watched her approach. Something else filled my heart, too, but I pushed the feeling aside, confused by the new sensation as I watched the beautiful girl astride the red mare. I would think on these emotions another time.

Wilmington's face was as dark as a thundercloud. He kicked the tired gelding into a trot as he neared the spectators, and then the big white horse almost went to his haunches as Wilmington reined in before the crowd, glaring at me. "You and the girl cheated me," he bellowed, his face contorting with fury. "I will not pay anything to a cheater." With a vicious jerk of the reins, he dragged the gelding away, riding toward his camp.

I scowled after the bitter man as the crowd surged around the skittish pony, congratulating Rose on the race.

Standing back for a moment, watching the hullabaloo, I realized I'd been holding my breath for the duration of the race, and I exhaled, my aching lungs filling with fresh air.

Rose caught my eye through the crowd of well-wishers and tugged on the reins, prodding her horse toward me. Slipping from the pony's back, she leaned against me, her copper cheeks glowing.

"Jason, we did it," she breathed in my ear, her warm breath tickling me. "He tried to push me off the starting line, but Strawberry was too quick. She moved away from him and shot off like a rabbit. He couldn't catch us."

She rested her hands on my shoulders as she leaned on me, and I could feel her happiness. It'd taken me a minute to relax from the intensity of the race, but now I leaned into her as well, contentment filling my heart.

"Rose," I began, finding my voice at last. "You did it. I'm so proud of you." I pulled her in for a hug. She came in closer, lifting her face to mine as her arms stole around my neck.

Our lips met, touching tenderly. A fire raced through me, my blood heating instantly.

Startled, Rose stepped back, her eyes wide. Her hand went swiftly to her full lips, and she stared at me, surprise reflected in her green eyes. Then she turned and melted into the throng around us, pulling Strawberry behind her.

The crowd drifted away, and I was left standing with Sergeant Reynolds. By the look on his face, I could tell he'd seen the whole thing.

What had I done? The kiss hadn't been intentional. I didn't mean to kiss her. Well, yes, I did. I'd seen her radiant face look up at me. Her eyes were so full of excitement, dancing with joy, her red lips parted. I'd lost my head in the heat of the moment.

Maybe he saw the shock on my face, because Sergeant Reynolds laughed and slapped me on the back. "Come back to Earth, young man. You just won five hundred dollars. I'll make sure you get your money before Wilmington pulls out of camp tomorrow."

He placed a hand on my shoulder and guided me toward his office. "Let me give you the gear I've rounded up for you. Or, better yet, I'll have a couple of troopers pack it to your camp. Let's look at the map to see what location you've chosen for your ranch."

He guided me into the coolness of his office and closed the door behind me. I dropped into a chair, feeling a little weak in the knees and anxious. The race and then kissing Rose marked an extremely significant day.

We spent an hour talking about trail conditions, geographic markers, water sources, and feed conditions. I showed him on his map where we'd located. The Arkansas River was plainly marked, so it was not difficult to point out the springs I would be claiming on my property.

"Remember that even though the river goes by your place, you should always claim a consistent water source near your house. Whoever controls the water will control the land around it." He pointed to my ranch with his pencil. "This water hole will keep your property valuable."

He showed me the saddles, bridles, and boots he'd promised, then told me he would visit my camp that evening with the money from Wilmington if he had not given it to me by then.

Somehow reluctant to return to camp, I visited the general store and made a list of purchases to take home with us. Food stuffs for the winter, lots of coffee, two hunting knives, some blankets, some more cooking utensils, and ammunition for Cal's old gun. I also included building supplies.

I wandered the store for over an hour making comments on various items to add to my list. The eager shopkeeper followed me, his paper and pencil in hand. Occasionally, he would ask me a question about quantity of something and then he'd lick his pencil and write it down.

Finally, I could stall no longer. Putting off the inevitable did not make it go away. I had to go back to camp and face Rose.

Trudging up the low hill toward camp, I thought the walk felt endless. I didn't remember it being so long.

As I came around the trees, I found Rose sitting by the fire, bending over a sizzling skillet. She looked up at my step but only stared at me, a question in her warm eyes as a crimson wave stole up her neck. I dropped on the fallen log as a brilliant idea came to me. *Just act like it never happened.*

"Sergeant Reynolds said he'd deliver the tack and our money this evening," I reported with a cheerfulness I didn't feel.

She didn't say anything but handed me a plate of potatoes and venison. We ate our meal in silence. The tension grew. I knew I needed to say something but couldn't find the words. Rose was courteous but aloof, shy yet stayed close to me. She kept her face averted.

The mood broke with the advent of two soldiers led into our camp by Sergeant Reynolds. They dropped a pair of tall boots, two saddles, and a pile of bridles before herding the grazing oxen toward the wagon train. "I was forced to go to Captain Wilmington's camp for the five hundred dollars, but I got it. Some of his teamsters threatened to quit him if he didn't pay up. He vowed he would not speak to you," the grinning sergeant reported. "He was so mad that this young lady beat him in that race," he added with a glance at the silent Rose. Reynolds shot me a curious look before handing me an envelope. "I look forward to doing business with you two. I've been very impressed with how you conduct yourselves and still believe this venture will benefit us both. Look me up the next time you visit the fort."

He turned and left our camp. As I opened the thick envelope, my stomach flinched with excitement, looking at the stack of bills. Counting them slowly, my fingers trembling, the agreed amount was there.

"Rose, we can pay for our things at the general store and leave tomorrow. If that's all right with you." I looked at her, wanting her to be a part of the decisions.

She smiled, her eyelids fluttering. I realized then I knew nothing of women, and this girl was a mystery to me. How did she feel, I wondered? Had I hurt her feelings? Was she mad at me?

I wanted to ask her so many questions, but they tripped over one another in my mind. I was pleased when she finally spoke.

"Let's ride them." She gestured to the quartet of grazing horses. "They need to run a little or they'll be difficult to handle. I'll only try the saddle on the gray and one pack horse until we get home."

She wrestled a hackamore on the bay mare and vaulted onto its back. Her face flashed copper in the sun as she glanced at me over her shoulder, beckoning me to follow as she rode swiftly away.

I threw a hackamore on the gray, my fingers fumbling with the knots, and gave chase. As I left camp, I glanced at the little red mare picketed nearby, her head down, grazing. That little horse won us a great deal of money, and I wouldn't forget it.

Rose must've been holding her mount in, because there was no way I would've caught up to her otherwise. I pulled my gelding alongside the bay mare. We rode side by side for a while, not speaking.

Finally, I could stand it no longer. "Rose," I began, my voice a little unsure. "I promised to take you to dinner at the café while we were at the fort. Could I take you there tonight?"

She smiled at me, a teasing glint in her eyes. "You can if you can catch me."

Laughing, she kicked the sides of her mount. The horse leaped into a run, and I was hard put to follow. When I caught her, I knew she'd allowed me to.

We returned to camp riding side-by-side. Rose coyly suggested she bathe in the river before dinner. I didn't think anything of it, but an hour later, I was stunned by the results of her preparation.

She stood beside the fire ring, intently watching my response, as she twirled and modeled the green dress we'd salvaged from the burned wagon. Her eyes glowed and her long, dark hair was pulled back and tied with a ribbon. The dress revealed the flattering curves of a blossoming woman, and I couldn't keep my eyes off her.

I stared, not knowing what to say. She'd taken my breath away.

"Do you like it?" she whispered, her long eyelashes fluttering. The faintest hint of a roguish smile played at the corners of her mouth. Did she know how alluring she was?

I could only nod dumbly, my heart pounding in my chest.

I was so proud of my partner that night at the café as I watched men turn and look at the beautiful girl who accompanied me.

The simple café amazed her. I wondered what she would've said about the Hays House in Council Grove. Her eyes darted about the room, watching the fat cook bring our dinner, the yellow lantern lights dancing on the plank walls, the other patrons who talked in low voices to one another.

Walking back to camp under the stars with the moonlight shining on Rose's dark hair, I was grateful she'd allowed me to catch her on our afternoon race.

CHAPTER 24

Despite my desire to leave early the next morning, it was not to be. Much to the pleasure of the shopkeeper, Rose had added a few purchases onto our list at the general store, so we took more time to prepare the horses for the return trip. Feeling like my business here was concluded, I was anxious to get going. I didn't like leaving Blue Heron, Scott, and Walter alone at the cliff dwelling. Eager to hit the trail that day, I was disappointed at the unavoidable delay.

The gray gelding arched his back when Rose threw a saddle on him. He knew what it was and didn't really seem too upset by the weight, but he swelled his belly when she reached to tighten the cinch. He exhaled and Rose tightened it good and fast. He fought the bit a little more than the saddle, but in the end, he accepted the tack.

The bay mare did not accept the saddle as easily. She arched her back and then tried to buck the saddle off. Rose worked with her for over an hour until the little mare would at least allow the saddle to sit on her.

"I'll not even attempt the bit until we're home and I can take time." Rose wiped the sweat from her brow with the back of her hand, watching the mare. "But we'll need to use the saddle for packing supplies and to lead her with a rope. The gelding can be ridden with the bit, if you are up to the challenge."

She eyed me skeptically, and I knew what she meant. It'd been a long time since the gelding carried a saddle. He might not like the extra weight. He could prove to be temperamental on the trip home.

"I'll chance it. It's better than riding bareback." I spoke from the edge of the fire where I began to prepare a meal. I stopped and faced her, tilting my head.

"Rose, let's go down and eat at the café again. I would surely love another piece of pie."

Her hands were busy with the saddle on the back of the bay mare, but she stopped and turned to me, her eyes brightening at my suggestion. "I would enjoy that, Jason."

She took only a moment to unsaddle the mare and picket her on the grass.

We talked then of horses and ranches and land as we walked to the eating house. Wilmington's wagon train had pulled out early that morning, and the sleepy fort was quiet.

We'd been absent from our ranch for about ten days. I was ready to head home, eager to reunite with the others. There was no real reason for haste, but I wanted to go. The cliff dwelling was the nearest thing I had to a home.

I thought of the Indians and smiled. They were the closest thing I had to a family.

Neither of us said anything about the kiss of the day before. I scarcely allowed myself to think about it. It'd been so impulsive and unplanned, but the memory of it made me blush. Just like the memory of Rose in that green dress.

"What's wrong?" Rose asked, seeing the color on my face.

I shifted uneasily. "I think it's going to be hot today," I replied evasively and gestured toward the thick clouds on the horizon.

She looked at the clouds, and then back at me, a questioning look in her eyes.

Opening the door for her, we entered the café and found seats on benches at an empty table. The fat cook wiped his hands on a greasy apron and brought coffee.

"What'll it be? Antelope or buffalo?" He swatted at a fly with his towel and then slung it back over his shoulder.

"No beef?" I queried, seeing an opportunity present itself.

The fat cook chortled, his heavy cheeks bouncing. "There's no beef out here. Maybe in Texas there are some cows, but not here."

"What would you say if I told you I had some cows?" I eyed the cook closely, keenly observing his response.

His bushy eyebrows arched. "I'd say that's amazing." He glanced toward the kitchen and then narrowed his eyes. "Some beef would go really well here. Would you want to sell them?"

"I'm starting a herd. I need most of what I have for breeding, but I might have a steer or two I could sell."

We talked about the possibility of delivering a cow before winter, then he left to fetch our meals.

Rose looked around the room with wide eyes as she had done on the previous evening. She'd been in so few buildings in her life. It's not like I'd been in many cafés myself. Pa and I would rarely go into such places, not having any money for food someone else cooked. The money Rose and I had won from Wilmington was earmarked for ranch purchases, but a meal or two at Fort Union was allowable.

While we waited for our food, I observed the other men seated in the room. Rose was the only girl. There were some soldiers and a blacksmith, judging by his leather apron and the size of his forearms. There were also three laborers, if I judged their appearance correctly, dressed in drab pants and nondescript shirts rather than the high boots of the teamsters or the uniforms of the soldiers. One wore buckskin pants.

These three men drew my attention and one of them—the one in buckskins, a clean-shaven man of about thirty-five—caught my look. Tipping his hat to Rose, he smiled. His manner was curious but not rude.

"Howdy, miss. It's rare to see a girl out here. My name's George Taylor, no relation to the old president." He wore boots with a faded blue shirt tucked into his buckskins.

Rose nodded politely at the stranger, and I felt very proud to be sitting with her. Not only were girls rare out west, but pretty girls were exceedingly so. Rose was beautiful and was sitting with me.

"I'm Jason Malone." I stretched to shake. "And this is Rose Mackenzie, my-uh-my partner."

Rose shot me a curious glance, and I smiled, pleased with my description of her. Although I wanted her to be more to me, a partner was precisely what she had become. I was content with the title. For now.

"Oh, we know you, Jason Malone," the stranger chuckled as he shook my hand firmly. "Everyone in Fort Union knows you after the beating your mare gave Captain Wilmington yesterday."

He nudged his partner and introduced him. "This is Randy. That there's Tom. They tag along with me. At the moment, we're footloose and hunting work, but I'd like to buy you two a meal. We made a bit from that race, and I'd be honored to repay a little."

I nodded my thanks and benches scraped as they stepped over to our table.

"I told Randy we needed to bet everything we had on that little red mare of yours, but he took some convincing." George straddled the bench and refilled his cup from the blackened coffeepot. He chuckled, remembering the race.

"Yes, sir," Randy spoke for the first time. "George told me to bet on your little mare against that big white gelding, and I balked. I thought there was no way that big horse could be beaten by that mare." He sipped his coffee and then looked from me to Rose. "George here knows horses. He said he could see that mare was a better horse and would run away from the gelding. He was right. We bet the whole eleven dollars we owned and made a goodly sum."

I glanced at Rose out of the corner of my eye after Randy finished his speech. Rose looked back at me. I knew what she was thinking.

We were served our buffalo steak and ate in silence. The whole time, I was praying and asking God for wisdom and discernment of his will.

"So, George," I began casually as I refilled my cup. I glanced at Rose, but she put a hand over the top of her mug. She didn't like coffee like I did. "You know horses. Where did you learn that?"

George finished chewing and swallowed. "I was a stable boy in a barn in Kentucky. Learned a lot about breeding and bloodlines and breaking stock for saddle and racing."

Rose kicked me under the table.

"What have you been up to since then?" I felt the excitement rising in me but tried to conceal it.

He hooked a thumb at his partners. "Randy and Tom here are good at building with logs and stone. We've been building structures whenever we can land a job. Otherwise, we hunt for the fort. Sometimes, I go up into the hills and try to catch some of the wild stock that runs up there. No luck, though. You have to be almighty crafty to trap those wild mustangs."

He looked up at the fat cook when the big man came and took our dishes away. "We'd like five pieces of pie, if you have 'em," he ordered and waved his empty coffee cup. "And some more coffee, please."

Rose squirmed in her seat, and I looked at George. "You say you're hunting work? Does the job have to be something quick or could it be long term?"

156

Here, Randy interjected. "We need something now, but I plan on heading back to the states for winter. Tom is thinking of joining me. I have a sister I want to visit in Illinois. George says he'll never leave the west."

George nodded. "This is my home now." He lifted the fresh pot and filled his cup. "I have nothing else, and I love it. I just hope I can find some place to winter in before the snow flies," he added, smiling at Rose.

She smiled and leaned forward, resting her elbows on the table. "We're building a ranch on the Arkansas River and we need help. Could the three of you come and build for us? Then, Randy, we can put you and Tom on an eastbound train by October. George, if you're willing, you can work for us and help us with the stock. It'll be a cold winter where we've settled, but the house you men build will help with that."

The horse handler grinned. "Well, missy, that's an answer to our prayers. We've been wondering how the good Lord was going to work this out for us, and this sure seems to fit us just right. Whaddya say, boys?" George turned to his partners. Tom and Randy nodded.

"Sounds just about perfect to me," Randy replied. "What kind of structures do you want built? And what kind of trees do you have locally?" Leave it to a builder to inquire about materials.

We talked another hour and then agreed to meet them in the morning for an early start.

CHAPTER 25

As the three men strode away, I was again reminded of God's perfect sovereignty. My plan had been to leave earlier. But because of an unforeseen delay, we crossed paths with men who I was sure would be important to our ranch. Funny how God orchestrates events we'd considered inconvenient. He is all wise and knows what's best for us. I wish sometimes I could just get out of his way and let him do mighty things without me always getting impatient or worrying about little details.

I thought out loud. "Rose, we'll have to order more food for the winter. Also, I'm thinking of pipe and windows and lanterns. We'll need to furnish a ranch house."

She laughed, and it sounded musical to my ears. "Wait a minute. We need to begin ranching with horses before we build fancy houses and barns. Patience, Cowboy Jason. All in good time."

We entered the general store and made a few additional purchases. I also ordered building materials that could be delivered later. Eventually, we'd put up a ranch house. We'd be feeding more hands, so the order included more staple items like beans, flour, sugar, rice, coffee, and salt.

The heat was unbearable that afternoon. Rose wanted to continue working with Strawberry and the bay mare, so I walked down to the Cimarron River to clean up—the last opportunity I had before arriving at the ranch.

Anxious to get going, I chewed my lip, making myself relax. Grabbing my towel and new clothes I'd purchased the day before, I ambled down the hill toward the shallow river. Although I wouldn't be wearing them on the trail, I'd better try them on before leaving the fort.

Finding a flat rock to hold my clothes, I stripped to the waist and bathed.

The river was only a stream this time of year, but water flowed and felt good on my dirty body. I put on my new shirt, and looking around first, quickly slipped from my worn trousers and put on my new pants. I would keep my moccasins to wear.

I thought about buying boots, but the ones Sergeant Reynolds gave us would work fine for breaking the mustangs, and I preferred the Indian shoes Blue Heron made me. They were so comfortable. Besides, I didn't want to spend the money.

After washing my dirty clothes in the river, I spread them in the sun to dry.

Dressed again, I sat on a rock, watching the river flow by and letting my hair dry. I'd have to hurry to get some kind of house put together before winter was upon us. George and his men should make it possible.

The warm sun at first felt pleasant on my back as I sat by the river's edge, but soon, the heat drove me to a shady spot under a large old pine tree.

The day-long delay had been worth it, but I felt pensive, anxious to head home. Sadly, there was nothing to do until morning. While Rose worked with the horses, I decided to force myself to think, to pray, to plan. Might as well use my time wisely.

The West was a wonderful place to be, and I was grateful to the Lord for bringing me out here. How good God is. The Mackenzie family proved to be a kind and helpful group—finding the cattle helped also. The capture of the wild mustangs was the beginning of our horse ranch and solidified the partnership between Rose's family and me.

A smile tugged at my lips as I considered Rose. She was never far from my thoughts. I knew I was falling in love with her. What did God have to say about this?

"Father, I want to thank you for bringing us to Fort Union with the oxen. The race money is an incredible gift. Help us be wise in how we handle this money. I hope the ranch is your intention for me. Until you open a door in another direction, I will pursue building the horse ranch. Guide me, Lord. My life is yours."

I paused, looking around again. I felt awkward praying about Rose.

"Lord, I think you know I have feelings for Rose. I believe you brought her into my life. Help me to honor her and love her as you would have me do. Guide our relationship, whatever that may be, and give me wisdom and patience. Amen."

I gathered my drying clothes in a bundle and returned to camp, thoughtful and clean.

Rose glanced at me and then disappeared, heading toward the river. She held a bundle under one arm, and she swiveled her head from side to side, looking for anyone approaching.

When she returned in an hour, sunlight glistened on her wet hair pulled back in a ponytail tied with a piece of red ribbon. Her new pants couldn't hide her figure, and the white blouse she wore contrasted with her dark hair and copper skin.

"Where is that lovely green dress you wore the other night?" I asked innocently, my blood warming at the memory.

She smiled, blushing. "That's only for special occasions."

We walked to the café that night, and she proved to be lively company. She asked a hundred questions about building ranch houses and barns and piping water to specific locations.

I answered her questions, but my mind was elsewhere. I watched the heads turn in the café as they stared at the beautiful girl at my table, and I became lost in the deep pools of her green eyes.

The next day, the sun was just rising as we rode north for the Arkansas River. George, Randy, and Tom were with us, their pack horses carrying much of our supplies and gear. They asked questions and talked pleasantly, making the time pass.

George asked Rose about the Cheyenne and wild horse chasing. "Everyone's heard of the incredible riders of the Cheyenne," he said, his words making Rose lift her head a little taller. "They're famous for their knowledge of horses."

I glanced at Rose when he said this and saw the pride shining in her eyes. The horse hunter could not have given her a higher compliment.

With no oxen to slow our progress, we made good time. This trip home, however, lacked the playfulness Rose and I had enjoyed on our trip south to Fort Union. George and his partners were good riders, and we covered many miles each day.

About mid-morning on the second day from the fort, I was surprised to see a wagon train ahead in the distance. Then I remembered. Wilmington had pulled out two days before us.

We rode past the slow-moving freight wagons, and each teamster waved a greeting to us. I recognized Baldwin atop his high wooden seat. He glowered sourly when we passed him. I did not see Thompson and wondered if he'd left the train in Santa Fe.

At the head of the caravan rode Wilmington on his big white gelding. We slowed our mounts to keep pace with him, but he looked straight ahead, ignoring us. He sat stiff in his saddle, his back ramrod straight.

"Howdy, Wilmington," George called, and the wagon master nodded coldly. "Jason Malone here, who I don't figure you'll soon forget, is starting a ranch on the Arkansas near Old Bent's Fort. He's hired us to build for him. I reckon he'll pay us with the money he won from you in that little race back at Fort Union."

George kicked his mount, and he, Randy, and Tom moved off, laughing as they rode. I looked at Wilmington's face, purpling darkly down to his neck, his lips pressed tightly, but he said nothing.

I pinched the brim of Cal's old hat, then Rose and I rode to catch up with George.

That night around the campfire, I confronted George. "Wilmington was very mean to leave me on the side of the trail, but I forgave him. If it hadn't been for him, I would never have met the Mackenzie's. You shouldn't have teased him that way today. He looked upset when we left him."

"And so he should be," George argued. "What kind of man kicks a boy out of his wagon train alone out here? He's lucky someone doesn't do more than just laugh at him."

"Regardless, I'm content with what's happened to me since that awful day. God has richly blessed me. I've found new friends, homesteaded my own ranch, I've a few head of cattle, and we're going to begin horse ranching." I listed the many positive things I'd encountered since landing on the banks of the Arkansas River.

"Don't forget the race we won and the money that provided," Rose added with a smile. "Also, we've a deal with the army to buy our broken stock. I'd say God has richly blessed us, indeed."

I walked away from the fire then. The night grew darker as the sun dipped in the west, but I already saw the evening star. A dove called for its mate, and the lonely sound touched my own heart. Would I one day have a mate?

I stood a short distance from the others and listened. The prairie was silent now. Even the constant wind had disappeared with the sun. The tall grass was thick and lush under my feet. Perfect for cattle and horses, I mused, pulling a handful of the rich stuff.

I gripped the bunch of grass and looked up, studying the dark blue of twilight in the sky. "If you can see me, Pa, I hope you know how much I wish you were with me now. This is a good land. I've claimed a place for us. Our ranch is coming together."

A lump rose in my throat, and I grinned, knowing Pa understood. I nodded, hoping he could hear the feelings in my heart as a tear rolled down my cheek.

Hastily, I wiped it away and turned toward camp.

As I strode to the fire, my steps muffled in the grass, I heard Randy speaking with Rose, the firelight flickering on their faces.

"You mean he was just dropped off out here by Wilmington, and then found your family? In all this open land, he found you, and then some stray cattle from a wagon train? Then you caught some wild mustangs? That's not luck, Rose. That's God blessing this young man. I'd stick to him if I were you. The Lord is with him."

I kicked my feet to make noise as I entered the firelight. Rose and I exchanged a smile as I passed the group, making my heart do a flip. Walking to the picketed horses, I fed the gray gelding the handful of grass I carried and rubbed his neck.

Was it true what Randy said? Pa always said we were never alone if we knew Jesus, but I had to admit that a time or two back there in Missouri and here on the plains when I stood beside Cal's grave, I'd felt mighty alone.

I drew in a deep breath and scanned the circle of companions around the fire. I wondered if Wilmington planned to get back at me, if revenge drove him to seek me out. But as I studied Rose and the men in camp, I could feel the fear slip away. I wasn't afraid of Wilmington or what he could do to me. I wasn't alone anymore. A cord of three strands is not easily broken.

I sought my blankets late that night but not before I saw the clouds come rolling in to blot out the stars.

I awoke in the gray morning light to a gentle rain. We'd ride wet.

CHAPTER 26

Our sodden and weary group rode into the mouth of the tiny canyon of the cliff dwellings the next day. Walter clambered down from the rocks where he'd been watching for us, the old muzzleloader in his hands.

"He's been up there for the past four days," Scott grinned when he saw his sister. My heart warmed as I watched them embrace. Blue Heron emerged from the stone shelter, and George tipped his hat when he saw her, his eyes widening. Blue Heron nodded at him shyly then hugged me. I'd not hugged a woman since Ma died, and I was somewhat embarrassed.

Rose laughed when she saw my awkward return of the warm greeting.

"Well, look at him, now," she accused, arching her eyebrows. "You wouldn't believe he was shy if you saw how bold he was with me the other day."

As Blue Heron led the blushing girl away out of the rain, she glanced over her shoulder. Rose's green eyes glowed as she looked at me. Giggling, the two women disappeared into the rock shelter.

Walter shot me a sharp glance, his old eyes narrowed, but he said nothing. Had he guessed my secret? Could he know I'd kissed his granddaughter? I was glad the rain hid my heated face. Turning to George and his partners, the old Indian said, "Welcome. Put your horses up anywhere and come in for some hot food."

I would not meet Rose's eyes that evening over the crackling fire. We ate on the open ledge of the cliff dwelling, the bright flames cheering the wet night.

"Choose a room to stow your gear," Walter instructed to the new men, indicating the dark mouths of the empty shelters behind him.

Randy shifted and tossed a stick on the blaze. "Well, it'll only be for a short while, then we'll have a real house for you to live in."

Blue Heron frowned and looked at me. "What does he mean, Jason? Are we going to move?"

I nodded. "I hired these men to build our ranch house and barn. Isn't that what we wanted?" I glanced from her to Walter, suddenly uneasy.

Blue Heron dropped her gaze and Walter looked from her to me. "We are Cheyenne. We do not live in white men's houses. We will stay here."

My intent was to make them happy, but their response was another example of something I'd not expected. I chewed the inside of my cheek and stared into the fire, not knowing what to say. I didn't want to press the matter. There was plenty of time before the house would be completed.

The following day the rain continued to fall. Despite the wet weather, Scott and I showed Randy, Tom, and George around the basin and the side canyons.

Randy was excited at the quantity of building materials close at hand, but George scowled when he saw our penned horse herd.

He shoved his hands into his pockets and hunched his shoulders. "You mean you're going to start a horse ranch with this bunch?" He nodded at the horses skeptically. "This isn't the best breeding stock."

I bristled. Didn't he realize the amount of work that'd gone into catching these few head? We were lucky to have them. "We know that," I snapped, looking over the shaggy, wild mustangs. "The army will pay for riding stock, not breeding stock. We hope to capture another wild mustang stallion known around these parts. We'll use him for our stud."

George shrugged and turned away.

We mounted again, and I looked at George. Rain dribbled from his hat brim, his face a mask of worry. In that moment, I felt doubt too. Could we do this? Walter had experience with horses, but he was old. Rose could ride, but she was very young. Could we put together a working, paying horse ranch?

Pa always said nothing was impossible for God. I believed that, but would he intervene with our venture? Did he really care if we built a ranch or not?

Rose and I were partners. I believed God had brought us together. I needed her and her family. But I also needed good horse stock. I needed Wildfire.

My thoughts whirled as we turned our mounts and rode back to the narrow canyon. There were so many details that had to be ironed out. Walter and

166

Blue Heron refused to move to the ranch house, and now George was not pleased with the quality of our stock. What other unforeseen difficulties would come our way?

Anxiety filled me as I found my blankets that night. I felt God had already given us so much. Would asking for more be right?

The next day Randy promised to help me pick a spot for the house. I took him to a knoll overlooking the river.

The location included a spectacular view. I could look over the river below, up and down the basin. The rise of land backed up against the mountains and then stretched out to a promontory for another hundred yards to a spot looking over the Arkansas River.

"I'm thinking of the house here," I gestured to the flat place near the mountain. "Then I'd like a bench built under that tree out on the point." I imagined myself sitting on that bench with a view of the valley and river at my feet while I prayed and spent time with the Lord.

He pointed to a wide, level place farther down the hill. "That looks like a good place for the barn and corrals."

"That's what I was thinking." I nodded in agreement. "What about water? I want it to be easy to get from here."

He turned and looked up at the mountain behind us. "Is there a spring up there?"

I didn't know, but I told him of the spring we'd diverted to water our second box canyon. He nodded, listening to my suggestions. I could tell he knew what he was talking about and enjoyed working the details out in his head as we spoke.

For the next month, we worked from dawn to dusk. I was good with tools, so I helped George and his partners construct the house and barn. Stones were so plentiful we used them for the bottom half of each structure and the interior walls. We cut logs from the nearby mountains and dragged them to our building site by saddle mounts. Their horses didn't like dragging the heavy logs, but they accomplished the task.

Walter, Scott, and Rose worked hard to saddle break the mustangs using the army saddles Sergeant Reynolds provided. Rose wore the tall cavalry boots when she rode the wild horses. She decided to keep the red mare for herself and even broke her to saddle and bit.

Despite the long hours of work each day, Rose and I seemed to always find time to slip away for evening walks or to simply sit and watch the stars. Our friendship grew.

I didn't kiss her again, although she allowed me to hold her hand.

Day by day, the buildings went up. George and Randy worked well together while Tom kept busy providing building materials to each work site. I was pleased to see how swiftly they built. I had a hard time keeping up when they were laying stone or trimming timbers.

Clay was readily available from the nearby river but took some effort to haul up to the house site. The barn was easier, it being on a lower level than the big house on the knoll.

I decided to build the house large and spacious. Building materials were plentiful, and I saw no reason to build small now and add on later.

The stone fireplaces Randy constructed from the rounded river rock impressed me. He put a huge fireplace in the living room which commanded a spectacular view on three sides. You could sit in front of the fire and see the plains in the east, the river visible from each window.

He added a wide, covered veranda that ran the length of the house and wrapped around on three sides. He added smaller fireplaces in the individual bedrooms, but an actual iron stove had been ordered for the roomy kitchen that might be months in arriving.

"I'll run water to these particular spots when you get some pipe," Randy directed. He showed me a spring he'd discovered on the mountain behind the house. "Until you get glass for the windows and pipe for water, I don't think you'll want to live here. It'll be too cold."

There was a slim chance the glass and pipe I ordered from Santa Fe would be delivered before the snow fell. I hoped to drive a couple of steers to the cook at the café in Fort Union soon but didn't know if there would be time. Winter had a way of coming early to these mountains.

"You'll need to order hinges and planks for doors, beds, and other furniture. I'll be gone before that stuff arrives, but George can finish the job," Randy explained, as he put the finishing touches on one of the smaller fireplaces.

I had already ordered many of these items, but little good that would do if they didn't arrive before winter. I resigned myself to moving into my new house sometime next spring.

Every day, Randy would stop working for a moment and look toward the east. From the knoll where we built the house, you could look right out onto the plains and see for miles. I knew he was trying to catch sight of a wagon train but none came.

By early October, we had three horses to sell the army, and I was anxious to deliver the two steers. We'd need meat for the winter, too, but game was plentiful. Walter or I went hunting occasionally and rarely came home empty-handed.

I decided the time was as late in the season as I dared a trip to Fort Union. We agreed Scott would accompany me on this journey.

The young boy was overjoyed at the prospect. His mother was not.

"You will have to take lots of warm clothes with you, Scott," Blue Heron fussed. "I don't want you catching cold out on those frozen plains."

Scott frowned. "Mother, we won't be gone that long. Besides, after Rose's experience when she visited the fort, I'm sure the excitement of the trip will keep me warm."

Then she turned her gaze on me. "I expect you to watch out for him, Jason. Take care of my son."

Leaving the next morning, I wondered if we were pushing our luck. It was already October, and storms could come at any time. I glanced up to the mountain. Snowcapped peaks shimmered in the higher elevations. We needed to hurry to the fort and return quickly.

Saying goodbye to these good people this time proved to be more difficult than I'd expected. Especially Rose.

She wore pants with the tall boots every day now, but her boyish garb couldn't conceal her womanly figure. She took my shirtsleeves in her hands and pulled me close. My breath caught as she leaned into me. I thought she meant to kiss me.

Her eyes glistened with tears as she pressed her body against me. I could feel her heart beating as she looked up into my face. "Come home to me soon, Jason," she whispered softly, her red lips trembling.

With a sob, she tore away from me and bolted into her room.

Blue Heron had been watching, and as Rose disappeared, I turned to look at her. Blue Heron's eyes held a soft, understanding glow. She nodded and smiled encouragingly. I mumbled my goodbye and went down the ledge to the waiting horses.

George, Randy, and Tom were to continue work on the house and the barn while we were gone. Randy had even suggested a large rock-walled corral near the barn. They hoped to finish this before winter.

I paid Randy and Tom what I owed them in case they left before my return.

Then, herding the two steers before us and pulling the lead ropes of the three horses behind, Scott and I left for Fort Union.

CHAPTER 27

Frost shimmered like jewels on the ground in the early morning but melted away as the sun rose and the day warmed. The plains were glorious in all their fall splendor. The colorful leaves in the trees along the Arkansas were painted yellows, reds, and oranges, preparing to drop. The vibrant colors contrasted with the dull browns and grays of the grasslands.

Higher up on the mountains, I glimpsed the white-barked aspens, golden leaves quivering in the early morning sunlight while the deep green of the pines clustered along the ridges and crags of their lofty thrones.

As we crossed the river and joined the old Santa Fe Trail, I heard wild geese above us, the dark triangles filling the air with their honk, honk. Winter was coming.

Flipping the collar of the buffalo coat against my neck, I was grateful for its thickness and warmth. Blue Heron had done a wonderful job making this coat, and I surely appreciated her work on this chilly morning.

Scott chatted incessantly, eager and excited for his first trip to the fort. He started a quick pace, but I had to hold him in, explaining that we didn't want to run the meat off the steers. They would be worth less if they were too skinny.

He laughed but settled down as we moved on.

The wagon ruts of the old trail made it easy to follow the road. The route was clearly marked, and we relaxed for the long journey ahead.

"I know you and Rose took a whole week to get to Fort Union," he began, a mischievous light in his eyes. "But be honest now, were you trying hard to get there fast?"

I shifted and the saddle creaked. "Well, no, we weren't anxious to push the oxen." I glanced at him from the corner of my eye. What was he getting at? "We didn't hurry, I suppose."

My mind went back to that trip with Rose, and I smiled. Riding with the lovely, dark-haired girl every day, camping under the stars at night.

Watching her race Wilmington on the back of the little red mare. That had been a fun trip I would never forget.

"I know you had eight slow oxen on that trip," Scott continued. "But it seemed that maybe you two dawdled a bit. I find it hard to believe it took an entire week to get to Fort Union."

Ignoring his accusation, I kicked the gray gelding and rode out onto the prairie for a look around, his laughter following me.

Maybe there was some truth to what Scott said, for he and I arrived at Fort Union in only five days.

We made camp on the knoll above the town under the very same tree where Rose and I had camped. Picketing the horses so they could graze and rest, we allowed the steers to stray, knowing they wouldn't go far.

We washed in the river while the sun hung low in the west. It would be dark soon. Eagerly, we walked to the café.

The fat cook was pleased to see me and even more pleased when I informed him of the two steers on the hill. I agreed to bring them to him in the morning, and he hurried to the kitchen to bring us some antelope.

Like Rose, Scott was all eyes, and he swiveled to watch customers coming and going. I grinned, enjoying Scott's excitement. Sipping coffee, I thought of my last visit to the café.

Unlike when I was with Rose, no one paid us any attention this time. The young Indian girl in the green dress had certainly drawn a lot more attention than this young buck. I smiled into my tin cup at the memory. Despite Scott's presence, I felt lonely, hollow somehow with Rose far away from me.

The antelope steaks were good and the pie better. I was on my final cup of coffee, ready to leave the restaurant, when the door opened and Sergeant Reynolds entered.

I stood to shake his hand, and he accepted our invitation to join us. Scott had never met a soldier and was impressed by the sergeant's blue uniform.

"Did you pass anyone when you rode in?" Steam rose as Reynolds filled a mug with coffee.

"We passed one big freight outfit going east," I replied. I briefly wondered if Randy and Tom had joined the train.

As Reynolds ate his meal, I explained about the three saddle mounts we'd brought. I could tell he was pleased about the horses, but the worry lines around his eyes told me he had something more to say. He kept glancing at me out of the corner of his eyes. Pensive, I squirmed under his questioning gaze.

I stood and stretched. "We're tired. Time to turn in. We'll talk tomorrow."

He looked at me then, and his concern was evident. "Jason, I need to talk to you of other matters tomorrow as well."

I nodded absently, not understanding what he meant and too tired to care. We left and began walking back to our camp.

"What did he mean about other matters?" Scott shoved his hands in his coat pockets. Cold wind whistled from the mountains, and I hoped we could conclude our business here quickly and return to the ranch.

Square yellow light shone from the windows of the military buildings around the parade ground. Stars twinkled overhead. I could tell the temperature had dropped with the sun. It would be cold tonight.

I shook my head and yawned. "I don't know. I guess I'll find out tomorrow."

We'd already gathered firewood while there had still been light. Putting a match to the piled kindling now, I watched as the tiny flame caught and spread. In a couple of minutes, we sat around a warm blaze, enjoying the heat and light.

After tossing on more wood, I rolled in my blankets and turned my gaze heavenward. The night sky was clear. I pondered the brilliant stars again in the dark canopy above me and thanked God for his creation. His work displayed around me, I thought how God was so creative, majestic, awesome—the Master of art and beauty. His handiwork was displayed around me, for all to see and marvel at.

I worshipped and praised him for his holiness.

The fire crackled and sparks danced. The sound made me drowsy.

The last thing I thought of was Rose. Her face, her dark hair. I missed her.

———◇———

At breakfast the next morning, the cook roared his approval at the sight of our two steers, and I grinned at his enthusiasm.

He purchased the animals for twenty dollars apiece, and I left them with his wife. Scott and I enjoyed another meal we didn't have to cook ourselves, then went in search of Sergeant Reynolds.

We found the big army man walking from the general store. He instructed us to bring the mounts around to his office.

Scott rode the individual horses as the big soldier stood by and closely scrutinized each animal. He stroked a horse's leg and picked it up, examining the hoof. He rubbed each animal's head and pulled its neck toward him to watch the response. Finally, he turned to me, a broad grin on his tanned face. "Good." He slapped me on the back. "Come into my office and we'll discuss price."

Telling Scott I would meet him back at camp, I followed the soldier into the stark office.

Reynolds seated himself behind his desk and faced me. "Unfortunately, the army sets a fixed price they'll pay for mounts from non-military horse providers. They'll only give seventy-five dollars a head. If you're in agreement, I can give you that amount."

The price was not what I'd hoped for, but it was a beginning. I knew Rose would have me take the offered amount, so I agreed. I signed my name on a couple of forms before he paid me the money.

I was stuffing the bills into my pocket when he looked at me across his desk with that worried look in his eyes I'd seen the night before.

"What is it, Sergeant?" Then I remembered the war and I squinted. "Don't tell me things have gone badly for the Union."

Reynolds frowned. "No, thank God. Nothing has changed since we last spoke. The weather is cooling, so I would guess there will be little fighting for the rest of the year. General Lee has returned to Virginia to lick his wounds."

I tilted my head, confused. "Then what has you so bothered?"

He touched his fingertips together and rested his elbows on the desk. He stared at me for a moment, his lips pressed tightly. Pulling open a drawer, he placed a thick envelope on the desk between us.

"A couple of weeks ago, the colonel asked me if I knew you. When I said I did, he gave me this and told me to handle it."

I looked at the envelope. "Handle what? What's it about?"

He shifted his feet. "It's from a lawyer named Mr. Tarleton from St. Louis. You ever heard of him?" He eyed me intently, watching my reply.

The mere mention of the Missouri city made me cringe. I could feel the cold sweat on my face, and my stomach lurched. Could the night riders know I was here? Had Wilmington reported my whereabouts to those who wanted compensation for the burned-out rental cabin? Or, did they want me?

I drew a deep breath and shook my head. "I've never heard of a Mr. Tarleton, nor do I know why he'd write me."

I stared suspiciously at the envelope and squirmed in my chair. Who was Tarleton?

"Oh, he didn't write you. This letter is not for you. He wrote to the people in charge at a few key points along the Santa Fe Trail. Points west of Council Grove. One letter was sent to the colonel here, and another was sent to Santa Fe. I don't know of any other locations. The text specifies in no uncertain terms that you are to be located and this information sent back to him in St. Louis."

I shrugged, feigning disinterest. No lawyer would be looking for me that I knew of, right? After all, I had done nothing wrong. "Maybe it's another Jason Malone," I suggested. "I'm nobody. Why would a lawyer want to know my whereabouts?" I relaxed, the logic of my remark calming me. It seemed a mistake, and I was eager to prepare for my trip back to the ranch.

Reynolds narrowed his eyes. "What'd you want me to do? I could, of course, not do anything. That would bother me, though, as I believe in efficiency and honesty." He leaned back in his chair.

I shrugged again. "Well, I have nothing to hide, but I'm sure this is all a mistake. Of course, be honest. Write this Mr. Tarleton and report that you know of a Jason Malone located on the Arkansas River."

My chair scraped as I got to my feet.

"Sergeant, it's good to see you again. I hope to deliver more stock in the spring. Travel during the winter might be too difficult." I shook his hand, and his grip was firm.

"I'll be seeing you then, Jason Malone," he said.

I turned to go. As I opened the door, I glanced over my shoulder. Sergeant Reynolds was staring at the envelope on his desk, a worried look on his face.

CHAPTER 28

Ready to set out immediately for home, I chewed my lip when Scott pleaded with me to take him to the general store. He insisted on seeing each of the different types of colorful candy in their clear jars on the counter and even suggested we take some home to his mother.

I laughed and shrugged. What matter could a short delay make? "Blue Heron would like licorice, I suppose, and so would Scott."

He grinned. In the end, I purchased a small bag of candy.

While Scott wandered the narrow aisles filled with various goods he rarely, if ever, saw, I asked the clerk about my order for glass, hinges, and lumber.

"There's still time for the late wagon train from Santa Fe. It only comes this far and then goes back. It's too dangerous to attempt a crossing over the plains in winter. Maybe in the next week or two, if we're lucky."

Giving the shopkeeper specific directions and distance to our ranch, I asked him to ship my order on ahead if it arrived. "I'll pay extra for the teamster who delivers." I was eager to complete the great ranch house on the knoll. The idea of leaving it vacant for the duration of the winter troubled me.

The owner scratched his head, then agreed to pass on my message. "Don't bet on it, though," he said, shaking his head. "Teamsters hate the cold, and it could be dangerous. You might have to wait until spring."

I left some money on deposit at the store for safekeeping and to pay for additional supplies upon our next trip.

After a filling meal at the café, we saddled our mounts and hurried northward.

Although reluctant to turn around and head home so fast, Scott wanted to see his family. This trip had been the longest length of time he'd been separated from them. I thought of Rose, Walter, and Blue Heron. I missed them too.

Traveling with just our two mounts enabled us to cover a great distance, and we made good time. By nightfall, we were far out on the road.

That night, as the sun disappeared over the Rockies, Scott pointed north and shook his head. "That doesn't look good."

I followed his outstretched arm and noticed large, dark clouds gathering ahead of us.

"A storm's brewing. We'll get it tomorrow," he added.

I nodded, a chill running down my back, recalling my promise to Blue Heron to look after her son. "Yes, I think you're right," I said softly, my eyes on the billowing, ominous clouds.

The sky had turned steel gray over us by the time we awoke, and we hurried breakfast and hit the saddle, not even waiting for coffee. By mid-morning, the wind blustered in our faces. By noon, the sky had grown even darker and a fine drizzle blew, striking us horizontally. The temperature had dropped, and tiny raindrops stung our faces like needles.

The horses didn't like it, either. Heads bowed against the gale, they plodded on, making a slow go of it. They were tough animals and accustomed to harsh weather, but their senses told them it was time to seek shelter.

I could tell Scott felt the same way as he kept looking to me to decide. The problem was, there was no shelter I could see. There was nothing around us except bare, open prairie.

Should we turn back to Fort Union? The wind would be at our backs, but we'd come so far already. I decided to push on, hoping I was making a wise choice.

The track turned to mud, the ruts of countless wagons filling with rain. We rode on the turf a few rods off the trail, carefully watching so we didn't lose our way.

We fought against the wind and rain until late afternoon when our situation grew worse. The rain had increased and was freezing now, a thin layer of ice forming on our shoulders. When the sun dropped, it would turn to snow.

I searched everywhere for something to use as shelter, anything to block the howling wind. My gaze swept the bleak landscape, hoping, praying for something. We found nothing, not even a stream bank or hill that would provide some relief from the angry storm.

Glancing at Scott, I saw he'd nestled down in the warmth of his buffalo hide coat, but I knew it didn't protect or cover all of him. His legs and hands must be as cold as my own. Nevertheless, he didn't complain. I'd discovered people out west were inclined to accept rough conditions as a matter of course.

With the wind screaming and the rain pelting us, my hands and face stiff, I finally saw something that might suffice as a bit of shelter.

Reaching out a frozen arm, I shoved Scott's shoulder. He didn't move and I stiffened, fearing the worst. Had he frozen to death? How could I break this dreadful news to Rose and Blue Heron? With a harder shove, he raised his head and peered at me, his nose and cheeks red from the extreme chill. I exhaled through clenched teeth and pointed to a stand of trees a hundred yards off the trail. It looked like an old stream bed. He nodded but said nothing. We turned our tired mounts in that direction.

Gaining the partial shelter of the trees, I stretched to help Scott from the saddle and braced myself as he fell into my arms. Shaking him roughly, I pointed to a spot behind a low bank where some deadfalls had piled. "Start a fire," I yelled above the wind.

I unsaddled the horses and tethered them tightly behind the deadfall near where Scott was busy gathering sticks. I could see his numb fingers struggling to grasp the matches as he finally lit a tuft of dead grass. He fed more kindling and started gathering huge armloads of fuel. It would be a long night.

I dragged other broken limbs and small trees near and attempted to improve our windbreak. Scott threw our blankets over the backs of the horses and I yelled against the wind to attract his attention. Gesturing to a large limb, he rushed to help me drag it near our fire.

It was completely dark now, with no stars visible through the dense clouds. I managed to put some coffee on to boil, more out of a need to get warm than desire for the strong drink.

We huddled together with only a single blanket wrapped around our shoulders to keep us warm. We dozed all night next to the sputtering fire, constantly feeding its hungry flames. Occasionally, one of us would leave the partial protection of the blanket to check the horses. If something happened to them, we'd be in worse shape.

What a long and miserable night. It reminded me of the three days after Pa died before I tied up with Cal. Those had been rough too.

We sipped the hot coffee to warm us, but neither of us felt hungry. Maybe we simply didn't have the desire to prepare food in this storm.

I spent a lot of time in prayer that night as I fed the fluttering flames of the little fire. I thanked God for wood. Without this fire, I don't think we'd have made it. God provided these small woods to shelter us in our hour of need. I praised him for his love.

I was reminded of the voyage St. Paul made where he and the crew had been shipwrecked and struggled to make it to shore on the island of Malta. If not for that small island in the Mediterranean Sea, all those men would have perished.

The fierce wind scuttled the tiny blaze. Keeping the fire alive at all costs became our sole purpose. When I checked on the horses, I gathered more fuel and dragged it near. We must keep the fire going. Our very lives depended on it.

Finally, a dull gray appeared in the east, and with infinite slowness, the day broke.

The rain and wind seemed to die down a little at dawn, so I shook Scott. Eyes wide, he stared at me from under the brim of his soaked fur cap.

"Scott, rain or no, we need to keep going. We should get home today if we can make some time."

There was little hope of us reaching the cliff dwellings this day, but I offered the thought to him anyway. Guiding people through situations wasn't easy, but I was learning that folks wanted a leader to make the tough decisions they wouldn't. I hoped I was doing right.

He nodded, his teeth chattering.

I rolled our wet bedding. The horses glared at me when I threw the wet and heavy leather saddles onto their backs.

Eager to get moving toward home, we skipped breakfast, mounted, and began our ride.

The storm lessened as the sun rose. It appeared the blustery mess had passed over us and our spirits lifted, hope surging within us. Had we made it through the storm?

Then, out of nowhere, the sky unleashed a torrential downpour with a vengeance. We pulled rein, watching the shower disdainfully. We were soaked to the skin.

Scott looked at me and shook his head. "We're crazy to be out in this. I pray God gets us home safely," he said hoarsely.

I echoed his prayer with silent ones of my own.

We camped in a better spot that night—an old buffalo wallow near a dead stand of elms and rotting willows.

The rim of the wallow protected us from the occasional wind, although the storm had become a deluge now rather than a winter blast. Water collected in the bottom of the wallow for the horses, and we dozed fitfully that night without a fire, huddling in our wet blankets and shivering, despite our buffalo coats.

Mud clung to my moccasins as I checked on the horses. Heads down, they stood in the hoof deep mire, eyes half closed to the relentless downpour.

We chewed jerky as the dawn broke. Then, shivering in the cold, we mounted for what we hoped would be our last day on the trail.

The horses were reluctant to run, but it did help them stay warm. We'd run them and then let them walk a little, never allowing them to sweat, which would freeze.

At the end of that awful day, we caught sight of the Arkansas River in the distance. We pushed our weary mounts, crossing the river, and rode the final miles to our cliff dwellings in the dark.

CHAPTER 29

George, Walter, and Rose ran to meet us when I called from the mouth of the canyon. The men took our horses while Rose, gripping my cold hand, led us back to the warmth and security of the stone shelter. A thrill raced through me at her touch, and I tried to squeeze her hand with numb fingers. Her wide eyes searched my face, and I read the concern in her gaze. But happiness swelled within me as I studied her in return—my beautiful friend.

Blue Heron met us, handing each of us a cup of hot broth. I gulped mine into my frozen body, its heat radiating throughout me, making my limbs tingle.

Scott, soaking wet and shivering, grinned at me. "We made it, Jason. God is with us. He brought us home." His mother draped a thick buffalo hide around her son's shoulders.

"Give him thanks, Scott. I think we tested him this trip," I replied, nodding in agreement.

Rose disappeared into my stone room and emerged a few minutes later. "Jason, I have a fire in your room. You need to get out of those wet clothes and eat something warm."

Nodding but saying nothing, I crawled through the small opening and replaced the stiff buffalo hide flap. My wet clothes were difficult to strip with numb and fumbling fingers.

Fatigue crept over me, and I was tempted to simply lie down and go to sleep in my warm blankets, but I knew the wisdom of Rose's words. I needed nourishment.

When I returned to the ledge, a large fire blazed. Blue Heron handed me a plate, and I started to eat.

Scott sat on the blankets beside me, telling of our journey to the fort. Even his chattering teeth couldn't dispel him from relating the dangerous return trip. His eyes glowed in the firelight as he told of the snow and ice.

"I wasn't afraid though. Jason was with me."

All eyes turned to me, and I shifted uneasily. Scott went on. "We sold the steers, and I ate apple pie. We also had potatoes, and we brought you some candy. The soldier liked our horses and bought them for seventy-five dollars apiece. Is that good, Mother?" He turned to Blue Heron and yawned. She smiled weakly, lines forming on her concerned face.

"You will eat and go right in to bed, young man." She patted his arm through the blanket. Scott yawned again. I knew he wouldn't argue with her this time.

Walter informed us that the day after we'd left for Fort Union, a wagon train going east had come into view on the plains. Tom and Randy rode out to join it.

"We passed that train on our way to the fort." I sipped my coffee, holding the hot mug with both hands. "We wondered if they'd hitch a ride with them. Hope we see them again one day. They did good work."

My eyelids drooped, and I could tell my speech was slurred. Laughing, Rose took my mug. "I hoped you'd tell us all the news, but I think you need to go to bed. We'll talk in the morning."

Saying my good nights, I turned and again entered my snug little room. I tossed more wood on the fire then lay on my bed, pulling the covers over me.

Rousing in the morning, I stared up at the smoke-stained rock of the overhang. How many other men had looked up at this same stone ceiling? I was just one, one of many, who had walked these lonely crags, hunted food, loved a woman.

I blinked, startled by my bold declaration, but it was true. I loved Rose. I thrilled at the memory of the recent trip to Fort Union. God had formed me into a leader. More importantly than my dream of a ranch, I felt myself becoming the man of God I was meant to be. Shaped, developed, tested through trials. I inhaled sharply, realizing I was only the clay, he the potter.

God had seen fit to bring us home safely, but I wasn't special. We could've easily frozen to death on the Great Plains as surely as others had over the centuries. But God was not finished with me, yet. There was still business I needed to attend to.

My thoughts drifted to Pa and the war and Missouri and slavery. Was I where God wanted me to be? Was my purpose here? I had to believe he'd brought me here.

I glanced at my cold fire ring, scowling at the gray ash—the fire out for hours. I lay back, listening to the falling rain pelting the trees of the canyon.

Sneaking an arm from under the blankets, I nudged the cold ashes until I uncovered a single glowing ember. Pushing a small stick into this red eye, I blew softly until I coaxed a reluctant flame.

An additional stick tossed upon the former one started a tiny fire burning. I fed the fire more fuel and allowed the tiny blaze to warm my rock room.

To my surprise, I did not feel hungry, despite only eating once yesterday. However, I realized with a grin, I dearly wanted a cup of coffee.

I dressed and banked the fire before removing the stiff buffalo hide from the door. Outside, the cold air rushed by but didn't bother me. I wasn't wet and didn't have to ride in this storm again. The cold was something to be tolerated, something that merely irritated or annoyed. Nothing more.

I knew I was home.

Standing on the ledge, I studied our small canyon. No snow. It was cold but not cold enough. Winter struck a quick blow but hadn't sent its full force against us—yet. It would hold off for a while.

Walter and George sat by the fire. They greeted me casually, but their faces showed suppressed excitement.

As I explained about the horses for Sergeant Reynolds and the steers for the cook, Walter and George shot meaningful glances at one another.

"All right, out with it," I finally demanded. "I can tell you have news. Someone tell me."

George looked at the old Indian. "This is your news, Walter. You tell him."

Walter turned to me, a grin spreading across his leathery face. "We have found mustang tracks by the river. I believe they belong to Wildfire."

"Wildfire," I breathed, tensing at the name. "Where? How many in his bunch? When was this? How far from here?"

The two men chuckled. "Hold your horses." George reached for the simmering coffeepot. "Walter thinks he's been in the high country, and the weather drove him down here."

Walter nodded, beaming happily. "Mackenzie and I saw this stallion around here years ago, but since we have been here, I have not. I got worried maybe he changed ranges, but now I know he is still here. We are trying to figure a plan to catch him."

"We found his bunch grazing in a high meadow about six miles from here." George shoved the pot back into the coals and blew on his cup. "The best we can figure, he has over fifty head with him, probably closer to sixty. Hard to say from all the tracks."

"I think I saw him." The words spilled from me. Both men stared.

"Who?" Walter tilted his head.

"Wildfire. I saw a red stallion leading a herd months ago up the river. I was afraid to tell you in case I was mistaken."

Walter nodded. "I think it's him. He's ranging to lower levels."

I bit my lip as my stomach muscles tightened. Wildfire—the horse the Mackenzies came here for. I wanted him. I wanted Wildfire for Rose.

George looked out over the brush-choked canyon, a slender tendril of steam rising from his tin cup. "The storm is showing signs of letting up, but it could be just a lull."

I thought of my cattle and the horses in our fenced box canyon. "Has anyone checked on the stock?"

Walter nodded, his hands busy with braiding another rope. "We made sure they are fine. The cattle found a place behind some boulders against the wall. They seem to like it there at night. They come out to feed during the day. The horses are fine too. They are used to this weather."

"The other box canyon you fenced is behind the hot springs. It's full of good feed. That was clever, Jason. You'll have to find some way to pump that hot water up to your fancy house." George got to his feet.

"I was sure hoping my windows and stuff would come this fall," I grumbled, poking at the fire with a stick. "Now I don't think they'll make it." I wanted to move into the new house before snow fell but doubted if that would happen now. This storm was probably the herald of winter.

George shrugged. "You never know. This might blow off, and the weather could hold another month. You never know," he repeated, shaking his head.

I nodded and prayed he was right. Then I thought back to his earlier comment about the hot springs. If the storm was gone by tomorrow, I'd visit the springs and take a hot bath.

The day passed with rest and good food, but Rose was once again shy around me. One moment, she seemed to like me, the next, not so much. I knew nothing about women and trying to read this young and spirited girl with flashing green eyes was about impossible.

I gave her the money from the sale of the saddle stock, but she protested. "This money belongs to both of us. We all worked together to trap those horses."

"I had nothing to do with breaking those mounts. Besides, we're partners. It's yours. We'll split future money, if we get any." I pushed the bills back to her. I knew this was the only money her family had, and I wanted to help them as if they were my own family.

The storm let up that night. The stars were out with fresh clarity again as a gentle, cool breeze blew down from the mountains, forewarning us that winter would come for real one day soon.

The next morning, I strode down to check on the stock, clean clothes and a flour sack towel tucked under my arm. The cattle and few remaining horses seemed to have weathered the storm without incident as Walter said they would. Only eight horses grazed with the cattle in the box canyon. The remaining mounts were housed in the barn below the house. There was plenty of hay cut and stacked, the grass on the ground not yet covered by snow.

I wandered over to the other canyon Scott and I had fenced. Inspecting the tall, round hay stacks, I was impressed by Scott and Rose's efforts. Dull, gray light shimmered on the pool of water fed from the spring above. Scott had worked hard to divert that water. I stood before the pool, marveling at it, at least two feet deep and eight feet across. The little spring flowed despite the cold storm. It would probably freeze soon.

Walking from the canyon, I studied the rock fence and gate poles we'd stacked beside the opening. We could use this corral for grazing if the need arose.

Satisfied, I headed toward the river and the hot springs.

My thoughts revolved around the springs and George's suggestion to pipe the water to the ranch house on the knoll. How to do it?

Nothing came to me, and I sighed, knowing it would be added to my never-ending list of future improvements to the ranch.

Dense foliage screened the hot springs from view, but I still took one last look around before stripping and sliding into the steaming water.

The smell of the sulfur annoyed me, but the pure joy of a hot bath compensated for the pungent odor.

Eagerly, I sank into the warm water, leaning my head against a rock. My legs floated in front of me and I relaxed, allowing the mineral water to do its magic. It did, and soon, I dozed, lost in a world of comfort and warmth.

I thought I heard the whinny of a horse as if from a great distance on the wind, but my mind refused to focus on the sound. The water steamed around me, and I felt my fingertips pucker, resembling prunes. My stiff muscles loosened their stressed, tightened grip on my frame while my whole body seemed to float on a cloud of warm liquid.

Again, I heard a whinny, this time much closer, but again I didn't stir. The total contentment of the hot bath made me not want to move or think. Drowsily, I thought it might be Scott or George on one of the horses.

Close by, a horse whistled shrilly, and this time my eyes shot open. The neigh sounded like the animal was right atop of me.

I turned my head and peered through the leafless bushes in time to watch the last of a stream of horses trot into our empty box canyon.

I couldn't believe what I was seeing. How many were there?

I rolled onto my stomach and craned my neck to get a better view, but they'd disappeared into the canyon. No doubt our stacks of cut hay attracted them.

Why hadn't they smelled me? They had to come right past me to enter the canyon.

I chewed the inside of my cheek and nodded. The pungent smell of the sulfur spring had masked my scent.

Trembling with excitement, I pulled myself from the water, trying not to make a sound. Hurriedly, I slipped on my moccasins, my heart beating wildly in my chest. Could this be happening?

A shiver ran down my spine, but I refused to think of the cold as I ran for the gate poles. What if they saw me? Would they run from the canyon or retreat farther into it?

It didn't matter now, because I pulled the first of the trimmed logs across the opening. My hands shaking, I tugged on the second one. This rail proved to be heavier, and I struggled to shove it in place. Dropping the log where it belonged, I turned to grasp the final rail. With a grunt, I heaved the pole into its holdings, almost shoulder high. Panting from the exertion and exhilaration, I bent over, my hands resting on my knees, my breath coming in gasps. I had done it. The gate was closed.

Then, I realized I was still naked.

CHAPTER 30

With a nervous glance all around, I sighed with relief. I was indeed alone. I hurried back to the hot spring and dressed.

Swiftly returning to the log gate, I slipped between the two lowest bars and trotted into the canyon, my neck craning for a view of the horses.

I heard them before I caught sight of them. Bending low, I inched forward.

A few horses were eating from the stack of piled hay. Many others fanned out and grazed across the wide meadow. They had no idea they were trapped.

A head rose sharply on a big horse far from me, sensing my presence. I knew I was well back behind the concealing undergrowth, but this animal stared right at me and lifted his nose high into the air. I marveled at his keen senses.

The big horse trotted forward but then stopped, prancing uneasily. The horse was a magnificent stallion, blood red in color.

I tilted my head, wondering as I bit my lip. Could this be the elusive Wildfire?

A tremble raced over me as I fixed my gaze on the great stallion. I felt my heart pounding with anticipation. Keeping my position, I studied the scattered herd as the big stallion returned to feeding.

Counting heads, my breath froze in my lungs as I went higher and higher. "Thirty-one, thirty-two, thirty-three …"

I couldn't get an accurate number as the young ones darted among the horses, playing near their mothers. Still, there were easily more than fifty head.

I couldn't believe my good fortune. Of course, it wasn't luck at all. I stopped right then and thanked God. He was responsible for this surprise success, and I was fully aware of it. Only God would perform such a feat. He deserved the glory.

Inching backward, I retreated from the canyon to the gate. Slipping through the cross bars once again, I ran for the cliff dwelling.

I glimpsed the hot spring as I ran, the strong odor of sulfur surrounding me, and I laughed out loud. Would the others believe my wild tale?

I crossed the shallow river, hopping on the rocks with careful steps. It took only a minute to scramble up the gentle slope of the opposite bank. Racing on, I laughed again, my heart full. I wanted to shout and yell my exuberance, but my heaving lungs prevented it.

Entering the narrow canyon, I raced along the well-worn trail until I came to the old sentinel sycamore tree and leaned against it, trying to catch my breath. I pushed on and skidded to a halt at the foot of the wall, peering up at the ledge above.

Walter and George were there, the old Indian gripping the rifle. They stared, anxiously studying my back trail.

"What is it, Jason?" George craned his neck, squinting behind me.

"I … trapped … mustangs …" I panted, my lungs heaving for air.

"Where?" Walter scowled, his brow wrinkling.

I leaned on my knees, straining to catch my breath. Pointing behind me toward the river, I indicated the general direction.

The two men clambered down from their perch. Rose and Scott followed as we all turned to wend our way back down the trail. They grouped around me in a tight circle as I tried to explain.

"I was taking a bath. I heard horses. They walked into the canyon to feed. I closed the gate."

I wanted to warn them I believed the herd was Wildfire's band of mustangs, but George laughed before I could explain further.

"Well, you old wild horse hunter." He punched my shoulder. "Here Walter and I were up early this morning, talking over plans to set a trap for wild ones, and you catch them while bathing!"

I could tell by the gleam in his eyes that he was teasing, but I frowned, shaking my head.

"I'll bet there're hundreds of them too," he added, slapping me on the back.

I glanced at Rose for support. She looked skeptical too. Would no one believe me?

"How many did you see, Jason?" Walter wanted to know, a big smile on his face.

"I'm serious," I protested, my breath returning. "It's a big bunch of mustangs. More than fifty, I'm sure," I finally got out, still wanting to say more.

I led the way into the basin. They followed, casting doubtful glances between them.

My breathing calmed, but I had to pay attention as we crossed the river. Scott and Rose skipped easily across the round stones, but George slipped, his boot splashing. They laughed as he shook the water out, grumbling about wet boots and cold weather.

Walter was surprisingly agile and made it across without event.

Making our way past the hot spring, I blurted it out. "I think I saw the stallion. It's a big, red horse."

I wanted to say the stallion was Wildfire but didn't want to get their hopes up. I'd let them see him first. Besides, I'd never seen Wildfire close up and they had. What if I was mistaken?

Rose stopped, causing all of us to halt. I looked at her. She'd gone pale and her eyes were large.

"Could he be Wildfire?" she whispered, a hint of hope in her soft voice.

George shook his head. "I'd doubt if that old king would get trapped so easily." He eyed Walter for confirmation.

The old wild horse hunter arched an eyebrow and pursed his lips. "He would bring his band out of the mountains for the winter. They need to feed. We saw his tracks last week. The hay piles would attract them. Maybe ..."

Rose stepped forward again, and the rest of us followed quickly, like sheep behind a shepherd. Horse hooves had cut a wide path in the turf— the trail of the wild mustangs. Again we halted, the tracks plain in the mud at our feet.

I could tell the others believed me now as they stared at the many tracks. I grinned at them, pleased to be vindicated at last.

With a rush, Rose broke from us and ran toward the bars of the gate. We trotted after her. Swiftly, she slipped through the gate and hurried into the canyon beyond, disappearing around a bend.

Climbing through the gate poles, we followed on Rose's heels, trying to move both quickly and quietly. Excitement made me tremble as we crept forward along the trail to the meadow where we met Rose again. She crouched behind a mound of rock and scrub oaks. Her eyes glowed as we approached, but her gaze locked on Walter.

"I think it's him, Grandfather," she whispered, and I noticed the thrill in her voice.

She usually called the old man Walter like everyone else, but on this occasion, the more formal title seemed appropriate.

We fanned out on either side of Rose and peered through the foliage, watching the wild horses graze. They seemed unaware of their plight.

I again started to count heads and was on twenty-two when Walter spoke.

"It is him." The old man's words left no doubt. "It is Wildfire. I have seen him twice before." He laid a hand on Rose's shoulder. "Mackenzie would have loved to see this. We have him, Rose. We have Wildfire."

Rose smiled, her lips quivering, as her green eyes sparkled in the morning sun. Tears streamed down her copper cheeks, and she nodded triumphantly at her grandfather, unable to speak for a moment. Finally, she cleared her throat.

"Oh, can this be true?" she whispered, wiping the tears with the back of her hand. "We've waited so long. I wish Father could be here to see this."

She gripped the old Cheyenne's gnarled hand with her own slender one.

I wanted to take her into my arms, to comfort her, but this was not the time. I was so grateful that God had allowed me to be the one to bring this joy to the girl I loved.

I looked again at the big red horse. His sleek neck bent regally as he fed on the grass at his feet. I watched his noble head as he chewed the long stems. Even from this distance, the deep lines and powerful muscles of his body were apparent.

We watched the herd feeding for a while longer, not wanting to end the moment, but we needed to not disturb the herd. Not yet. That would come later, Walter promised.

"We want to take our time getting acquainted with this bunch. Do not want to spook them. There is time to be patient," the old man said with a glint in his eye. My heart warmed, knowing he loved this. His vitality and purpose had returned. Walter was happy.

We retreated to the gate, excitement and realization filling our senses. It was true. The great stallion was ours. What Mackenzie had wanted when he brought his family to this lonely place where the Rocky Mountains kissed the Great Plains had come true.

I was amazed at my lack of faith. I knew God could do anything he wanted, but somehow, I'd believed this was too difficult for God. He brought me here at this right time, to meet Rose and join her hurting family. God brought me a family to love just as he brought a wild mustang from the mountains to our boxed meadow. Anything is possible with God.

In just a few short months, I'd gone from a lost boy with nothing to a young man who'd found friends and a place to live my dream. God had done amazing things in so little time. I knew right then and there he was with me. Even when I didn't feel his presence, he was still working and maneuvering events for our good and his glory.

We spent the rest of the morning checking and strengthening the fence that blocked the canyon. We would be delinquent to lose these horses now that we had them. Besides the great stallion, there were many horses in the herd for riding stock we could sell to the army, and many of the mares would be ideal brood mares.

Blue Heron prepared a special feast at hearing our incredible news, and George volunteered in assisting her. The day felt festive and joyful. That night, after the delicious meal, Walter called for a time of thanksgiving.

Wrapped in blankets and buffalo robes, we sat around the fire ring on the ledge of the cliff dwelling. We prayed and sang praise songs to God. My new friends surprised me as they sang old Scottish and English worship hymns they'd learned from Mackenzie. Even George knew a number of the songs and joined in the prayer time.

I began to understand what King David meant when he wrote that his cup runneth over. My heart was full, and I knew contentment. Not simply because God richly blessed me but because those I loved were also happy.

That night, after the prayer time ended and each person drifted into their dark stone rooms, I left the ledge and strode to the basin by the river. There, upon the open ground between the towering mountains around me, I wanted to spend time alone with my creator.

My thoughts went to Pa. I smiled, thinking how proud he would be to have this land I now stood upon. The ranch we wanted was going to happen.

God had brought me through many tough and hazardous events to finally stand where I was now. What would be the next steps? Was I to continue building my ranch and live here, seeing the fulfillment of my dreams? Or was there something more?

Cal challenged me to think deeper, to determine what else I was to do and how to accomplish it.

The answers flooded over me—filling me—but not surprising me. Man is not to be alone. I loved Rose and would ask her to be my wife. However, I didn't want to hurry her. I sensed she returned my feelings, but we hadn't spoken of them.

Eagerly, I looked forward to an opportunity to share how I truly felt about her.

CHAPTER 31

For the next two weeks, the weather turned mild once again, winter keeping its distance for a while longer. Each day, we worked with the horses. Our final count of horses in Wildfire's band was sixty-three, more than I had expected.

We culled fifteen head from the herd to start. Some of these were too old, others injured or unhealthy. One by one, they were released from the boxed canyon into the basin.

We divided the remaining horses into two groups. Those we planned to saddle break for the army were moved to our other fenced canyon. Those selected for breeding were kept in their current enclosure.

Wildfire's band proved to be such a better quality of horseflesh, and this made us re-evaluate the first herd we'd captured in the dry watercourse. Some of them we now determined to be unfit for breeding but certainly adequate for saddle stock.

George's abilities had been sharpened in Kentucky and proved essential for our needs as we roped and broke the wild mustangs. He had an easy and gentle way with the horses but also possessed a natural quality of kindness within him.

God truly assembled a winning team of horse wranglers in the trio of Walter, Rose, and George.

Scott and I did as instructed and helped in many ways to hold animals and ride broken stock. Hundreds of tasks a day followed for each of us as we strove to build a paying, working horse ranch.

More corrals were needed, but the ground was too hard for digging in this season. We would have to wait until spring.

We discussed another trip to Fort Union before the snow fell to ensure enough hay for our large number of stock, but reminders of our last trip from the fort ruled that out of the question. We would have to find more feed.

I'd given up the idea of living in the big house on the knoll until spring when lumber and glass could be delivered, but on November first, three wagons appeared down on the prairie at the river's edge. I saddled the gray gelding and rode down to meet them. The freight wagons held my order from Fort Union.

"We have everything except the pipe," the burly teamster—a tall, bearded man in a woolen cap—explained to me. "My name's Jorgenson. Delivered freight to Fort Union and was told we were done for the season unless we were game to deliver these wagons to you. Most of the teamsters said we were crazy to try, but I'm from up north and can tell this is Indian summer. No snow for a while longer, I think."

For five days, Jorgenson and his teamsters built doors and tables and installed glass in the windows of the big house. A black iron stove was carried into the kitchen. Fires roared in all the fireplaces in the house to chase out the cold.

A thrill went through me as I watched the white smoke curl from the rock chimneys. Randy knew his craft well and built solidly. The house remained snug and dry.

The three empty wagons left five days later as George and I moved our meager gear into the stone and log house. Furniture and lanterns filled the rooms while deer hides covered much of the flagstone floor. Tall stacks of firewood lined the back porch in preparation for a long winter. The rooms were comfortable and spacious in contrast to the little stone rooms of the cliff dwellings.

I think Scott and Rose looked at my house wistfully, but to their credit, said nothing. They chose to remain with Blue Heron and Walter in the cliffs.

Our days were filled with making furniture, hauling water, and cutting firewood and hay. Some of the higher meadows still had grass. We cut and hauled the hay to various piles outside the enclosed meadows. The ranch was working well, and we had plans for driving at least a dozen head of saddle stock to Fort Union come spring.

We built stone water troughs just inside both enclosures for water from the hot spring when the other water froze. The horses didn't like the ill-smelling sulfur water but would drink it.

Snow crested many of the higher mountains, but none came our way until late November.

George was roping a bay mare and I was helping Rose wrestle a halter over her head when a snowflake fluttered from the leaden sky and landed on Rose's dark hair. I saw it first as I usually had an eye on Rose. Other flakes followed and soon a flurry swirled.

Laughing at the snow, we tried to ignore it, but a white canopy descended and drove us from the corral and into our homes.

For three days, the snow fell, painting our world silver and clean. Soon mounds covered the ground and piled inches deep. All the boulders and piled debris near the river were concealed by this white blanket.

On the second day of the winter storm, I bundled into my thick buffalo coat Blue Heron had made, trudged through the snow, and crossed the river to the cliff dwellings to invite everyone to my house for dinner. I invited Rose and Scott to help prepare the meal. The two siblings agreed and accompanied me back to the warmth of the big house on the knoll.

Blue Heron and Walter were all eyes as they entered my house that evening for the first time. We sat around the large dining room table and ate fresh venison. George had killed a deer, and the meat was tender and tasty. With it, we enjoyed potatoes the teamsters from Fort Union had delivered.

After dinner, we moved our chairs around the large stone fireplace in the spacious living room and discussed future ranching ideas. We hauled water daily now so water piped from various springs in the vicinity would reduce our workload. Also, corrals and another barn would help. The gray gelding, Strawberry, George's horse, and a few others were the only residents of our barn now.

"We will need to trap more horses," Walter began, starting the age-old story of every wild horse hunter. "We will need to increase our herds if we want to continue to sell to the army and go into large scale breeding."

"The better the animal, the better the price you can demand for them," George agreed, puffing slowly on his pipe.

I turned to him and saw him staring through the blue cloud of smoke at Blue Heron. He seemed unconscious of his observation, but I certainly noticed. Glancing around the room, I caught Rose's eye. She noticed George staring at her mother too. Rose arched an eyebrow and smiled knowingly.

Later, Walter, Blue Heron, and Scott bundled into their heavy coats, preparing to depart for the cliff dwellings. Tentatively, I placed a hand on Rose's arm.

Her eyes widened, curious. "Stay a while?" I asked.

A soft glow came into her green eyes, and she nodded. Turning to my other guests, I promised to deliver Rose safely home soon.

Scott grinned mischievously, but Walter only scowled, his old eyes narrowing. "Bring her home soon," he commanded as he ushered his daughter and grandson from the house.

Rose nudged me as Blue Heron smiled softly at George before stepping onto the wide porch, her dark eyes glowing.

The door closed behind them. As we returned to our seats before the great fireplace, I glanced out the front window. Dark had come outside, but a lantern was unnecessary. We'd all traveled this region many times and knew the way home even at night.

Little conversation ensued as the three of us stared awkwardly into the dancing fire. Finally, George knocked the ash from the bowl of his pipe and retired to his room, and Rose and I were alone. The snow continued falling as Rose and I watched it from behind the protective pane of the window glass.

Sitting together on the couch, we shared a buffalo robe spread across our laps. The lantern was extinguished to conserve fuel, and only the fire's ruddy glow lit the big room.

Both of us acted like we were watching the fire, neither of us spoke. The nearness of the beautiful Indian girl made my heart beat in my ears. I hoped she couldn't hear.

Reluctantly, I untangled myself from the comfort of the warm robe to replenish the fire. Sparks fluttered as I tossed logs on the flames.

Rose lifted the edge of the robe and smiled, inviting my return. She'd scooted over, closer to where I was sitting.

Pretending not to notice, I slipped beneath the robe, snuggling close to Rose. I felt the warmth of her. This is where I belonged. We'd grown close these last seven months. I knew she was the girl for me.

Taming my anxiety, I faced her. Staring for a moment, I summoned my courage as I studied her bronze cheeks and the long lashes over her sparkling eyes.

"Rose," I whispered. "I'm in love with you."

Her eyes flickered and widened. A gentle smile tugged at her red lips. "I'm in love with you, too, Jason. I have been for a long time."

I blinked. A long time? How come I wasn't aware of this?

"You are?" My voice cracked. I felt embarrassed, but she only smiled.

"Yes. Mother saw first, and then Walter. He says you are a good Christian man and will make a good husband."

I felt for her hand under the robe and held it, our fingers intertwining.

My heart full, I looked back at the fire. What had I done to deserve this happiness? I left Missouri with nothing and now felt like the most blessed man in the world. God blessed me more than I'd ever dreamed possible, more than I deserved. The weight of that made me feel more responsible, more mature.

If this girl loved me, and we were discussing marriage, I would need to be more than a rancher of a dozen cows. I would need to be a real rancher, making money to provide for a wife and family.

I drew a deep breath. Family? I would have children one day and didn't want them to be raised by an unwise, unprepared man. I would be a man of example, a Christian leader for my children, one who was responsible, diligent, hard-working.

I wouldn't marry Rose until I was established. I would do things right.

"Rose?" I turned to her, holding her hand firmly. Her green eyes glowed softly in the firelight. It took all my will power to say what I must.

"Mountain Rose Mackenzie," I started, needing to get the words out. "I want to marry you. I want to be your husband. But I cannot until I'm somebody established with a paying ranch. I came out here to create my father's dream ranch, and I've been blessed with property and some breeding stock and horses. But I need hundreds of cattle to get this ranch up and running. I need capital to invest in the place. It will take years to get this ranch producing. I want to do things the way God would have me do them. Responsibly."

I paused, my heart in my throat. I struggled to say these next words. "Rose, will you wait for me to build my ranch so I can provide for you as the Lord would want? I don't need to be rich—I feel rich having you—but I need to honor you. I want to show that I respect and value you."

I paused again, my love for her washing over me like a wave. She meant everything to me.

"You're special and a gift from God, and it'd be wrong to take that lightly and invite you into a marriage that I'm unprepared for," I finished, grateful to have my say, but fearful of her response.

I could feel the panic rising in me again. What if she wouldn't wait? What if she didn't think I was doing the right thing?

"I want to honor you and be prepared for a wife," I repeated, studying her eyes intently, searching for her reply. "Will you wait for me?"

I held my breath. This girl held my heart. She could, with a word, destroy me or lift me to the heights.

Rose smiled.

"Jason, you're the man God has brought for me to love forever. I will wait for you. You make me love you even more that your thoughts are for my comfort and peace. You have shown me real love. We'll marry when you've asked Walter for my hand and you've properly prepared a place for me."

CHAPTER 32

Rose and I walked together every day and discussed the future as I pondered how to ask Walter for her hand. Rose teased me about my hesitation to ask Walter's permission, but I wanted the timing to be perfect.

The horse portion of the ranch grew in a favorable direction, but we'd need more buildings and corrals come spring. Capital was a real issue, and the little money we hoped to get from the army for the sale of more saddle stock would be used on these necessities. Not to mention the day-to-day costs of running a ranch with numerous people to feed and clothe.

"I can't get away from the fact that we're still too small. We also need more tack." I kicked at a rock in the frozen ground, my frustration mounting as I considered plans and costs. Would we never be able to marry?

"Patience and faith, Cowboy Jason," Rose reminded me with a smile. A fur hood surrounded her lovely face, her eyes shining brightly. "God brought us together. We need only to be faithful, and he will provide. Trust in him. He has not let us down, and he'll not start now."

Her words calmed me. I knew she was right. I drew a deep breath and nodded, praying for patience.

That night in my room, I studied Scripture, seeking the Lord in his holy Word. God always spoke to me if I would allow him to.

The Spirit soothed me as I read, and I knew God wanted me to stay close to him, to wait on the Lord. Rose was right, God would provide in his perfect timing.

A week before Christmas, Scott argued with Blue Heron that since he was doing a man's job, he wanted to live with the men. I'd given my permission when he'd asked if he could move into the house with George and me but said the move was contingent on Blue Heron's blessing.

Walter gave his approval and encouraged his daughter that the move would be good for Scott, to help him mature as a young man. Blue Heron reluctantly consented, but she looked at me, her gaze narrowing while she gripped Scott's shoulder.

"Jason, I'm entrusting my son to you. He is young and impressionable. I expect you to take this responsibility seriously and watch over him—like a big brother. Help him develop into a Godly young man. I am counting on you," she said, her voice stern.

Agreeing with all solemnity, I promised to do my best. Scott whooped his delight, and I helped him cart his few belongings to my house on the knoll. He was given a room of his own and couldn't have been more pleased.

"Besides," Walter explained while Blue Heron watched her son gather his belongings, a tear shining in her eye, "we need more space anyway. This room was too crowded."

I knew Walter was only trying to soothe Blue Heron's fears, but I appreciated the support.

We agreed we'd celebrate Christmas Day with a feast at my house. Blue Heron came over the day before and helped Rose cook. Despite several things that needed attending, George hovered in the kitchen, refusing to budge, eager to assist Blue Heron with food preparations. The house smelled of roasting venison, cornbread, and potatoes.

Pine boughs and candles decorated the big house for Christmas Day. Everyone was excited for the wonderful meal. I, however, was a wreck as the hour neared. I'd decided tonight would be the night I'd ask Walter for Rose's hand. What would he say?

The Christmas meal brought a warm and cheery time of family and friends. The living room glowed brightly with the candles and the roaring blaze on the hearth, the peeled yellow logs of the upper wall shining merrily.

George complimented Blue Heron, saying he'd never tasted a more delicious meal. Blue Heron blushed and dropped her gaze before shyly smiling at the horse wrangler.

We laughed and talked of the past many months since we'd met and the events that shaped our year. We'd worked with the mustangs—only working a few hours each day due to the cold—and had made tremendous progress. Despite the cold weather, five more horses now wore saddles.

We even observed a moment of silence in memory of those loved ones no longer with us to share our joy. With fondness, I remembered both my father and Cal. How good to know they were now in heaven, and I would see them again one day.

The evening went on, my nerves stretching with anxious anticipation as the evening passed. Rose shot me encouraging glances, knowing I'd chosen this day, but I grew more uneasy as the day wore on.

Finally, she caught my elbow as I was leaving the kitchen, fetching my sixth cup of coffee. "Quit stalling, Malone, and go talk to my grandfather," she urged in a stern whisper. "You're starting to make me nervous too."

She pushed me toward the old horse hunter. Walter watched the snow-covered basin from the living room's big window, but I felt as if he expected me as I approached. I wiped my sweaty palms on my pants. "Walter," I stammered. "Will you come with me to check the stock in the barn?" I glanced over my shoulder to where Blue Heron stood beside Rose, the two of them watching me closely.

He waited a long moment before shaking his head. "No. It's cold out there, and I'm warm. Take Scott."

I tensed. I'd planned for this moment. What if I couldn't get him to come with me?

"Walter," I urged, placing a trembling hand on his shoulder. "I really need your help. Someone with your experience, not Scott."

He scowled and sighed but didn't sound sincere.

I caught the old Cheyenne sharing a meaningful glance with Blue Heron as I shrugged into my heavy coat. Closing the door behind me, I stood on the wide porch, my gaze traveling the length of the valley as I prayed for the right words.

I waited. My cold hands were shoved deep in my pockets, and I watched the steam from my mouth as I shivered. Looking to the east, the endless prairie stretched to the horizon. I shifted uneasily and chewed the inside of my cheek. Finally, I peered through the window's clear glass.

Walter stood behind the door, watching me. His eyebrows arched then, and he hastily opened the door and joined me on the porch.

We thumped down the steps, taking the trail to the barn, our moccasins crunching last night's fresh snow.

Walter remained silent as he followed me to the stone building. I glanced at him and pulled the door open, heat washing over us as we hurried in and closed the door behind us.

Reaching for a pitchfork, I fed the horses. The atmosphere was pleasant here with the comforting smells of hay, fresh manure, and leather. I always loved being around the barn when I wanted to think—it relaxed me. But not today.

Walter watched me, his arms crossed over his chest, as I finished the chores. He studied me with a piercing gleam in his eye, waiting.

I was waiting too. I didn't know how to begin. My mind felt muddled, and I bit my lip, wondering what to say.

He frowned at me as we left the barn, but I was too nervous to consider his look of disappointment. We headed back up the trail. My mouth was dry as we stomped our snowy feet on the porch. As he gripped the door handle, I reached for his arm.

"Walter, we've been through a lot this year. We've hunted and worked together and learned about each other. You know me now—I'm not a stranger any longer. I've tried my best to be wise. I'm a good worker, and I have hopes for the future. I plan on making this ranch a fulfillment of the dreams of both my father and Mackenzie. I believe it's no coincidence that God brought us both here with the same desire and goal."

I paused to catch my breath and organize my thoughts. The old Indian stood there, listening, saying nothing. I thought I detected a soft warmth in his eyes.

"I've come to love your family as my own. I've especially come to love Rose. I think the Lord has brought us together. I want to ask you for permission to marry Rose when the ranch is stable and providing a living. I won't bring her into this until I'm in a position to take care of her properly."

I paused again, released his arm, and then stepped back and nodded. "I wanted you to know my intentions and to ask for your blessing."

My speech seemed to rattle from me. By the time I'd finished, I'd stumbled over my words in a hurry to get them out. A great sense of relief washed over me as I finished, and then it was my turn to stand there, not speaking.

Walter stared at me a moment, and then put a hand on my shoulder. "Jason, it has been a pleasure to get to know you. I am honored by your asking for Rose's hand in marriage. Blue Heron and I have spoken many times of this, and we have been hoping you would do so. We are proud of you and the man you have become. Your father, too, would be proud of who you are."

He smiled, letting his words sink in. "When you are able to provide a living for Rose and yourself, you have our blessing to marry her. Only don't wait too long. The struggles of life are best shared with another. I know Rose loves you and that you love her. Honor her, be good to her, and always seek the Lord's will."

I wanted to hug him but didn't know if that would be appropriate, so I grasped his hand and wrung it fiercely. "Thank you, Walter. You can't imagine how happy this makes me."

His dark old eyes misted. "Yes, Jason, I can imagine. I was young once and loved a beautiful girl too."

We opened the door as the sun was setting. Rose caught my eye as I entered. I nodded once, unable to keep the smile from my lips. I thought my heart would burst.

She walked to her grandfather and hugged him. "Thank you, Grandfather. I am so happy."

He nodded, a tear rolling down his wrinkled face. Blue Heron joined us, tears welling in her dark eyes as she hugged Rose. Then, surprising me, Blue Heron turned and hugged me too.

That was probably the best Christmas of my life.

CHAPTER 33

The winter months passed. I worked long hours and gave my best to do what I could to make the ranch a better prospect. We located another box canyon farther up the valley and spent weeks building rock walls to close the entrance. Then, we moved my small herd of cattle and some of the horses to the new canyon to lessen the tax on the hay in the old one.

George, Walter, and I often spoke about the need for hay conservation and water availability. We kept the animals safe and fed through the winter.

Storms came and went, and we weathered each of them in our homes. George, Scott, and I lived in the house on the knoll. Walter and Blue Heron with Rose were committed to the cliff dwelling, but Rose admitted to me that she looked forward to moving to my house.

After February, I checked the trees daily, searching for the first hint of spring. Nothing appeared on the skeleton branches of the trees along the river, and I started to think spring would never arrive.

Despite my impatience, the day came when the first leaf opened, and then, as if by magic, the magnificent handiwork of the Creator burst forth, splashing colors across the canyons. Green grass carpeted the valley, and the trees filled with foliage.

Spring was here. The changes were almost imperceptible, but finally, the cold weather pushed behind us for another year and the ranch leaped into activity with the impetus of a falling rock.

Cows calved and new foals and colts kept us up late at night. We wanted to be on hand for each delivery in case complications occurred. Scott and I built more corrals and we moved stock from pasture to pasture. New grass grew, and the animals were ready for fresh, nutritious grazing.

George and Blue Heron began taking evening walks along the river. Mutual loneliness had drawn these two very different people together. By May, they'd announced their engagement. They would wait for the next delivery of horses to Fort Union and seek a preacher to perform the ceremony.

Rose pouted. "Why do they get to be married before us? We've been engaged longer. What are we waiting for?" She looked at me, pleading, her eyes full of frustration.

"Rose, patience," I cautioned. "We have committed ourselves to a situation that would provide for you. I cannot bring you into a marriage that might not sustain our livelihood. You deserve better. Besides, what kind of a Christian man would I be to place that kind of burden on you? I don't want you to always live a life of poverty and worry. I want to be able to give you a firm foundation for the life we wish to build together."

I paused, watching her closely. Then, I bit my lip and continued. "When the children come, I want to be a Christian father they can respect. It's important."

Her eyes widened. "Children?"

I smiled when she blushed, shyly glancing away. With a sigh, she nodded at my words.

She didn't like waiting, but she relented. The Lord guided us, and she knew it. We had only to be patient.

I spent long hours in prayer and Bible study. I sought the Lord's will and was sure he was with us. He would provide in his perfect timing.

Seeds were needed to add to Blue Heron's carefully hoarded wild plant seeds she'd collected in the fall, and an extensive garden was planned to help supplement our needs. We agreed that George and Blue Heron would go to the fort at the end of May. I would accompany them to complete the transaction with Sergeant Reynolds. Walter and Scott would stay and keep the ranch running, preparing the tilled soil for the garden, but an argument arose about whether Rose should go or stay.

"I want to be there when my mother gets married," Rose complained. "Besides, I can help with the stock. You're delivering quite a lot of horses to the fort."

She was right. We had fourteen horses we wished to deliver, and they were only half-broke wild mustangs. Green broke, Walter called it.

"We don't have enough saddles for four riders," I protested, looking for any excuse to keep Rose at the safety and comfort of the ranch.

She crossed her arms over her chest and glared at me. "I don't need a saddle, Jason."

"I wouldn't use a saddle anyway," Blue Heron interjected, draping a supportive arm around her daughter's shoulders.

I shrugged and nodded, knowing I'd been out-numbered, but I really didn't mind. I loved having Rose along. I only wanted to spare her the difficulty of another rough trip to the fort, but I knew she was up to the challenge.

We hit the old Santa Fe Trail and followed the path south toward Fort Union. I noticed the freshness of wagon tracks in the road. Already, freight trains had traveled here this year. I dimly wondered if we would pass them on the trail.

The small herd proved challenging as we moved them down the track, alternating between running them quickly and walking them. They demanded constant vigilance, always looking for an opportunity to bolt. By time the sun leaned far to the west, we were all exhausted and searched for a place to camp.

As we topped a rise, I saw the wagon train we'd followed stretched out below us, hugging a small stream that wound down from the higher peaks. Teamsters waved at us as we moved above them, choosing the upstream side from the wagons to make our encampment, about two hundred yards away.

Twilight descended as George and Rose worked together to picket the mustangs. Blue Heron walked between them, handing braided leather ropes to each of them as the pair secured the horses for the night.

As I gathered wood, my gaze scanned the wagons down the slope from us, remembering Cal and the days with the freight wagons. That seemed so long ago now—about a year, I guessed. I thought of Cal's grave site on the knoll above Bent's abandoned fort and I frowned, recalling the trials of that journey. Then I shrugged, remembering the many blessings too. Cal was a good friend.

Returning to our campsite, I arranged wood and started a small blaze. Darkness enveloped me, and I could only hear the others wrangling the horses in the gloom, brushing them and making sure their hooves were clean. After pushing the coffeepot into the fire, I rustled in my pack for a skillet when I heard footsteps approach, boots moving through the grass.

"Do you need something, George?" I called as I sliced bacon into the pan, not bothering to look up from my work.

"Jason Malone."

My blood chilled when I heard that voice, and I snapped my head up as I searched the gloom for the intruder. There, just at the edge of the firelight, stood a shadowy figure, eyes glittering in the dark, and I knew it was him. Slowly, I stood and faced Captain Wilmington.

CHAPTER 34

My fingers gripped the knife as I watched him, wondering at his intent. I didn't have long to wait.

"Teamsters told me of riders camping near us. I wondered if it'd be you." He chuckled without humor. "And look what fate has delivered to my doorstep."

He took a step closer, and the firelight revealed the scowl on his face and the cruelty in his eyes. "I've dreamed of a chance like this. You cheated me at Fort Union, and I intend to get a little of mine back or take it out of your hide. Which will it be?" He whacked his tall boots with his riding quirt, the sharp sound loud in the quiet night.

I stared at him, marveling at my lack of fear. I was not a boy anymore, lost and desperate for somewhere to belong. I'd grown this past year, in responsibility, in my faith, and in my relationships. God had shaped me for times like this, and I straightened, taking a deep breath before I replied.

But before I could speak, another figure loomed from the darkness. I felt my eyes widen as I recognized the burly form of Thompson.

He nodded at me, then turned his gaze on Wilmington. "I saw you leave the wagons and head this way. I figured this was what you were up to."

He paused, and I heard a horse whinny a short distance away.

"And what business is it of yours?" Wilmington demanded.

Thompson continued. "You're a bully, and I thought I'd seen the last of you when I left the train in Santa Fe. I hired on with another caravan returning to St. Joseph, but something told me to tie to you again, to keep an eye on you. Everyone's heard about how this young man bested you at Fort Union. I knew you'd not let it go."

He paused again, and Wilmington shifted his boots, glaring at Thompson. "I heard he's selling horses to the army. If something were to happen to Jason Malone, I would have to alert the authorities at Fort Union. They wouldn't look favorably on anything interfering with their horse dealer.

Not to mention, the military contracts you hold to freight supplies for the forts would disappear if they knew you threatened this man." He hooked a thumb in my direction.

Wilmington shifted again and glowered, his wheels turning as he considered Thompson's words.

I sensed movement around me, and George and Blue Heron stepped from the darkness, lining up beside me. Rose stood on my left side, her hand slipping into mine, squeezing it fiercely.

I smiled, feeling good. I was not alone. "Wilmington, it's over. You were not cheated, just beaten." I glanced at Rose. She peered up at me, and I studied her. So lovely, so strong. I looked at Wilmington again. "You were beaten by a better rider."

The wagon master narrowed his eyes, his lips pressed in a thin line as he glanced at the others around me. Then he whacked his high boots again and spun on his heels, striding from our camp.

I turned to Thompson, but he held up a hand. "Jason, I did nothing when Wilmington kicked you out of the train last year, and it's stuck in my craw ever since. I've had time to stew on it, vowing to make amends if the chance came. I'm sorry about Cal."

He turned to go, glancing at me over his shoulder. "If I'm this way again, would it be all right if I stopped by your ranch and said hello? The news is out about your holdings on the Arkansas."

I smiled. "You'd be welcome, Thompson." I hesitated and gestured to the vacant spot where Wilmington had stood. "And thanks."

He nodded once and disappeared in the darkness.

———◇———

Horses move faster than cows, and despite the number of horses we had to drive, we made the fort in only four days.

Blue Heron, true to her word, didn't require a saddle and often would leap astride different mounts while we rode. The Cheyenne were superb riders.

Sergeant Reynolds greeted us warmly, and the purchase of the riding stock was completed with little delay. With the captured Wildfire as our stud on the ranch, the magnificent stallion promised to sire generations of horses for the army.

After paying me, Reynolds pulled me aside from the others, worry lines crinkling the corner of his eyes. Frowning, he whispered, "There's a lawyer here named Mr. Tarleton who's been waiting and hoping for you to come to the fort. It's the same man I received the letter from last fall."

I'd forgotten. I cringed as I recalled the mysterious letter the sergeant reminded me of. Were the Missouri men still after me? What was Tarleton here for? What had I done? I drew in a deep breath and resolved myself to not worry about it. Whom should I fear if the Lord is with me? I informed the sergeant I would see the lawyer on the morrow.

"And the war, Sergeant? Any news from the east?" I'd been thinking of Pa. Missouri was far away and the war far off, but did our beliefs matter? I wanted to think they did.

Reynolds nodded. "It looks like the Confederacy has gone into defense, hoping to outlast the Union. Maybe the war began over state's rights, but President Lincoln is shrewd and now the conflict is over slavery. With that, England will no longer support the South, regardless of cotton. The Confederacy is losing, and the war cannot last much longer. Everyone knows it."

I smiled, unable to speak.

Exhaling deeply, I turned and walked away. Pa had been right.

That night, the four of us had dinner at the café, where we were informed the army cook at the fort was also a chaplain and performed weddings.

"Then tomorrow, I get married." George beamed at the blushing Blue Heron. "And we'll not be living in the cliff dwelling."

Blue Heron smiled. "No, indeed, husband. Your house is my house. We will live where you say."

Rose shook her head. "Walter will never move to the log and stone cabin. He'll live out his days where he is." A sad look came to her eyes, and I gripped her hand. "I wish he would live with us."

"He is content where he is. We'll still see him every day," I reminded her, glad he would be near.

We stayed up late that night, excited about the amount of money the sale of the horses had brought us. We also talked of the coming wedding. George and Blue Heron were happy. I was glad they'd found each other. I, too, was eager to get married, but I would wait until I'd built a successful operation for Rose. The short ceremony was full of laughter, joy shining in the happy couple's eyes. The old army cook-chaplain was accustomed to the suddenness of his services being needed and was ready to oblige. Rose and I acted as witnesses.

After the event, I ushered George and his new bride along with Rose into the general store to enjoy some shopping before we left for the ranch the next morning. Blue Heron and Rose were so excited to look at calico, cooking utensils, and clothing. George grinned and turned to me. "You run along, Jason, and take care of your business. I'll keep an eye on the women."

My feet dragged as I started for the sergeant's office. Was I walking to my own destruction? I glanced heavenward, praying for strength. Whatever happened now, I would face it. The time of running was over.

Pursing my lips, I straightened my shoulders and walked on. My faith had grown a lot this past year. My leadership skills, my submission to the Lord's sovereignty, my reliance on the Holy Spirit. Come what may, God was with me. Together, we could handle anything that came my way.

Sergeant Reynolds brought me into his little office and introduced me to Mr. Tarleton, the St. Louis lawyer. He was a man of about fifty and had a keen, shrewd eye that studied me closely. "I'll be outside if there is anything I can assist you with," Reynolds said as he left the room, closing the door behind him.

Mr. Tarleton scowled suspiciously at me, making me squirm under his penetrating gaze. His scrutiny made me nervous, like the schoolmaster catching me doing something wrong.

"Young man." He ruffled the papers in his hand, glancing at them and then peering over them at me. "Are you Jason Malone? The same Jason Malone who accompanied Calvin Stuart on a wagon train last spring across the plains?"

I blinked. Cal? Was this about Cal? I chewed the inside of my cheek. "Well, I was with Cal, but I never heard his last name."

"Do you know the whereabouts of Mr. Stuart now?" he demanded, and the chair creaked as he leaned forward.

I nodded. "Yes, sir. I buried him on the side of the trail near Bent's Fort. I think that was last May. Why? What does this have to do with me?"

Mr. Tarleton paused. He leaned back again, relaxing. "I have known Mr. Stuart for these last twenty years, and I have never known a more clever and stubborn man. I have conducted his business affairs and investments, and he always came to see me, giving me additional funds to invest or suggesting businesses to purchase. He has no home, no family, and no vices. He handed his money from his lucrative freighting job over to me each year and instructed me in how to best handle his growing capital."

He wiped his brow with a white linen handkerchief. "He was seen by numerous physicians in the last two years, who all corroborated the diagnosis that he was fatally ill with a cancer and his life would soon be spent. He vowed to me that he would rather die on the wagon trail than in a hospital bed. No amount of pleading would dissuade him from his decision. And, I must add, I was not surprised."

He paused again, smiling slightly at me. "I'm here to conclude Mr. Stuart's affairs. Last summer, I received a fascinating letter from Mr. Stuart mailed from Council Grove on the Santa Fe Trail. In this letter, he informed me that he had come to know Jesus Christ as his Lord and Savior. Also, he instructed me to hand all his earthly possessions over to a young rancher named Jason Malone. Naturally, I had to meet this most influential person who so impressed and impacted Mr. Stuart's last days. Upon receiving the response letter from Sergeant Reynolds, I endeavored to catch the next stage west to meet you."

He leaned on the desk, his elbows resting on the scarred surface.

I frowned. What did all this mean?

Mr. Tarleton must've sensed my confusion. He smiled. "You are a wealthy man, Mr. Malone."

I couldn't believe my ears. Could this be true? I had no idea Cal had anything or that he'd leave it to me. He was so sick when I met him back on the trail in Missouri. I remembered how he gave me breakfast and a job. How that chance meeting so powerfully changed my life.

After a few more words, I stood and shook the lawyer's hand. Stepping from the small room, I closed the door behind me and looked up.

Cal had found me. Just like he said he would. I smiled, remembering the old teamster's final words. And he was right about needing a partner.

Rose and her mother met me as they came from the store. I felt dazed by the enormity of this news from the St. Louis lawyer.

Puzzled by my obvious bewilderment, Rose tilted her head. "Is everything all right, Jason?"

I explained the gist of the lawyer's visit to Fort Union. "Rose, he dispatched a buyer to Texas to purchase a herd of cattle and drive them to my ranch.

They should be here by end of summer. And that's not all. There's more. I'm rich. The ranch will prosper."

Rose gasped, her eyes widening as her hands flew to her mouth. She leaped into my arms, hugging me fiercely. "Jason, this is the news we've been praying for. God is so good. Now we can be married."

And so we were.

That afternoon, the army chaplain performed an identical wedding service for Rose and me as he'd done for George and Blue Heron that morning. Now, George and Blue Heron stood to be our witnesses.

Rose was beautiful in her green dress, her long dark hair pulled back and tied with a ribbon I'd bought from the store—a green ribbon matching both her dress and her dancing green eyes. She was the perfect bride for me.

My joy was now complete.

Cal found me like he promised. I hadn't understood him then, as he lay under a heavy freight wagon in the dark, but I did now. His memory would forever be with me on our ranch.

Also, the dream of my father and the dream of Mackenzie had brought a group of lonely, lost travelers together. Now we were joined forever by marriage and love. I had a new family, one to take care of, to love, and to create new dreams. Like Scott said, our connection bound us together. Horses and Jesus. With Rose by my side and with Wildfire, the magnificent stallion, the ranch seemed destined for greatness.

Life is hard, I realized, but patience had seen me through. God had been with me through the tough times, and he was with me still. His sovereign hand guided events and maneuvered them to bring about the workings of my life. That day on the Santa Fe Trail when Wilmington so callously threw me off his train had not been an accident.

Like Joseph in the Bible, whose brothers sold him into slavery, and that what they meant for harm had turned out for good—was all ordained by a loving Master. The Master of my fate. Jesus Christ not only saved me but also saved others through me. I was eternally grateful for the Lord's provision and guidance.

I knew Pa and Mackenzie were in heaven. I wondered if they ever met up there and saw the fulfillment of their individual dreams come true through the working of the Lord in their children. I hoped so.

Pa always said you were never alone as long as you knew Jesus. I had to agree, after the unfolding of the events surrounding me on the plains. Jesus had obviously been with me through it all. He provided the adventure I'd been searching for, the ranch Pa and I dreamed about, and Wildfire for Rose.

ABOUT THE AUTHOR

ANDREW ROTH taught American History for twenty-two years at the middle school level before beginning his literary career. He lives in Bakersfield, California, with his wife and is a proud father and grandfather. A native of Kansas, Andrew was raised with a deep love and appreciation for history, particularly the Old West. A Christian for more than three decades, Andrew's hope is that his writing will encourage readers and rebuild lives. The passage he feels is his guiding verse is Jeremiah 31:4, "I will build you up again and you will be rebuilt."

Made in the USA
Monee, IL
13 December 2019